# CAMELOT'S MISPLACED SON

## PAT PAXTON

Hydra
Publications

ISBN: 978-1-940466-71-2

Goshen, Kentucky 40026
www.hydrapublications.com

*For Polly, Katie, and Ben – everything is.*

# CHAPTER ONE

HAVE YOU EVER DIED, lying flat on your back under a sky full of shimmering stars just as the dawn sun was poking its nose up out of the Atlantic Ocean? I did. When your time comes, that's the way to go. It happened for me on a Sunday morning.

Obvious, but still strange to realize that there are only seven possible days that a person can die. Think about Tuesdays. Most of them are as dull as watching metal rust, but how would you feel if you knew you had lived your last one? What if Tuesday came and went this week, but there was going to be no next Tuesday? Like most people, I never gave it much thought.

Anyway, my leaving couldn't have been more beautiful. The lovely earthly surroundings; the tingle of pain draining out of my body; then the sight of loved ones there to greet me. All of it so beautiful, it even eased some of the sadness of having to go.

My name is Phil. Phil McCracken. Wait. Not really. It's actually Murphy. Phil Murphy. Not only was I leaving this life a week before my thirtieth birthday—that's thirtieth, not thirteenth, as my attempts at humor might indicate—but more tragically, I was leaving behind my three-year-old son, Willie. Even worse, he had no mother to care for him. And worse yet — well, maybe not worse, but still really shitty—I was leaving the most caring, intelligent, and beautiful woman I'd ever known.

I hope it doesn't happen to you. I'm not talking about death. That one's barreling down on all of us. What I mean is, I hope you don't have to go with so many things undone, leaving the people you love in such a bind.

I can't tell you not to do the things I've done. Even if I knew how you ought to be living, I wouldn't preach it at you. I can't stand when people do that. Everybody needs to figure that out for themselves. I'm satisfied with the choices I made—most of them. I'm sure you've heard people say how you regret the things in life you *didn't* do, as opposed to the things you did. Well, you may think you regret the things you didn't do because you're oh-so-sure you know what the outcome would've been had they happened. But no one really knows; not really.

I believe the biggest regrets come from the things you *did* do. Choices made and actions taken with known, damaging consequences that hurt people—others and yourself. If you can limit that kind of regret, you'll feel better about having to leave.

Well, I did it anyway, didn't I? Telling you how you should live. Shame on me.

You know, I'd love to tell you all about what happened to me, but I don't think I've got the horsepower. I'm just too worn out. Somebody else is gonna have to do it.

# CHAPTER TWO

THE RING of his cell phone jarred Phil Murphy out of a slumber. He'd drifted off with his back against the headboard and the TV on mute. The Weather Channel was good for that. The alarm clock's blue neon glowed 10:31 PM, 4/8/00. It had survived the millennial scare and was able to display the year in double zeros, after all. Computers hadn't crashed. Planes hadn't fallen out of the sky.

He grabbed his phone off the nightstand to make it stop ringing.

"Is it time?" he asked, knowing it was his sister, Kara.

"Yeah," she answered.

"Okay, I'll be there in a few minutes."

"Just bring Willie's things with you," she said.

He'd been waiting on this call. He had Willie's clothes all rolled up in a plastic Kroger bag, ready to go. Phil's budget forced a "function over form" mentality. He had convinced himself that using plastic grocery bags as a suitcase for his three-year-old son was a form of recycling—saving the planet one overnight stay at a time.

Within a few minutes, Phil had the little guy, still in his jammies, into his car seat and was rolling through the Dover, Delaware night toward Kara's house in their little white truck. He left security at his place in the paws of Otis. He was a dog and a half, really—a slow-moving seven-year-old half lab, half shepherd, half-assed cur. God forbid if anyone actually broke in. The only risk to an intruder was being suffocated by Otis's loving tongue.

Kara met them in her driveway, taking the bag from Phil's hand as he carried the sleeping Willie to the front door and handing him off to Kara's husband, Gary. Phil and Kara wasted no time in getting back on the road.

"Who called? Dad?" Phil asked.

"A nurse. I'm not sure Dad's able," Kara answered.

"We probably shouldn't have left him there alone," Phil said.

"It wasn't for long," she said. "I was there until 7:30."

The hospital was only fifteen minutes away, but getting somewhere you're anxious to be always seems to take longer. They both were showing signs of wear. Kara was only two years older than Phil, and too young for the dark crescent moons under her eyes. Hopefully, they'd clear up when this was all over.

Phil punched the button on the contraption that spits out a ticket and raises the parking garage gate, then steered his little white truck up the ramp. At this time of night, there were vacant parking spaces near the door.

The clip clop of Kara's shoes ricocheted off the walls of the empty garage as they approached the automatic sliding door that opened into the hospital lobby. Phil and his sister found the elevator, pressed "4", and stood mute, absorbing the sounds of an all-piano rendition of The Beatles', "Why Don't We Do It In The Road?" on the Muzak. Oh, the humanity.

Finally, they exited the elevator and began their trek down the long hall, past the nurse's station, where they took in a warm smile from the night shift ladies whose faces had become all too familiar over the last few weeks. Phil had a new appreciation for what they did. He'd seen firsthand how hard they worked and how much they put up with from pushy family members. No wonder the burnout rate among nurses was so high. Phil's family had gone out of their way not to be such a family.

Kara's shoes were at it again in the long empty hallway. The brother and sister wanted to get there and they didn't want to get there, but now they were there, like it or not.

"Hi, Dad," Phil said softly from the doorway. His father managed a tired smile back to him from his chair next to the bed.

In the bed, connected to life-sustaining equipment—if that's what you wanted to call it—lay Phil's shrunken mother. Four months earlier, the family had received the news that her breast cancer had metastasized, and it had been a barreling ride downhill since. She'd last been conscious eight days ago, but Phil's dad couldn't give the order to disconnect the equipment until now. None of them could. Although it was unbearable to see her this way, no one could let go.

"Are we ready?" asked the nurse. Phil could almost see the regret in her face after the words left her lips, like she was giving them another chance to change their minds. The staff all knew this moment was past due.

"I guess so," Phil said. Kara stood next to her still-seated father, one hand on his shoulder and the other gently holding her mother's hand. From the other side of the bed, Phil held his mother's other hand while a nurse removed the oxygen mask and turned off the machines that had been running her kidneys and lungs.

"How long?" Kara asked.

"Probably just a minute or so," the nurse answered.

Phil's dad sat silently as the heart monitor's beep slowed. A minute had passed, and the heartbeats were now five seconds apart. Everything else was sullenly still.

It was then Phil felt a sudden squeeze on his hand, accompanied by rapid beeps from the heart monitor. Her eyes shot open.

"What's happening?" Kara shouted.

"I'm not sure," answered the nurse, doing her best to present a calming front. The frantic shifting of her eyes gave her away.

"Connie!" the nurse yelled toward the door as she hastened to turn the equipment back on.

Before any help could arrive, time seemed to halt and everything became eerily quiet to Phil. The chaotic bustling of the nurse, the erratic chatter of the heart monitor; it all fell into the background. His mother's eyes connected to his. She again squeezed his hand, smiled a calm smile, and then she spoke in a raspy whisper through vocal chords that hadn't been used in eight days.

"My sweet Halloween baby."

Phil, stunned, could only return her smile and search her hollow eyes for answers.

And that was it. Her grip loosened. The rapid beeps from the monitor turned to a single-toned drone. Her eyes closed.

# CHAPTER THREE

THE NEXT FOUR days were a blur. Despite his dad's insistence that no one need "babysit" him, Phil decided Kara, with her husband and two kids, had more of a fort to hold down at her house than Phil did. So, he and Willie entrenched themselves at his dad's house until after the funeral. They even brought along Otis. The dog was a chip off Phil's block; eighty pounds of unrealized potential. Aside from the circumstances, it felt good to sleep there again, all of them under one roof.

Phil even got to slip out one night and go back to his own house during a light rain for one of his favorite activities—tormenting his snobby, henpecked next-door neighbor, Stanley. Once a month, when he knew it was about to rain, Phil would sneak out in the middle of the night to fertilize Stanley's yard. The night-time clouds not only provided the moisture to activate the fertilizer, but also gave cover from the moon's spotlight. It was a fruitful investment that paid great entertainment dividends when he would slurp a cold beer from the front porch, watching Stanley mow his yard three times a week and languish under the tongue of his nagging wife. Better than television and cheaper than the movies.

With the funeral done, it was back to work for Phil. His daily routine was dull, but welcome now. He'd take monotony over mortuary any day. It was early Wednesday morning and Phil found himself in his truck at Oglethorpe Chevrolet, out by Dover Downs. He watched as his co-worker, Angela Boatwright, came bouncing across the parking lot toward his little white truck, then open the passenger door. She was perk personified.

"Hey there," Phil said, as she daintily lowered herself into her seat.

"Thanks for picking me up, Phil."

"No sweat. Do I get to give you a ride home, too?"

"No, thanks. They said my car would be ready around noon, so my sister is taking me to lunch and bringing me by here to pick it up."

As they headed east from the parking lot toward the expressway portion of DE-1, the spring sun was low in the morning sky, staring Phil squarely in the face. Conversation was sparse.

"You know," Phil said, "my dad always told me you should try to live east of where you work. That way the sun would never be in your eyes on the drives to and from the job. I should've listened."

"What a surprise. Phil Murphy didn't listen to his parents."

"Watch it, there," he said with a grin. "I haven't delivered you to the office yet. If you get too clever, we may see what kind of hitchhiker you make."

"You're too much of a gentleman to dump me along the side of the road. And if you did, I'd have to report your bad behavior to Mr. Adams," she said with a shy grin, brushing away a strand of her short ebony hair that was tickling her eye.

She was referring to Wilton Adams, the President and CEO of First Collateral Bancorp, Phil and Angela's employer. Angela was Adams' lone administrative assistant.

She was right. Like a lot of teenagers, Phil had paid little heed to the guidance of his parents. But now, as a dad himself—a single dad at that—his father's words were becoming more and more logical with the passing of time, much to Phil's annoyance.

Phil hadn't been sad to see the Twentieth Century depart. The last bit of it had knocked him around a bit. Now that the new millennium was just a few months old, he hoped to be turning a corner. A decent night's sleep would be a good start. Not only was he losing sleep on nocturnal shenanigans at his neighbor's expense, but lately something had him waking up drenched with sweat. He had better things to do than wake up in wet sheets, particularly if it was only his own sweat, and not the "his and her" variety. That variety was a scarce commodity these days. No fault of Angela's, though. If it were up to her, well, you know.

They'd been on one date a few weeks earlier, mostly due to the urging of mutual friends. It ended with a benign peck at her front door, and it all meant much more to Angela than it did Phil. Not that he was without regard for her feelings. He actually thought Angela was very nice. And she was. Very nice.

So Phil's recent lack of companionship was not an issue of supply, but one of demand. He wasn't in the market for a romantic relationship. He just didn't know how he might ever again be able to muster enough trust. For now, the extent of his world was Willie and Otis. Phil kept them all fed by spending his days as a credit analyst at First Collateral in downtown Dover.

"You've got a birthday coming up soon, don't you?" Angela asked.

"I guess I do. With so much going on, it's easy to forget."

"You can't forget about a big one like this, though," she said. "The big 3-0. You'll have to tell me what it's like," she snickered.

"You'll know for yourself in a few years."

"So how do you like working for Charlotte, Phil?"

"Don't ask."

"Too late. I already did."

"I actually *was* listening when my parents told me, 'If you don't have anything good to say…'."

"Well," Angela said, "just leave out the bad parts."

"Okay."

Then ensued a dozen seconds of silence.

"So after leaving out the bad parts, that's what's left?" she asked. Phil just smiled, keeping his eyes on the road.

"I will say that she is a stickler for just about everything," he said. "I suppose there's bound to be something good somewhere in that statement."

"Just give her some time," Angela said. "It's just been a few months."

"I guess so," Phil said. "I think I got a little too comfortable when Jerry ran things. I wish he hadn't retired."

"Well, Mr. Adams thought enough of her to bring her in from a big bank in New Jersey," she said. "So I guess she must have something going for her."

"Who are you, her publicist?" Phil asked with a grin.

"No. I've really only spoken to her a few times, but she seems nice."

"Oh, Angela. How many times did you take candy from strangers when you were a kid?"

"I'm not that gullible, Phil Murphy."

"You've only seen the ass-smooching, 'What can the president's assistant do for me' side of her," Phil said. He took a swig of coffee from his travel mug. "Well, it appears I've disobeyed my parents again, haven't I? I should just keep my mouth closed."

As they continued toward work, Phil glanced at the dashboard clock to find he was running ahead of schedule. Having to pick up Angela at the car dealer had forced him into punctuality.

"How's Willie?" Angela asked.

"He's great. Growing like a water maple."

"He is kind of tall for a three-year-old, isn't he?" she said. "With his mother so tall, and you being such a sturdy guy, he may really turn out to be a big one."

"Yeah, I've heard the mom's height is a big factor," he said. "I'm six-one, and Belinda nearly looked me in the eye—whenever she could bring herself to."

That one brought a few moments of uncomfortable silence to the cab of the little white truck. So Angela veered the subject off in another direction.

"How's Willie liking his sitter?"

"Oh, he loves Stephanie."

"That's so sweet," she said. "Do you think he sees her as kind of a mother figure now?"

"I don't think so. She is very matronly, I guess, especially with her rules and all. But I think he may see my sister, Kara, more like that. He spends a lot of time with her, too. I'm really lucky to have two great people to help me take care of him. But as great of a daycare provider that Stephanie is," Phil said, "she's wound pretty tight about her hours of operation."

"What do you mean?"

"Well, I can drop Willie off at her house anytime in the morning, but by God, I'd better be there by 6:00 that evening to pick him up. I mean, at 6:01 you don't want to be on the business end of her wrath."

"I can understand that," Angela said. "She does keep—what, a couple other kids—plus she has three of her own?"

"Yeah," Phil said. "Other than that, she's the best. She came very highly recommended. I'm lucky to have her. She genuinely cares for Willie and is very warm toward him. The little guy loves it there."

Up ahead, pulled over to the right in the emergency lane, there was a middle-aged woman standing behind a light blue Ford Taurus. Phil flipped on his blinker and guided his truck into the lane behind her.

"She looks kind of helpless, huh?" Phil said.

"Yeah."

"I see her, or any lady her age, and I picture my mom stuck along the side of the road," he said as he opened his door. He approached the woman with a smile.

"Need some help?"

"I think I do, thank you. It just started making the worst noise, so I pulled over. The noise quit when I parked the car."

"Can I have a look?" Phil asked. He hated working on cars, but his budget encouraged him to rely on himself for maintenance and minor repairs.

He opened her car door, reached in, and gave the key a turn. Started right up. Engine purred quite nicely.

"Sounds like it's running fine," he called back to the woman.

Since it didn't sound like an engine problem, he put one khakied knee on the ground and looked under the car. There was the culprit. The tailpipe was dragging. A bracket had rusted in two near the rear of the car, dropping the pipe to the ground. That probably was a hell of a noise, he thought.

"Here's the problem," he said. "I can tie the pipe up to get you through the next few days."

"That would be nice. Thank you."

"I've got a coat hanger in my truck. I'll be right back."

Phil hoofed it back to his truck, opened the driver's door, and flashed a shit-eating grin at Angela. Pushing the back of the driver's seat forward, he reached into the extended cab and grabbed a wire coat hanger. Procrastination with regard to vehicle cleaning can be a good thing. He also pulled out a blanket to lay on. Now back at the Taurus, he rolled up his sleeves, spread out the blanket, plopped down on his back, and shimmied up under the rear end.

He straightened the metal hanger, then bent it into a "U" shape. He let the tailpipe rest in the "U", then grabbed the wire and lifted it up to tie each end around a nearby bolt. Good and tight. It wasn't going anywhere for a while. He pulled his arms back down.

"Aw, Jesus!"

He'd wedged his right forearm between the gas tank and still burning-hot tailpipe. Phil's forearms were substantial, and working it loose took a good three or four seconds—long enough for him to feel like a branded steer. By the time he freed his arm, he could only see white spots. After a few deep breaths, he slid back out from under the car to find Angela standing with the stranded woman.

"Are you okay, Phil?"

"Yeah, I'm fine. I might just need to get some ice on this when I get to work."

"Let me see that," Angela said, grabbing his big paw and turning it over to get a look at the underside of his forearm.

"Oh, my God," she said. His arm was a mess—red and yellow spots, with a couple of charred accents.

"Maybe you should see a doctor," the woman said. She was probably right, but Phil, in an effort to keep his budget under control, had chosen the highest deductible his employer's healthcare plan offered. Any trip to the doctor would be out of his own pocket. What would a doctor do anyway? Probably just clean it, put some kind of ointment on it, and give him some Tylenol or the like. He could do all of that himself.

"I'll get it cleaned up at the office," Phil assured her, trying to mask the urge to wince. She thanked Phil, got in her Taurus, and merged back into traffic.

Phil and Angela walked back to the little white truck, where he opened her passenger side door, and she lightly landed in her seat.

"Are you okay to drive, Phil?"

"Sure."

He trudged around the back of the truck and up to the driver's door. As he opened the door, something caught his eye. He stood still, peering over the roof of his little white truck toward Dover Mall.

From his position on the slightly elevated freeway, he saw a glare about a quarter mile away, blinding him for an instant, then stopping altogether. Just when his eyes had refocused, it would flash again, making it hard for him to see what was drawing him to look. It—whatever it was—was pleading with him to look in that direction. He squinted, focusing more acutely.

"Do you see that, Angela?"

"What?"

"That flashing down there," he answered.

"Yes. It's probably just a car mirror or something reflecting the sun."

At least she saw it. He'd thought maybe he was still seeing spots due to his seared appendage. Now the pauses between the flashing became long enough to get a decent look. His attention was drawn to the parking lot of the Dover Mall, which was mostly empty this time of morning.

"I don't think it's anything, Phil."

There was something, all right. Looking over from the four-lane, there appeared some debris in the most strangely familiar configuration. The flashing seemed to be a collection of beer cans or the like, shifting with the wind. Finally, the debris settled, allowing Phil to see the distinct shape of some characters in a very specific formation:

THE INSTANT PHIL had recorded a mental image of it, the wind scattered it into an unrecognizable mess, and the flashing ceased.

"We should probably get to work now, Phil. We're cutting it close. You need to get something on that arm, too."

"Sure," he answered, still focused on the debris. Not knowing what to make of the episode, he got back in the truck, scribbled down the characters in the formation as he saw them, and then headed toward downtown.

"You didn't see that?" he asked.

"What, the flashing? Yes."

"I mean those dots and dashes. This," he said, holding up the napkin he'd scribbled on.

"No. You saw all of that?" she asked, looking concerned. He didn't answer, his mind still churning for meaning in what he saw.

First Collateral Bancorp owned and occupied Dover's lone "skyscraper", a seven-floor building on Loockerman Street, the town's heart of commerce. The bank was around the corner and a couple of blocks down Federal Street from Kent County courthouse and the state capitol building. This location made the First Collateral building the perfect nest for lawyers and lobbyist, who rented space from the bank. They could be seen slithering all about Loockerman Street.

Up the ramp and into the parking building, Phil squeezed the little white truck into a tight spot between a navy mini-van and a dark green BMW convertible with the vanity plate, "NV ME". This display of insecurity on wheels belonged to Russ Curry, a co-worker of Phil's who was a bumbling amalgam of condescension, unfounded vanity, and social clumsiness.

Until recently, Curry had been a credit analyst like Phil. Rumors had circulated that Curry was the boy toy of the aforementioned Charlotte Timpkin, the new Vice President directly supervising the credit analyst group. The flames of this rumor were fanned when Charlotte created a new position for Curry and recommended to the higher-ups that they make him an Assistant Vice President. He was now under Charlotte, providing a buffer between her and the credit analysts.

Charlotte still ran things, and no one really knew how Curry was spending his time. He feigned busy bee behavior by constantly pecking at his computer and walking around the office at a brisk pace with papers in one hand. He also went to the restroom a lot.

Phil hopped out of his truck, made his way around to the other side, and had Angela's door open before she could gather her purse and jacket. The two made their way from the third floor of the garage down to the ground level and entered the bank. Crossing through the lobby, they passed through the open doors of the bank's elevator and punched "3" and "7". Angela was going all the way to the top floor.

When the bell rang, the opening elevator doors revealed the third floor, where Phil Murphy spent his days. Lately, it felt more like a sentence than a career. He lumbered grudgingly across the large open room, lit brightly by abundant floor-to-ceiling windows, found his way to his desk, dropped his portfolio on the carpet, and sank in to his chair with only one thought in mind: coffee.

# CHAPTER FOUR

"MURPHY, WHERE THE HELL IS AUSTIN?" Charlotte barked from her office. It was nearly ten thirty, and Gus Austin, Phil's co-worker and best friend, was nowhere to be seen. Typical. Phil was a little envious of Gus's disregard for, well, everything. Gus's proclivity for folly might have been partially due to a lack of mouths to feed.

"I'm pretty sure he was going over some numbers with the owner at the Stumble On Inn. If not there, maybe Wilson's. Somewhere, I don't know."

That was a big lie. Phil was doing his best to cover for him.

"Not buying that, Murphy," came the terse reply from Charlotte. The sound waves drifting out of her office seemed to lower the temperature in the room each time she spoke.

"Pretty sure, Charlotte," he said, as he eased up out of his chair and went to refill his coffee cup from the machine across the room, temporarily avoiding further discussion on the topic.

Phil and Gus had been best friends since middle school and grew up on the same street in Dover. However, when it was time for high school, Phil's parents had sent him to Delmarva Country Day School, a local private prep school.

This was not because Phil's parents were well-to-do. They weren't.

It was for the opposite reason. Phil was the beneficiary of an outreach program in which Delmarva brought in working class kids on scholarship with the intent of providing diversity.

Curious that the school deemed a WASP like Phil requisite for providing diversity. Only a few such ninth graders were brought in each fall, for a variety of reasons, mostly academic. However, in Phil's case, athletic prowess and extracurricular activities were his ticket.

He was reluctant, but his parents felt they couldn't pass up the opportunity for him to prepare at Delmarva for admission to a prestigious university. Only problem was that Phil underachieved and just muddled through. The lesson learned, for Phil's whole family, was that mediocrity at a high-level prep school still only yields mediocrity in college choices.

On some level, Phil had relished seeing his parents' plan to force him away from his natural high school backfire on them. He was only now realizing that his parents had their best hopes for his future in mind. Pangs of regret for his absence of appreciation of their efforts were becoming more commonplace, especially since his mother had taken ill.

Phil and Gus had remained best friends even while attending different high schools. After graduation, they'd both enrolled locally at the public Delaware Bay College, where they played on the school's baseball team—Gus the tall, lanky lefty first baseman, and Phil the speedy center fielder with a bazooka for an arm.

They also spent their spare time, and too much of what should've been study time, on a tireless safari for coeds. Socialization was part of the college experience, after all. Gus was as loyal as they came, and Phil trusted him completely.

Just as Phil arrived back at his desk from the coffee maker, Charlotte's voice rang out from her office again.

"The long lunches are bad enough, but he'd better start getting here on time in the mornings."

Her voice stung nearly as much as Phil's arm. He'd used an ointment he found in an office first aid kit to dull it a bit.

"I know he's not sleeping in, Charlotte. He's with one of our customers."

At the bank, Phil sat two desks away from Charlotte's office door, the first desk being reserved for her administrative assistant. The credit analysis department housed a dozen analysts, all in a large open room. The setting was antiquated, reminiscent of a mid-twentieth century office, with each analyst pinned between a desk and a credenza. This was Charlotte's brainchild, as she insisted that no cubicle wall would obscure her view of her employees, and their lack of privacy would discourage loafing.

She was now standing in her office door.

"You're a good pal, Murphy, but Austin's walking on thin ice. If you're going to join him on it, you're both going to fall through."

Charlotte was fortyish, and if one didn't know her, she might appear quite attractive. However, to know her was to loathe her. She stood five feet nine, of slender build, but moderately busty. Her hair was so dark that it appeared to be colored. It was usually pulled back by some sort of band or claspy contraption, fully exposing her forehead and cheeks, curving around her face, and almost touching the tops of her shoulders. She wore high cheekbones, pouty lips, and dark brown, narrow eyes, perfect for employing an intimidating glare.

Charlotte basically looked pissed all of the time. And not in the good way that a woman can look more beautiful when she's angry. Hers was a look of irritation; constipation, even. She'd been at the bank for only three months, but had already left a heavy footprint, redesigning the Credit Department office, securing a generous promotion for her right-hand man, and ruling with a firm hand.

She turned from her door and retreated back into her office. Phil picked up his phone so it would stop ringing.

"Credit. Phil Murphy."

"Has she released the hounds yet?" asked the familiar voice of Gus Austin.

"I told her you were going over some numbers with a client, but she wasn't buying it, so think of something before you come in."

"For once in your sad life, you weren't lying. I was doing just what you said, at the Stumble On Inn. Meet me at the Outpost for lunch," Gus said.

Just then, a loud thud came from immediately behind Phil. He turned to find Charlotte had dropped a thick legal-sized envelope on his credenza, causing him to nearly jump out of his seat.

"Get this up to Mr. Adams' office ASAP."

After Charlotte walked away, Phil agreed to meet Gus at the Outpost, a local café, at 11:30. He grabbed Charlotte's envelope and headed toward the elevator, a place where he sometimes hid out, just to get away from his desk. He would occasionally ride it up and down for ten or fifteen minutes just to unwind a little. No one was the wiser, except for the building security office that monitored the elevators with hidden cameras.

He didn't mind running Charlotte's errands to Adams' office. The CEO of First Collateral was seldom in, so it gave him a chance to visit with Angela. Over the course of the nine months she'd been at the bank, she had become a bit of a confidant to Phil after his wife wasn't in the picture. She offered eager ears to whatever Phil had to say.

Upon exiting the elevator on the seventh floor, he opened the door into the hushed lobby of the CEO's office. In his best cowboy twang, he commenced with a bit of goofiness.

"Pardon, little woman, my mule's double parked out front, and I'm plum out of quarters for the meter. Would you barter me a parkin' validation for some jerky? Or maybe a rabbit pelt?"

Phil knew how Angela felt about him. He had genuine affection for her, too, but not in the same way. Although he didn't really have further intentions with her, Phil couldn't help himself when it came to flirting. He did it without even knowing.

"So what brings you here?"

"I done told ya my mule is double parked."

She snickered aloud. Angela was a receptive audience for his cornball shtick. For that reason alone, he probably should have clung to her. But he liked her too much to lead her on.

"Did you get something on that arm?" she asked.

"Yup," he snorted, still in cowpoke mode, displaying the wound to her.

"What's that on it?" From her desk, she pointed toward several brown specks splattered throughout the redness.

"Dunno," he answered. "Varmits. Critters, maybe."

She smiled and said, "Really, Phil, you need to make sure that doesn't get infected."

"Okie doke."

With the delivery of Charlotte's envelope done, Phil headed back down to his desk to get some more work in. In a while, it was time to meet Gus for lunch.

Getting out on the street was good medicine after a morning of financial drudgery. Having made his way down Loockerman Street, he entered the front door of the Outpost where he told the hostess he'd be lunching on the patio. Today was an outdoor day to be sure, with the lunch time sun warming up a mid-spring day quite nicely. Once he hit the patio, his eye caught Gus occupying a table near the sidewalk on Loockerman.

Leaned back in his chair with his trademark cheesy mirrored sunglasses on, Gus appeared genetically predisposed to being a used car salesman. He was definitely a fish out of water in the bank's commercial credit department. Six feet three, lanky, wavy blond hair, and always wearing a big shit-eating grin, Gus lived alone in an apartment a few blocks from Phil's house.

"Where ya been?" Gus jabbed, his usual greeting for Phil, even when he wasn't late. The waitress took their orders and eventually brought their lunch.

"So what's up at the Stumble On Inn?" Phil asked Gus.

"Bars are cash cows. Who knows how much more they're actually takin' in beyond what their books are showin'. But they could still be a lot more profitable if they would just modernize a little bit. Shit, they've got a house band on salary. Salary...," his voice trailed off.

"But that's one of things that makes the place so great," Phil said. "You, of all people, should appreciate that."

Phil was referring to Gus being a performer of sorts at the Stumble

On Inn. It was just a downtown joint on Loockerman that served alcohol, wings, and sandwiches, and did it all in one big open room with an actual three-feet-high stage in the back. The owner employed a house band of four: guitar, bass, piano, and drums, whose main purpose was to serve as a backing band for customers who wanted to perform.

"You know," Gus said, "I'm thinking about getting an agent."

"No shit?"

"Oh, no shit. I've got a guy coming down from South Orange to catch my show before long. I sent him my Christmas album, and he was...intrigued," he finished in a whisper.

"South Orange, New Jersey? That *is* the entertainment hub of Bergin County, isn't it? Or is that Sussex County?" Phil asked.

"You know, you oughta be nice to me now, so I'll remember to let you backstage when I'm playing the Garden," Gus said.

"Yeah, I guess I should," Phil said with a smile.

"So what the hell's wrong with your arm?" Gus asked, with a mouth full of burger. "You know if you'd just wear a rubber, this shit wouldn't happen."

"Something really weird happened this morning," Phil said as he took a bite of his burger, then leaned back in his chair and lazily looked around the outdoor cafe.

After a quarter minute of silence, Gus said, "Well, are you gonna tell me?"

"Heh, I love doin' that to you," Phil said, leaning forward in his seat. "Okay, but you're gonna think I've lost it."

"Oh yeah, you've just *now* lost it." Gus said.

"Angela and I stopped to help this woman with car trouble on DE-1, and..."

"That's not weird," Gus said, interrupting. "You do that all the time, Dudley Do-right. What victim did you save this time?"

"No, that's not what I'm talking about. I burnt the shit out of my arm on her tailpipe. After I went back to my truck, I saw some weird formation in the mall parking lot."

Phil went on to explain the event to Gus, and then showed him what he'd sketched after he had gotten back in his truck.

"Big deal, so you thought you saw some dots or letters or some-thing," Gus said. "They don't *spell* anything. People see crap like that all the time."

"I know that, but this wasn't like a cloud in the shape of a bunny or somethin'. The formation was really clear."

The drone of clinking glasses and chattering silverware was pierced by a smooth, lilting laugh from across the patio. It was a soft bit of a giggle, but still cut through the low rumble of the crowded restaurant.

"Oooh, there's Jill Wheaton," Gus said.

"Where?"

"Over in the middle, with those other people from Trust. "

Jill was a new employee in the bank's Trust Department, where she had started a month or so earlier. She was also the younger sister of Thad Wheaton, a high school classmate of Phil's at Delmarva. Thad was a teammate on most of the high school's sports teams, but they weren't particularly close. Thad went on to play defensive back at Rutgers.

Jill was five years younger, and beautiful. Five feet six, naturally blonde, with big, round, soulful brown eyes, soft features on a full, cheeky face, and a warm, easy smile.

She was Ivy League educated, having just recently returned to Dover with an MBA in hand. Phil never had any interaction with her in his youth, as they never were in the same school at the same time, but they knew of each other. She was known for being kind-hearted. With the April sun glistening on her gently falling golden locks, it was hard for Phil to take his eyes off her.

"Man, would I like to *plow* her," Gus said, snapping Phil out of his fawning daydream.

"You're not worthy," Phil answered.

"Well, that goes without saying," Gus said. "But, nonetheless..."

After lunch, Phil and Gus moseyed back to the office, muddled through the rest of their Thursday, and then headed home. Phil found himself at the babysitter's door right at her six o'clock deadline.

"You're cutting it close, Phil", Stephanie said while glancing at her watch.

"What's life without a little excitement, Stephanie?" She wasn't amused. She never was.

In just a moment, the smiling little guy came bounding out the door onto the porch, where Phil grabbed him and tossed him up into the air, catching him, then carrying him under one arm like a loaf of bread for the walk out to the truck.

"Tell Stephanie goodbye," Phil said, to which the toddler responded by silently waving to her with a big grin. She blew him a kiss.

Willie was a chunky, nearly mute child, with a head of short, dirty-blonde hair. Owner of a hoarse little laugh and heir of his father's blue eyes, the kid hardly ever spoke. Not that anyone would expect a lengthy oration from a three-year-old, but it had concerned Phil enough that he occasionally "tested" him by having him repeat words. He always passed with flying colors.

Seemed he was perfectly capable of talking but must have been born with sense enough to know he had twice as many ears as he did mouths for a reason. Anyway, Phil wasn't about to force the kid to be a chatterbox, especially when he seemed to be a perfectly happy little guy.

"Let's go find out what Otis did today," Phil said to Willie as he fastened him into his car seat.

Phil, Willie, and Otis were tenants in a little two-bedroom house on McHenry Street, with a covered porch that extended across the entirety of the front elevation. The back yard had two nice maple trees, one in each of the back corners, all enclosed by a six-foot-high wooden privacy fence. Otis could come and go at will into the back yard via a dog door Phil had installed.

As Phil exited the truck, his snooty next-door neighbor, Stanley, called out, "Phil, I think Otis did his business in my yard again this morning."

"Couldn't have been him, Stanley. I didn't let him out front this morning. Besides, Otis only does a tooskie in our back yard, inside of the fence. It's his way of marking what's his, you know?"

"Well, there's no other dog around here his size, capable of leaving that big of a dropping."

Stanley was constantly finding something to whine about. If it wasn't Otis's excretory manifestations, it was autumn leaves blowing from Phil's trees into his yard. He had a gripe for every season.

Phil had always suspected Stanley, in his mid-thirties, was merely the mouthpiece for his wife, Donna, who was a fussbudget supreme and constantly on Stanley's back about everything. Stanley wasn't in possession of the requisite spine to stand up to her.

"Your yard's looking nice and green, Stan. What's your secret?" Phil tried not to grin.

"I don't know, just keeping it neat is the key. I hate mowing, but Donna likes it short."

"She'd have to, wouldn't she?" Phil asked.

"What?"

"Nothing."

When Phil and Willie mounted the porch and opened the front door, the Murphys were greeted by Otis, his tail beating against the little table by the door, coming dangerously close to taking out a picture frame sitting upon it. Phil and Otis were cut from the same cloth, physically sturdy, underachievers, tough-minded and soft-hearted at the same time. Phil considered Otis his first-born.

After a plate of spaghetti and a romp with boy and dog in the back yard, it was bath time for the Willie. Later in the evening, as Willie and Otis played with a toy truck on the carpet, Phil lazily plucked his guitar on the couch while the Phillies game played on a muted television. Darkness had fallen on McHenry Street.

Phil hopped off the couch and into the kitchen for a can of tuna, a nightly ritual he and Otis had come to enjoy. Upon his return to the small living room, he noticed Otis was no longer accompanying Willie in the floor.

On the other end of the room stood Otis, motionless, staring down the hallway. Phil couldn't see the other end of the hall from his position near the kitchen.

A motionless Otis was not an uncommon sight. However, he was usually motionless in the way a beached whale or road kill is motionless. This was different. He was fixated, staring intently on something down the dark hallway.

"What is it, buddy?"

Otis answered his owner with a low growl, never shifting his eyes away from their focal point down the hall. As Phil slowly moved around Willie, he began to see a soft glow coming from the shadowy hallway. By the time he made his way over to Otis's side, he could see a flickering light escaping his partially open bedroom door at the end of the hall.

He'd left no light on in his room. The television hadn't been on, either. The only sound to be heard was Otis's baritone warning that something wasn't right.

Carefully, Phil crept down the dim corridor toward the light, with Otis following closely. Now standing outside the portal to the bedroom, he raised his left hand, placed it on the door, and slowly pushed it open.

On the other side of the room, he found the television on, but oddly the cable box on top of it was dark, with no channel number displayed. The screen showed what appeared to be the inside of someone's garage. The view was through the eyes of an unseen person, surveying the room. There was no face on the screen, only what this person was seeing.

The view then looked downward, and a pair of bloodied, gloved hands came into frame, working feverishly tying the top of a garbage bag closed. There was no audio, only silence. The right hand then lifted the bag, and the view raised back up and began to move toward a doorway. The left hand entered the screen, turned the doorknob, and pulled the door open.

Through the door went the covert trash hauler, into a darkened back yard, all the while the view darting in every direction, scouting the back yard as if trying to stay out of sight. The pace was hastened as the owner of the perspective zeroed in on its target: two plastic garbage containers up against the house. Once there, the gloved hands entered the screen again as lefty removed the lid and righty tossed the bag inside, rocking the container back and forth. The lid was then reattached.

With that, the television screen went black. Phil hurriedly flipped on the overhead light switch, did a quick search of the room. Closet, nothing. Under the bed, nothing. The lone window in his bedroom was still closed and locked. With a drum corps pounding in his chest, he quickly turned out the light, fetched Willie from the living room floor, and locked the front and back doors.

After their nighttime routine, Phil sat on Willie's bed with his back against the headboard, reading a story to his son, with Otis at their feet. Phil would just camp here for the night. Before long, all three Murphys were sawing logs.

# CHAPTER FIVE

Every other Thursday for the past year, Phil and Willie put themselves in the little white truck and drove three and a half hours down the coast to the Norfolk Federal Detention Center to visit Willie's mother. Odd, Phil thought, that Thursdays were the only day of visitation the facility allowed. Maybe it was part of an inmate's punishment to make it inconvenient for their families to see them. Maybe they figured the fewer the visitors, the less chance of a hacksaw blade being smuggled in by way of a Trojan horse cake. Whatever the reason, today was such a Thursday and as much as Phil loved a road trip, he had grown to only tolerate these visits. He thoroughly enjoyed the time together with his son, but dreaded the time having to see his ex. Phil felt a moral obligation, though, to keep Willie in contact with his mother. He would've taken him to see her more often, but these trips had drained his accumulation of vacation days at work, and he couldn't afford to take unpaid days off.

Out of Dover, they took US 13 the entire way, passing through the length of the Delmarva Peninsula. The trip south culminated with a dramatic crossing of open water by way of the Chesapeake Bay Bridge-Tunnel from the southern tip of the Delmarva Peninsula to the mainland of Virginia. It was a twenty-three-mile stretch cutting through the bay and the ocean, comprised of causeways, bridges, four small manmade islands, and two one-mile tunnels that dove down beneath the choppy Atlantic.

Phil and Willie had two traditional stops they enjoyed. On the way down, they always made a point to pull into the mom-and-pop convenience store, Peanut's Pantry, in Nassawadox, Maryland, to have a Dr. Pepper and some beef jerky. The other stop in their routine was at a little restaurant called The Sandpiper on one of the causeway's manmade islands. The Murphys almost always got their evening meal there on the way back from their visit.

Having left the house at 10:30 AM, and visiting hours being from 3:00 PM to 5:00 PM, they could enjoy a leisurely drive down Route 13. Phil, usually a bit of lead foot, just set the little truck's cruise control to the speed limit and eased it southward, shoving in his "Spanish For Dummies" CD to eat up a little time.

About two hours in, they were in the parking lot of Peanut's Pantry, sitting on the hood of the truck watching the cars pass while they slurped on a Dr. Pepper and gnawed at their beef jerky. Willie always tended to wear a good bit of what he tried to consume, so Phil always made sure to bring an extra shirt for him.

"Buster, do you think we need something new to drive, or should we hang on to the old truck?" Phil asked Willie as the whine of the cars approached on Route 13, then faded in to the distance after they had passed.

"Truck," the three-year-old answered.

"Smart man. Truck it is."

Peanut's was a good place to reinforce Willie's potty training, a process the single dad had been forced to launch by himself over the last six months. So, Phil lifted the boy off the hood of the truck, carried him in his left arm—his right arm still sensitive from the burn—and they headed for the restroom. After a successful number one, they were back on the road and navigating the mesmerizing series of causeways and tunnels. The tunnels were particularly entrancing, illuminated with a seemingly endless string of street lights attached to the walls.

Upon reaching the prison, Phil and Willie made their way on foot from the parking lot to the visitor's lobby. Norfolk Federal was a minimum-security facility, housing mostly white-collar criminals.

After an emptying of pockets and a stroll through the metal detector, Phil and Willie were guided to an outdoor green area, similar to a small park, about fifty yards square, surrounded on three sides by a fifteen-foot-high chain-link fence that separated the visiting area from the parking lot. The fourth side was the prison building itself, from which Phil and Willie had come.

A guard guided them to a picnic table and asked them to wait there. Thursday's were the only day for visiting, so there were two dozen other people milling about the grassy area, with children on the playground equipment. When weather didn't permit, there was a much more dreary and restrictive visiting area inside. On rainy or particularly cold days, the two-hour indoor visits passed like eight hours of a German documentary subtitled in Polish.

Within thirty seconds, a heavy metal door across the way opened. Through it walked Willie's mother and Phil's ex-wife, Belinda. Escorted by a guard, she was adorned in jeans and a tee shirt, over which she wore a standard-issue light blue smock, the shoulders of which were tickled by her dark brown hair. Phil was thankful that Willie didn't have to endure seeing his mother cuffed, shackled, or through a thick pane of glass, as would most likely be the scene at a more secure prison.

When she was fifty feet away, without a word, Belinda dropped to one knee and held out her arms with a big smile. On cue, Willie leapt from the picnic table seat and ran into his mother's embrace. As deceitful and misleading as she had been prior to the divorce, Phil still got a warm feeling when he witnessed Willie nuzzled in his mother's bosom. Whatever wrongs Belinda had committed, Phil knew that she genuinely loved and cared for Willie. But with that said, her actions had shown that she couldn't be a reliable mother.

She picked Willie up, then rose from her kneeling position and walked toward the table with Willie's arms wrapped around her slender neck. Belinda was tall, just a few inches shorter than Phil, and kept a rather elegant look about her, even in her bland prison-issue smock. Her face was angular, with high cheekbones and a straight nose.

The guard faded into the background and assumed a position near the fence, surveying the yard.

"Hello, Phil," Belinda said quietly as she sat down, placing Willie beside her on the picnic table bench.

"Hi, Belinda," Phil replied. Their tone confirmed the fact that this meeting was not for themselves, but only for Willie.

"Thanks for bringing him."

"He needs to see his mom," Phil said.

"It'll be nice when I'm out of here."

"That *will* be good," Phil said, adding, "How much longer?"

"I have a parole hearing in six months. Things have gone about as well as possible in here during this last year, so there should be no problem getting released then."

"I hope so, Belinda."

"You know," she said, "they're piloting a new program here for only the most model of inmates. For mothers who have small children, they're letting them come here and spend a couple of days."

"Their kids?" Phil asked, trying to mask his alarm.

"Yeah. They have special, homelike quarters set up that we can use. Willie could come and stay up to three days and nights with me in our own little apartment."

"Inside the prison? Willie would stay *inside* the prison?"

"Yes," she answered, "but he wouldn't be exposed to any other inmates."

"Wow, that's a lot to take in," Phil said. "Why would they go to all of the trouble?"

"To encourage good behavior. It's a reward," Belinda said. "I've already qualified, so he could stay right now, if you gave the okay."

Belinda could really sound sweet when she wanted something.

"Well, I didn't bring any of his clothes or anything, Belinda," Phil said, trying not to sound too relieved.

"I guess that's true," she said.

"Maybe some other time, though," he said.

"Just remember he can come anytime, and there's no notice required," Belinda said. "Very few of us have qualified, so you can basically show up unannounced and drop him off."

Phil said nothing.

"Okay?" Belinda said, trying to wring a response out of Phil.

"Okay," he answered.

A lull in the conversation ensued. Topics were scarce. There was one more thing she wanted to talk about, though.

"You know," she said, "having all of this time to think has really changed me, Phil. I honestly believe that we could be a real family again someday."

"We've been over all that before, Belinda. Too much has gone wrong," he said. "We aren't the same people we were, neither one of us."

The *wrong* Phil was referring to was the events that led to Belinda's incarceration. While working as a cashier at the local greyhound dog racetrack, she developed a gambling addiction. She had found a race-track patron who funded her bets, enabling her addiction, and she accumulated a large debt with him.

The final nail in the coffin that contained their corpse of a marriage was Belinda getting too cozy with the man who carried her debt, then sleeping with him in the hopes he'd forgive it. He didn't, so she stole to repay it, skimming cash out of her cashier's drawer each evening until she was eventually found out.

Phil was completely blind-sided by all of it. He thought he and Belinda were a team for the long haul. While she constantly pressured him to be more ambitious at the bank, he didn't take it as the warning sign he should have. Looking back, Phil could now see she was right about his lack of enthusiasm toward his career. Though they were very young and just starting out, nothing seemed good enough for her, including their little rented house on McHenry Street. After she was arrested, Belinda blamed Phil for it all, saying that he'd been a poor provider for their family. Even though it felt like a dagger in the back to Phil, on some level he felt she was right, and he wondered what he could have done differently. Maybe he *could* have put forth more effort to be a better provider.

Phil could only imagine that her motivation for wooing him now was financial. As a time-serving felon, she probably knew gaining decent employment after she got out would be a tall order.

"I hope you'll reconsider, Phil," she said. With Phil rebuffing her niceties, she took a more direct approach. "That may be the only way you'll get to live with Willie once I get out of here. Why make things hard?"

Even though her words were venomous, she kept the tone pleasant, so as not to upset Willie. Although she'd never been this direct before, Phil had seen this coming for a while.

"Just get on with your time with Willie," Phil said coldly.

As she got up from the table and helped Willie off the bench, she said, "Just think about it. There's no hurry." Then mother and son turned and walked, hand in hand, toward a swing set across the yard.

Phil knew he would have his hands full when Belinda got out of prison. Even though she was a convicted felon, she had been a model prisoner and was preparing to present herself to the family court judge as a reformed woman, now even more capable a mother than before because of her new perspective on life. One thing that she wouldn't have to pretend about was her love for Willie. Phil knew that was real and would shine through at the hearing.

As he routinely did, Phil had brought some reading material with him to pass the time while Willie spent the remainder of the two hours with his mother. Today's selection: the printed guide for his Spanish For Dummies CD. At the conclusion of the visit, they said their good-byes and parted ways.

Two fender-benders made for slow going on the way out of Norfolk. It was nearly six forty-five by the time the Murphys made it through the first tunnel of Chesapeake Bay and into the open arms of the Sandpiper Restaurant. Father and son enjoyed a relaxing, but slowly served, dinner while they sat in a booth at a heavy, rough-hewn dark wooden table next to a window overlooking Chesapeake Bay. The Sandpiper was Phil's favorite kind of eatery: very casual, with inexpensive fresh seafood. He had indoctrinated Willie early about the joys of seafood, and the two put it away heartily.

After re-entering the little truck, Phil noted the time displayed on the radio to be 8:18 PM, and being in the eastern part of the eastern time zone, darkness had fallen on this late April evening. He was full and relaxed. Soon after they began their voyage home, Phil found his co-pilot to be fast asleep in his car seat. Radio pickins were slim, but he eventually found an AM sports talk station, then settled in for the remaining three-hour drive home.

The combination of a filled belly, weak-signaled radio talk show, and a day of driving were causing Phil to glaze over. After several miles over the causeway, the little white truck approached the entrance to the second and final mile-long underwater tunnel. The sight of the roadway in front of them disappearing down into the water was an eerie spectacle, particularly at night.

As the little truck entered the tunnel and began its descent, the radio signal faded to static. The series of lights on each side of the tunnel walls made for a mesmerizing experience, as one after one, they passed in rapid succession. The enclosed tube, ever declining, entrapped the drone of the tires on the pavement, making the sound all-consuming, particularly in a cheap little truck like Phil's.

Full, comfortable, tired, and bored, Phil was quickly becoming the subject of the hypnotic effect of his surroundings. Without knowing it, and with eyes still open, his mind began to drift. The series of fast-passing tunnel lights blurred into two solid lasers, not unlike airport runway lights converging into a point on the horizon. The roar of the tires saturated his head.

But then, an out-of-place sound caught his ear—the soft laughter of a woman. Looking to his left, he found not the interior of the tunnel out of his truck window, but the graceful contour of a beautiful brunette woman sitting next to him in the middle row of a small plane—a six-seater, accelerating down a runway at the cusp of darkness. Another young woman sat alone behind them in the back row, while a male pilot and an elegant, thirty-something blonde woman occupied the front two seats of the plane. What was happening? This felt too real to be a dream.

Just as Phil had envisioned moments earlier, the runway lights became a blur as the small, single-engine craft neared the end of the runway, then lifted smoothly upward into a warm night sky. The young woman beside him reached over to gently squeeze his hand as she continued to look straight ahead.

Phil's mind was a swirl. Where was Willie? Where was the little white truck? He knew none of these people, but oddly, they felt familiar, particularly the pilot. He was not dressed in any sort of official flight suit—only a headset, tan khakis, and a light blue dress shirt, with no tie. This seemed to be a personal trip, with this perhaps being the pilot's own plane.

In a glance to his right, he found his reflection in the window glass. To compound his confusion, the reflection was not of the Phil Murphy he'd watched develop for almost thirty years, but of an entirely different man.

What he saw in the window, backlit by the soft lighting of the lush cabin's interior, was a classically handsome man, perhaps in his mid-thirties, with a thick head of neatly trimmed dark brown hair, a linear nose, high cheekbones, and dark eyes.

Even his clothing was foreign to him, as he found himself adorned in an expensive navy-blue business suit with a starched white shirt, with jacket removed and crimson silk tie loosened. While he had no idea why or how he had gotten into this situation, he felt strangely at home.

Suddenly, the words, "Who's going to be up there this weekend?" escaped his mouth, Phil having no control over them, and not recognizing the New England flavor of his own words.

"Mom and Dad. Some of the cousins. Just everyone you'd expect at a wedding," the pilot answered, his words reflecting the same regional dialect as Phil's.

Phil turned to the beautiful brunette to his left, looked into her deep green eyes, and said, "Hope it's not too crowded. We'll need some privacy." Leaning in, he planted a short but passionate kiss on her full lips.

It was at this moment that Phil realized he wasn't calling the shots here. Phil was inside of this man's body, feeling, hearing, and seeing everything he was experiencing, with no control over what was happening. He was both a participant and a spectator.

"Yes, Davis, you'll have privacy. Nobody wants to see your vulgar public displays of affection," the pilot said with a laugh.

Realizing something bizarre was afoot, and wanting desperately to learn the whys and hows of his situation, Phil tried his best to soak in everything he could. Although he was experiencing all of Davis's senses, he could only see what Davis was looking at. Fortunately, he was still able to hear everything.

Davis had nestled into the soft, tanned leather of his seat, facing forward, but with his head turned toward the window. The young woman beside him reached up with her right hand to gently massage the back of his neck as he peered out over the tremendous expanse of urban sprawl. In the background, miles away, was the Manhattan skyline, complete with the Empire State Building and World Trade Center Towers. In his hand, he discovered a short, heavy glass, a quarter full with a dark liquor, and it was being raised toward his mouth. His lips tingled as it passed through, resting on his tongue momentarily before sliding down his throat. Single malt scotch. Top drawer quality.

There was a lot to learn. All he knew so far was, evidently, his name was Davis, he wore expensive suits, lived or worked in or near Manhattan, and jetted around with the beautiful people. And these women were *beautiful*. Drop-dead, first-class beautiful. Long and leggy. They even smelled good. Really good. Phil had never had reason to think much about perfume, and had never been in such close proximity to people of this social status. At least now, though, he knew the fragrance of expensive perfume. Soft, understated, but tantalizingly sweet.

While the women on board were pleasing to the senses, he felt no particular connection with them. However, the pilot was a different matter. Although he'd only seen the back of his head, with an occasional flicker of a profile, he somehow felt a strong kinship to him.

With the passing of time, light, sporadic fragments of conversation ensued among the occupants. There was very limited use of names, and they weren't a particularly talkative group. The only name he'd learned was that of the brunette beside him. Her name was Kristen Minnows.

There was hardly any back-and-forth between the pilot and the blonde woman seated next to him, although they appeared to be a couple. From the use of the word "Daddy" between the blonde woman and the similarly aged young woman in the very back, they seemed to be sisters.

A sneeze popped out from the rear of the cabin. Then another.

"Here, Lauren," the blonde woman in the front said, holding out a silk handkerchief toward the back of the cabin for Davis to relay to the woman in the back. As he was passing the hanky back, he paused to look at its monogram, *cKb*.

Complete darkness had fallen and the five travelers ventured northward, if the compass could be trusted. From his seat just behind the blonde woman, Davis had full view of the cockpit controls. He must have had an interest in aviation, as he spent a good deal of time looking at the plane's dashboard. This was both a blessing and a curse for Phil, who was picking up useful information, but at the same time, being a nervous flyer himself, stressed about seeing the fluctuations on the dials and meters.

As the voyage progressed, the group became quiet. About the only conversation heard was the pilot talking to air traffic controllers, complaining of his radio settings, particularly not being able to get the right frequency for Martha's Vineyard. Finally, at least some clue about where they were headed, Phil thought.

Along the way, Davis had consumed scotch sufficient to make him very relaxed. He had spent a good bit of time leaning slightly forward, peering at the cockpit, but now he was leaning back in his soft seat, his head turned toward the window. His eyelids growing heavy, they slowly began to close.

From Phil's perspective, his view was like a lone actor on a stage with the curtain lowering down in front of him. He felt the relaxation that the scotch had induced upon Davis's central nervous system, yet Phil's mind was still sharp. Davis was going to sleep, and while Phil could no longer see his surroundings, only the darkness behind Davis's eyelids, he could still hear everything.

"Piper 9253, come in," a female voice intruded over the cockpit speaker. "This is Providence International. We're going to have to reroute you, due to temporary flight restrictions in this area."

An eerie chill crept in to Phil's mind upon hearing the voice on the speaker.

"Copy that, Providence. What's the issue?" the pilot asked.

"We've got Venus in the immediate vicinity doing some touch and goes."

This voice was somehow sickeningly familiar to Phil.

"Criminy, you mean Air Force One is doing practice landings?" asked the pilot.

"Yes, Piper 9253, sans the commander in chief, and we've had to restrict air space in a fifty-mile radius around Providence to only those crafts landing or departing this airport. This happens occasionally. Our apologies. What's your destination?"

"Martha's Vineyard. I've been following the lights of the coastline."

"Well," said the controller, "I've got you currently at twenty miles due south of our fifty-mile boundary. We're going to have to reroute you either inland, due west, or you can just veer northeast over the Atlantic, pretty much directly to Martha's Vineyard. It's only a short distance over the water."

"Okay, Providence, rerouting on a northeast course immediately."

After the exchange with the controller, the blonde woman asked the pilot, "Johnny, is this going to delay us?"

"No, dear," he answered, "it's actually going to make it a shorter flight."

"Why didn't we go this way to start with?" she asked.

"It was a little easier to just follow the lights of the coastline, but this will give me a chance to work on my instrument-only piloting."

"Is that safe?"

"Absolutely, and it's only about fourteen miles across the water. We'll be there before you know it."

Phil had listened intently to everything said and wanted with every fiber of his being to tell the pilot not to trust the voice on the radio. While he didn't know exactly why, the pilot needed to ignore the instructions and stay with his initial, conservative flight plan.

As the little plane turned northeast and ventured out over the Atlantic Ocean, Johnny the Pilot noticed a haze forming over the water. The darkness was manageable, but the haze made matters more difficult. He was losing altitude. His altimeter didn't show it, but he could feel the pressure in his ears building. To make things worse, now the altimeter had begun to jump around, so he couldn't be sure how far above the water he was flying.

Becoming disoriented in the haze and darkness, but not wanting to upset the passengers, the pilot said nothing. He picked up his radio handset and spoke in a calm and poised voice that belied his anxiety.

"Providence, am I still on your radar?"

"Yes, Piper 9253," the woman's voice answered.

"What's my altitude? There's a heavy haze over the water, my altimeter is acting up, and it feels like I'm losing altitude pretty quickly," the pilot said.

"I've got you at 4,500 feet, Piper 9253. You've dipped down from about 6,000, but you're safely above the water."

"Okay, Providence, I'm going to go ahead and...."

Suddenly, Phil's eardrums felt as though they'd exploded, and Davis's eyes opened to find spinning chaos inside the cabin as the little plane hit the dark Atlantic, sending it cartwheeling on the water's surface wing over wing. The spinning stopped with everyone hanging upside down, water gushing into the fractured, wingless cabin, which was being quickly swallowed up by the rocking waves of the ocean.

As the craft drifted downward, through Davis's eyes, Phil saw the horror of Kristen frantically, fruitlessly struggling to free herself, while the other occupants sat motionless. Phil felt nothing from his waist down, which meant Davis felt the same. The plane quickly struck the ocean's bottom, jarring his entire seat loose from the cabin floor, its back falling all the way off. Just like the flight attendants on commercial airlines always say, Davis's seat cushion broke away and became a flotation device. Untethered by the seatbelt, he drifted upward toward the fracture in the hull.

When he reached the opening, his armpit caught its edge, suspending him upside down to view the gruesome scene below him. Though in the darkness, he was still close enough to see that Kristen's efforts had ceased now, and she, too, became still, her limbs no longer moving at her own will, but at that of the currents on the ocean floor.

It can take a while to die, Phil was learning. Though Davis couldn't move his legs—most likely due to spinal cord damage—and he hadn't taken a breath in nearly sixty seconds, his heart was still beating, albeit very slowly.

The current shifted ever so slightly, freeing his armpit from the jagged edge of the breached hull, and releasing him from the doomed craft. He began a slow drift upward, clinging to the seat cushion as it ascended toward the surface. Too little, too late, it appeared.

His eyes were still open, but the sight of the wreckage on the ocean floor quickly disappeared in the darkness. The curtain was lowering again. The time between heartbeats grew longer. Longer, still. Then darkness. The curtain had fallen.

Suddenly, there was a flash of white light, and after his eyes adjusted, Phil could see again. He found himself in his little white truck, dripping with sweat, parked in his own driveway on McHenry Street. Willie was sleeping soundly in his car seat next to him. The radio clock read 11:22 PM.

His dehydrated calves twitching, Phil sat motionless, trying to gather himself, wondering how he had made it safely home. He knew the voice on the speaker in the plane, and it did not belong to an air traffic controller. It was a sinful voice. Perhaps being in the darkness of Davis's closed eyes had heightened his auditory awareness. He didn't know why or how, but what he did know was that the voice on the speaker, the voice that drove the little plane and the five lives within it smashing into the Atlantic, belonged to Charlotte.

# CHAPTER SIX

THE NEXT MORNING, Phil muddled through his and Willie's routine, then dragged himself into the office. He'd felt like he'd been squashed flatter than a man hole cover; stiff, sore, and still exhausted, even though he'd gotten the best night of sleep he'd had in a while. After getting Willie to sleep the night before, he'd managed to make it to his bed, get his shoes off, then crash, fully clothed, until morning. When he woke up, he was troubled to learn that he hadn't just dreamed the plane crash episode on the way home from the prison.

But today was Friday, and his scorched arm was a little less like a hanging salami than it had been the day before. Even though his healing arm could probably use the air, he thought he'd keep his sleeves cuffed today, rather than rolled up, so as not to invite gawkers.

When he got to work, Phil found he had received a message on his computer from the bank's bookkeeping department, announcing that he had overdrawn his checking account—again. That would be bad news to anyone but was particularly unwelcome to Phil. Employees of First Collateral were required to keep a checking account at the bank, not only for loyalty purposes, but mainly for direct deposit of their pay.

Phil was no stranger to an overdraft notice. A few months earlier, he had made bidding them adieu his number one resolution for the new year of 2000. He was fairly thrifty but not enough so, as he had yet to completely adopt the spending habits of a meagerly paid sole provider. Although he held a bachelor's degree in Finance, banking just wasn't a high-paying industry for the majority of those employed in it.

While Belinda's income was now gone, some credit card debt she'd kept hidden from Phil was not. Compounding his troubles was his absent mind. Specifically, he just couldn't seem to keep track of how he used his debit card, and it was now getting him in hot water at the bank. Before he had time to fret, his attention was drawn to Russ Curry, who was standing just outside of Charlotte's office door.

"Murphy, Charlotte and I need to speak with you."

Curry wasn't a bad-looking fellow, but blandness was his dominant physical feature. He wore a long face, with all of its components lacking any prominence. The possible exception was a small, vanishing jaw that produced a chin nearly blending into his neck. Six-feet three, gangly, and in his late twenties, he just seemed to try too hard: Cliché sports car; top-of-the-line suits; the latest haircut; designer eyeglasses. All of it was just mascara on a monkey.

He could afford it all because he was the lone heir of a significant estate left to him by his parents, who had been killed in a car wreck a few years back. No siblings, no friends, and he didn't care. Tough to feel sorry for a guy who alienated everyone he encountered—Curry was excruciatingly adept at simultaneously offending, boring, and humiliating others and himself, and not having any clue he was doing it.

He had been off to a slow start at the bank until Charlotte arrived. Not bad at crunching numbers, but there was an amber alert on his people skills. He was now supervising the same group of people whom he had just been working alongside. Usually that's a recipe for disaster because most find it difficult to supervise their former friends. No such problem in this case, as Curry didn't consider anyone at the bank to be his friend — and he was correct.

"Come on, Murphy," Curry said, still perched outside of Char-lotte's door.

Phil knew something was coming — something bad. He wearily

pushed up on the arms of his chair, raising himself up to begin the death march toward Charlotte's office. As he put one foot in front of the other, he lamented spending what he probably shouldn't have and not keeping track of it. He reached the office door, paused to peer in, and found Charlotte behind her desk. After Phil passed through to threshold, Curry followed, and moved swiftly to a flanking position, standing beside her chair. Phil took a seat in one of the two chairs in front of her desk.

"This is a formal reprimand, Phil," Charlotte said. "Overdrawing your checking account can't be tolerated, especially by someone whose job it is to review the financial records of our customers. Frankly, it's an embarrassment to my department." Curry nodded, silently showing his agreement with Charlotte. Upon first hearing her voice, Phil felt a literal chill, confirmation that it was indeed Charlotte's voice on the small plane's radio the night before.

"And you've been slacking," she added. "You're behind on your reporting. You're late getting to work half the time, and you're never at your desk."

"Never," Curry parroted, attempting to add emphasis and create some real purpose for himself in the conversation.

"Do you even want to be working here?" Charlotte asked him.

"You're over-blowing all of this," Phil said. "My overdrafts have nothing to do with the quality of my work. You know my situation. I'm down to one income now. I'm not late that often, and no one in this office has better relationships with our clients than I do."

"Well, all I can say is if you want to stay here, you'd better pick up the pace."

"Noted," Phil said in a disgusted tone. He raised himself from his seat and trudged out to his desk.

As he fell back into his duties, the rest of the work day passed without episode. Lunch with Gus and Angela. He was itching to tell Gus about the weirdness of his drive home from Norfolk the night before but thought better of mentioning such lunacy in front of Angela. After lunch there was an afternoon treat provided by Geneva, a fellow analyst in the department.

Of particular amusement to Phil and Gus was a ritual in which Geneva — who was a tad masculine and a bit cantankerous — was an unknowing participant. Like many in the office, she would occasionally refill her cup at the water cooler. The spigot for the cooler was around waist-high, and Geneva, who sometimes complained mild back pain, would stand erect in front of the cooler while holding the cup in one hand, and operating the spigot with the other. From their view directly behind her, it looked exactly to Phil and Gus as if she were standing in front of a urinal, relieving herself.

Add to that the sound of the water streaming into her cup and her burly appearance, and the spectacle became a wonderful tickler of their adolescent funny bones.

"Here's to cheap entertainment," Gus said.

"Yep."

When five o'clock rolled around, Phil and Gus were winding down, looking forward to a Friday night. Not sure exactly what he would be doing, Phil figured he and Willie would spend a laidback evening at his sister's house. Kara had two kids of her own; a boy about Willie's age and a girl, two years older. She and her husband, Gary, had been a great help to Phil since he had become a single father.

Just then, the elevator doors opened, and Jill Wheaton entered the room like a dewy, warm breeze drifting in off the sea. Carrying a folder in one hand, she was crossing the credit department floor, heading toward the Trust Department on the opposite side of the building.

Jill and Phil had exchanged glances on a couple of occasions during the last month but had yet to speak. On this occasion, however, she was about to walk right past his desk.

First came eye contact. Then mutual smiles. As she got closer to his desk, he ventured a "Hello," to which she answered with a soft, "Hi." Sadly, in the scope of the last twelve months, this exchange was the new pinnacle of Phil's love life.

Out of the periphery of Phil's vision came a shadow, followed by a loud thud, as Charlotte dropped a box of client financial records on Phil's desk.

"Here you go, Murphy. If I were about to lose my job, I don't think I'd be going home just yet."

Phil's embarrassment was thick in the air. Jill kept walking on past his desk, but Phil was certain she could still hear the conversation. Phil mumbled lowly to Charlotte that he had a deadline to pick up Willie at the sitter's. But Charlotte, who had seen Jill coming and timed her interruption intentionally, spoke even louder so Jill would hear her.

"Priorities, Phil. Where does your paycheck come from?"

Jill didn't look back, denying Charlotte any satisfaction.

Charlotte slipped back into her hole, and Phil leaned back in his chair. Holding in what he wanted to say was eating him alive. Gus, who had been on the phone during the episode, saw the whole thing.

"Whaddya gonna do?" Gus asked after hanging up the phone.

"I'll call Kara, I guess. Hopefully she can go get Willie."

"If she can't, I will," Gus offered.

"Thanks."

So, Phil called his sister and explained his predicament. She was more than happy to pick up the little guy.

"Why don't I just keep him here tonight?" Kara asked. "You can come and get him tomorrow. He could use a sleepover with his cousins, and it sounds like you could use a Friday night out."

"You're the best, you know," Phil said.

"Always glad to be able to help my little brother," she said, and Phil knew she meant it.

Upon hanging up, and the office mostly empty, Phil took the opportunity to fill Gus in on his drive back from the prison and the plane crash experience. Phil was appreciative of the fact that he could divulge such a psychotic-sounding story to his best friend without fear of judgment or humiliation. Gus always seemed to take whatever Phil told him as being true. Just as they finished that discussion, they saw Charlotte exit her office with coat over arm and purse in hand, leaving for the day.

"Her leaving a room is like a fart fading away," Gus said. "Don't worry. I'll stay here a while and help you knock some of this work out. When you get done, come over to the Stumble and witness my artistry.

I've got some new material I'm trying out. Angela's going to be there with some friends, too. We'll blow off some steam."

After a productive ninety minutes, the two took a breather.

"So, do conjugal visits really exist?" asked Gus, his one-track mind evident.

"Couldn't tell ya. Not in the market for one. All she is to me now is Willie's mom."

"You don't want any of that now, anyway," Gus said. "I'd imagine after Willie came barrellin' through, it's probably like tossin' a tuna into a tunnel."

"Oh, yeah," Phil said, tongue in cheek, "Once that damage is done, it's time for an entirely new woman. Dipshit, haven't you ever done it with a woman who's had a baby? It's all good."

"Only one, but she'd had a C-section," Gus said. "And they say *dog* is man's best friend. It's really an ass-first baby."

"I don't think we'll ever see that saying on a coffee mug," Phil said. "What about Janet Quinn? Didn't you get with her? I heard being with her was like doin' it with a pickle jar."

"Yes—I did get with her. No—she has no baby. And yes—pickle jar to everybody else. Who do you think made her that way?" Gus asked as he leaned too far back in his chair, causing the wheels to flip out from under him, spilling him over backwards onto the floor.

"Smooth." Phil said.

"Don't worry about me, dill hole," Gus said, picking himself up off the floor. "We need to get you laid. Maybe Angela will invite you to her house for a dip in her Jacuzzi."

"Nah, I'm not ready for that yet," Phil said. "Speaking of that, you still wearin' a rubber every time you get in a hot tub?"

"Hell, yes. I'm not lettin' any of that microscopic stuff crawl up into my junk," Gus said. "Plus, I'm always ready for action that way."

They eventually returned to their work, and an hour later, Gus parted so he could prepare for his show at the Stumble. Another hour and a half went by and Phil had hammered out the last of the work that Charlotte had dropped on him.

He leaned back in his chair, reached for the ceiling, stretched out the tight muscles in his back and arms, and wearily lifted himself from his seat and headed toward the stairwell door. Although the elevator was operating, the bank's lobby doors were locked at this hour of the evening, so he'd need to take the side exit.

He lumbered down the three flights of stairs and leaned on the heavy metal door that exited into the alley beside of the bank. Darkness had just beset downtown Dover, as Phil made his way up the alley toward Loockerman Street for his walk to the Stumble On Inn.

An extended day of mind-numbing financial work had Phil's mind in a bit of a haze. Fifty feet before reaching Loockerman, he paused in the lonely alley to look at his reflection in the dark window of a closed store.

As he loosened his tie and slipped it off over his head, he drew in a deep breath, then let it bleed out slowly. Blankly, he stared into the reflection of his own tired eyes. As he did, everything around him seemed to darken, with only his reflection in focus. He could feel his senses dulling.

Inside of his head, he began to hear the low, muffled rumble of what sounded like a cheering crowd. In the window's reflection, his face began to fade, slowly fusing into the darkness that surrounded it. His eyes were open, but they only found the dim windowpane reflecting the soft glow of a distant street light.

A warmth came over him, completely encapsulating him from head to toe, as if he were submerged in an emollient bath. An ever-so-mild vibration massaged his body and comforted him, the way the gentle jostling of a car ride soothes an infant. Complete relaxation and safety surrounded him.

Unable to see anything now, and with the muffled crowd noise still providing the soundtrack, he now began to hear the muted words of a man in close proximity. They were followed by the even nearer voice of a woman, whose words he literally felt. Her words were comforting and reassuring, even though he couldn't quite make them out. He felt as if he were floating in a state of suspended bliss.

But sharply, suddenly, his peace was interrupted.

A loud bang rang out, followed by two more in quick succession. He felt the screams of the woman's voice jolt his once resting body.

Quickly, he was thrown to one side, then back to the other. He heard the revving of a car engine. The benign drone of the cheering crowd had now been replaced with muffled screams and the voices of men yelling. He was being tossed about like a row boat in a hurricane. He could feel the vibrations of the woman's sobbing voice.

Her stress was palpable to him, as if he were part of her, and it was causing his entire body to tighten. His heart raced faster and faster until it felt like a drum roll on a tightly stretched snare head. Unable to withstand any more tension, he felt an explosion in his chest. And then his tension and pain were gone.

In an instant, the darkness of the windowpane became a flash of brilliant white, enveloping him. The sight was short-lived, however.

The abrupt sound of a blaring horn penetrated Phil's skull, shocking him back into the here and now, as a motorcycle swerved to avoid him in the alley. He found himself still facing the darkened store window, his reflection now visible again. Gasping for breath, with a bead of sweat rolling down each temple, he felt like he'd aged twenty years.

# CHAPTER SEVEN

AFTER HE'D GATHERED HIMSELF, Phil emerged from the alley and wandered down Loockerman Street with manic notions banging off the walls of his mind like seeds inside a maraca. Best to put his troubles away for a while. So, he worked his way through several people standing on the sidewalk outside of the Stumble On Inn, opened one of the two heavy, oversized mahogany doors, and stepped inside, pausing to have a look around.

The smell of stale beer smacked Phil in the face like the object of one of his drunken college come-ons. He found a familiar comfort in this forest of dark-stained wooden walls and floors. All stools were taken at the long bar on his left, and every table appeared at capacity as the house band did its business on the stage at the back of the large room.

Phil navigated his way over to the bar, placed his order, then turned to scan the room for his friends while he waited for his beer. He spotted them at a table next to the opposite wall, about halfway between the stage and the front entrance. They were a welcome sight.

Phil had a problem with alcohol. He wasn't an alcoholic. He really didn't drink very often, mostly on weekends, and not even every weekend. He might go three weeks without a beer. The problem was that he never got sick when he drank too much. His drinking buddies envied him for it. Because of that, however, he didn't have the built-in sensor that would tell him to call it an evening. He just didn't seem to know when to stop once he'd started, and it was common for some sort of idiocy to ensue.

"Good timing, Murf," Gus said as Phil sat down, joining Angela and her two friends.

"Really? You've already done your show?"

"Smart-ass," Gus said with a grin, "You're actually just in time. I'm feelin' it tonight. They'll be shovelin' the wet panties off the stage after I'm done." If synchronized eye-rolling was an Olympic sport, the ladies at the table would be gold medalists. All but Angela, who knew Gus for the lovable buffoon that he was.

Anybody could take the stage at the Stumble, and there was a sign-up list to determine the order. Whenever there were no takers, the band would just do covers of popular songs, mostly rock, old and not so old. The closest description to what Gus did, would probably be scat singing. He had a very unique act, in that he would "sing" popular songs, but without using words. Mind you, it was not the occasional *scooby doo* inserted into a song that a jazz singer might employ, but the entirety of his vocal emissions was gibberish.

The music and melody would be instantly recognizable, but the lyrics were made up entirely of bops, ba ditty ops, lang de langs, and the like. All genres and tempos were fair game, too, from raucous upbeats to dramatic ballads. It was at once hilarious and rather remark-able. He was good at it.

The owner of the Stumble let Gus sell his recordings after his performances at the bar. Surprisingly, he sold quite a few units, mostly to alcohol-impaired customers curious about the novelty of it all. Gus chose to think otherwise, and his friends let him do so.

"You wouldn't believe what just happened to me," Phil said.

"More bunny-shaped clouds?" Gus asked.

Phil paused. It was one thing to confide in his best friend privately, but to do it in front of co-workers was a no-no. Thinking how ridiculous it would all sound, Phil's inner filter put his tongue under arrest. He'd keep a lid on his bizarre experience in the alley.

"It was nothing," Phil said. Quickly changing the subject, he asked "What are you singin' tonight?"

"Startin' out with a little KC and the Sunshine Band," Gus answered.

"Does the house band keep that horse in their stable?"

"Oh, yeah. They can play anything," Gus answered. "You know, we always just call them 'The House Band'. They should give themselves a name."

Phil took a swig of his beer, then casually spoke.

"Oh, they did, just the other day, I heard."

"What is it?"

"Episiotomy," Phil said, lifting his beer bottle to his lips in an effort to hide his grin. Angela's mouth fell open but said nothing.

"What the hell's that mean?" Gus asked.

"It's got somethin' to do with the Greek alphabet or some shit like that," Phil answered.

"Phil," Angela said, "let me see your arm. Is it any better?"

"I haven't seen it since I got dressed this morning, but it's fine."

"Well, roll up your sleeve, mister," she said, "and let me make sure. You always understate things."

So, he unbuttoned his cuff and dutifully rolled up his sleeve. He paid his arm no mind, looking around the room instead. Angela grasped his thick fingers and pulled his hand toward her, examining his wound.

"Well, a lot of the redness is gone, but that thing must have got you good. These charred spots...they're like writing or something."

"Writing? What are you talking about?"

"It's like that hot pipe branded you," she said.

Then Phil finally got around to having a look at the arm he hadn't seen in fourteen hours. What he saw caused his mind to race.

"SHIT BALLS!" Gus let out. "That's what was on your napkin."

"Yeah, I know."

"What napkin?" Angela asked.

Phil pulled out his wallet and unfolded the napkin to reveal an exact match to what was etched into his arm.

"So, you're saying that what's burned into your forearm is the same thing you saw in the parking lot when all of that flashing was going on?" she asked. "Are you sure you didn't just see this on your arm and then write it on the napkin?"

"You saw me write it down in the truck, before this showed up on my arm."

Then Gus chimed in. "And I saw the napkin yesterday at lunch, when his arm still looked like a dissected frog. That stuff wasn't there yet. It's like Morse code or something." Gus took a swig of his beer and pondered a moment. "That had to be on the tail pipe for it to be branded onto his arm. Murf, you must have seen it on the pipe, and then somehow just imagined that you saw it in the parking lot."

"What's it mean?" Angela asked.

"Nothing," Phil said calmly. "I think Gus hit the nail on the head." He was playing it down. Last thing he wanted to be was some freak show. But he was worried. Too much weirdness afoot. He *hadn't* seen any of those markings on the pipe because he was laying on his back, facing the underside of the hot pipe. It was the top side of the pipe, which wasn't visible to him, that caused the burn.

"Another mystery solved by Gus Austin," Gus said. "Private Eye. That's just one more potential career after I get fired from the bank."

Just then the band finished their song and the front-man announced, "Ladies and Gents, please welcome Gus Austin!"

The drummer launched into a thumping disco beat as Gus made his way past the tables along the wall, up the four stairs at the side of the stage, and finally under the lights. Upon taking the microphone from its stand, Gus pointed back toward the band and addressed the crowd.

"Let's hear for Episiotomy!"

A collective groan of female voices came from the audience, with a few stray male cackles. Sports that they were, the band played on, and Gus plowed into his scat version of "Shake Your Booty".

Instead of starting it the way KC does, "You can...you can do it...very well," the audience got "doo dow...doo dat doo dow...baw bat baw..." with Gus sliding his feet, pointing his toes in and out while flapping his elbows. He looked like a stork having a seizure. The crowd simultaneously tapped their toes and fought off the urge to dial 911.

"Quite the spectacle, isn't it?" Phil said to the ladies. "I never get tired of it."

While Gus continued to strut his stuff on stage, Phil finished his beer and flagged down the waitress, telling her to bring a bucket of six more on ice. He'd start paying closer attention to his budget tomorrow. Gus brought the song to a climax, and the audience erupted when he finished it up. He took a bow and made his way back to the table.

"Why can't the bank pay me to do that?" Gus asked his friends.

As the evening went on, one full bucket of beer replaced an empty one several times as the five talked of the week's ups and downs. Gus did two more songs, one a soulful ballad he'd written called "She Awaits Me," which of course contained only gibberish for words, making the title all the more odd. The band had now played ten songs in a row due to a lull in audience participation. So the MC called out, "We're gonna hafta recycle some songs, if we don't get some help up here."

"That's your cue, Phil," prodded Angela.

"I'd say it's Gus's turn again," answered Phil, who was seated tightly next to Angela due to there being five occupants at the small table.

"No, I'm done," said Gus. "You always say you're going to sing, and you never do. Don't be a chicken shit."

"Peer pressure, eh?" Phil said with a smile. "Okay then, here I go."

Her inhibitions lowered by alcohol, Angela put both hands on Phil's cheeks and planted a quick peck on his lips. Phil had always felt their one date a while back had meant more to Angela than him. He never told her so because he didn't want to hurt her feelings. He now realized he'd probably been unintentionally stringing her along.

Gus raised a hand and yelled toward the stage, "Here comes Murf!"

Unbeknownst to Phil, as he made his way along the wall toward the stage, Jill Wheaton had just entered the Stumble with a date.

"In his Stumble On Inn debut, ladies and gentlemen, Phil Murphy!" announced the MC.

This immediately caught the attention of Jill, who was taking a seat at a table in the back, far from the stage. As Phil started his climb up the stairs at the side of the stage, he stumbled. Sensing more embarrassment looming for Phil, Jill slid down in her chair a little to make sure he couldn't see her. She could hardly watch, but at the same time, found it hard to look away. It was like watching a natural disaster on the evening news.

"Another drunk takes the stage," quipped her date, a fellow she hardly knew but had agreed to see at the urging of a mutual friend. She had found herself wanting to go home halfway through dinner, but forged on, fulfilling her obligation to see a movie with him. He had convinced her to end the evening with a quick stop at the Stumble On Inn. Having never been there before and being the silver-lining kind of person she was, she decided to look upon the visit as new experience.

Phil, still with beer in hand, set the bottle down on a stool near the microphone stand at the front of the stage. He strapped on an acoustic guitar that had been parked in its stand while the band's ax man employed the electric guitar.

Phil turned to the band, and said, "How about 'White Sport Coat and a Pink Carnation'?"

Then the drummer counted out the tempo, and the band struck it up nicely. The electric guitar meshed perfectly with the piano and bass, while the drummer kept it all in time with a snappy beat.

When the music reached the point where Phil was supposed to start singing, he was quiet. He stood motionless in front of the microphone, his left forearm resting on the neck of his guitar, and his right on top of its body. The band played on, continuing with the intro, waiting for Phil to begin.

The stage lights were bright, and he couldn't see past the first few tables. He knew the song well yet searched for the first words. Nothing. His mind began to wander. Oddly, he felt no sense of panic, so he just stood there. The band played on, in a holding pattern.

Jill hardly knew Phil at all, but here and now, she felt embarrassed for him. This had train derailment written all over it, she thought. But in actuality, she was much more worried about it than him.

*Just sing!* she thought.

And like a telepathic arrow shot straight from her to him, the lost lyric came bubbling up from the depths of Phil's grey matter. He closed his eyes, drew in a deep breath, then exhaled the first words from the back of his throat. Softly, cautiously, he made his way through the first half of the first verse, still with his eyes shut. The pleasing vibration of the bass guitar and bass drum playing in unison pulsed through Phil's body. He now employed his once idle hands to strum the song's chords, quietly at first. Finally, he opened his eyes. With his voice and strumming growing stronger as he entered the first chorus, his relaxed grin had managed to free itself.

As Phil cut loose a little and moved about the stage during the instrumental portion, Angela's friends questioned her about Phil and what kind of relationship they had. Wanting to say more, Angela could only reply that they were friends.

"Why does he let Charlotte treat him that way?" Angela asked Gus. "He doesn't let anybody else."

"I guess having an ex-wife in federal prison can be life-altering stuff," Gus answered. "His custody of Willie is pretty shaky. When she gets out of prison, she's going to petition the court to get Willie back."

"I understand that," she said. "But what about the way he lets Charlotte treat him?"

"Well, he has to keep *this* job. The family court judge lectured him at the custody hearing about long-term stability and job jumping specifically, so he's afraid to change jobs. Plus, there aren't many decent jobs in Dover right now, anyway. Charlotte knows his situation and gets a twisted kick out of screwin' with him. There's something genuinely shitty about her."

"But his ex is a convicted felon," Angela said. "She's not going to get custody."

"She's still his mother," Gus said, pausing to swig his beer and watch Phil. "That carries a lot of weight with most judges. She's quite the actress, too, so she'll probably be pretty convincing about how reformed she is, with a new perspective now, and all that crap."

By now, Phil was completely relaxed, entirely in his element. His voice was only serviceable, but with the band sounding so good, and Phil obviously having a great time, whatever he lacked in voice quality was made up for by the good vibe coming from the stage.

Meanwhile, back at Jill's table, she was enthralled. She sat quietly, staring at the stage, pupils fully dilated, while her date droned on about his job. She had no idea what he had been talking about, only throwing out the occasional "uh huh" and "hmm," to feign attentiveness.

On stage, the song approached its crescendo with Phil facing the band. As they hit the last chord in unison, he spun around, knocking over the stool at the front of the stage and sending his beer bottle down onto the closest table, tumbling the drinks of its occupants. The place erupted.

Jill told her date she was tired and needed to go home. They slipped out, and Phil was none the wiser.

# CHAPTER EIGHT

ONE EYE OPENED to reveal only a pillow. The other eye was shmooshed into the mattress. For just an instant, Phil wasn't sure where or when he was. But relief fell over him after he raised his heavy head to see his own bedroom and realize it was Saturday morning. A decent night's sleep, but he still felt like an alcohol-saturated turd.

He'd had too much again last night, but somehow found himself in the comfort of his own bed. He remembered something about Angela driving him home. Not sure if his truck was still downtown or not.

"Why didn't you stop me, buddy?" he asked Otis, who was at his feet as always. Otis had no answer, lying upside down, curled into the shape of a "C" with his tongue hanging out of the side of his mouth. He looked like the dead deer that adorned the side of the interstates in nearby rural Pennsylvania.

It was 9:30 AM, and the sun was streaming in through Phil's bedroom window. He trudged into his living room, taking a glance outside to find his truck parked in his driveway, and the keys on the little table by the door.

He revived himself with a shower, grabbed a couple of bananas and Otis's leash, then headed out into a glorious Saturday spring morning. He opened his truck door, allowing his four-legged shadow to hop in, and they headed out on the short drive to Kara's house to pick up Willie.

Kara was smart, with the unusual combination of book smarts and common sense. She graduated Cum Laude with a history degree, then went to work for a local branch of a large insurance company handling injury claims. Soon she figured out she could make much more money as an independent with her own firm, handling claims for several different companies. She didn't even need an office. All of the work was done by phone, fax, mail, and computer, so she worked out of her house.

She'd met her husband Gary, an attorney, when he was fresh out of law school, and she was up against him on an injury claim. As often happens when a new lawyer meets an experienced injury adjuster, she schooled him something fierce, basically taking his lunch money. From that moment, he was smitten. They married after a short engagement, and she convinced him to do defense work for her company. They made an effective team. When Kara was occasionally unable to negotiate a claim to settlement, Gary defended her policyholders when they were sued. The whole arrangement allowed Kara to have rewarding career and be at home for their two children.

Phil and Otis rapped on Kara's front door. She answered with her usual wide grin.

"Hey, Sleeping Beauty! Did she finally get up out of her fluffy little bed?" she teased, sticking her bottom lip out.

"Not all of us are up with the chickens, Beavis," Phil said.

"Well, come on in. We slept in ourselves here today, and we're just now having breakfast. I think we just may have something for this guy, too," she said, bending over and grabbing Otis's fat face with both hands.

Otis led the way to the kitchen, with Phil and Kara just behind. You could almost stir the thick aroma of bacon and maple syrup in the air. Everyone was around the large table, with Willie in a booster seat next to his two cousins.

"Where's my buddy?" Phil said loudly as he entered the kitchen.

Willie beamed from ear to ear, raising his hand and yelling, "Here!" in his hoarse little voice.

The two bananas on the way over hadn't made any kind of dent in Phil's appetite, so he was ready for some real food. After a good, noisy breakfast, the kids adjourned to the living room for some Saturday morning cartoons. The adults relaxed among the dishes at the kitchen table.

"Things any better at the bank?" Gary asked.

"They would be —if they weren't worse."

"Worse?" asked Kara. "Didn't think that was possible. You hate it there."

"Yeah," Phil said, "but there's nothing like a little reprimand and threat of probation to make a good thing even better. Seems I don't keep track of how I use my debit card, and I've overdrawn my checking account too many times. The bank makes all of us keep a checking account there. It's where they deposit our pay. I've just got to get more organized."

"Yeah, organization is always good," Kara said, leaning back in her chair. She took a sip of coffee, then asked, "Anything in the handbook about having an account at a different bank?"

"No. We just have to have one at our bank to accept our pay deposit."

Another sip of coffee by Kara, followed by silence.

After a pause, Phil said, "I guess I could open an account at a different bank, and just withdraw my pay as soon as it goes in, then deposit it in my new account. At least if I overdraw the new account, it won't get me in trouble at work."

Kara smiled. "But you still better get a handle on what you're spending." She had a talent for cutting through all the noise and static to find simple answers. "Why don't you and Willie come over for dinner tomorrow?"

"Can't think of a reason why not," Phil answered, then paused. "Hold on...still can't think of one...Gimme a minute..."

"Don't hurt yourself, little brother," Kara said with a chuckle, "Just say yes."

"You talked me into it," Phil said.

"So, what's on your agenda today?" she asked.

"Thought I'd head over and check on Dad, maybe take him out to one of the parks."

"Good. We had him here for dinner last night," she said. "I just can't stand the thought of him all alone over there."

After a pause, Phil said, "I miss Mom."

"Me, too"

"What do you think she meant when she called me her 'Halloween baby' at the hospital? My birthday's in May, nowhere near Halloween."

"I don't know," Kara answered with a solemn tone. "She'd been in a coma for eight days, so she couldn't have been thinking right, or at all."

"I know," Phil said. "But she was looking me straight in the eyes when she said it. I felt so connected to her."

"I guess we'll never know," Kara said.

"Guess not."

They soon said their goodbyes, and the boys were off. They swung by the elder Murphy's home, where Phil attached his father's trailered canoe to the hitch on the little white truck. Then it was off to Ted Harvey Wildlife Area, south of Dover, past the Air Force base. They enjoyed a lazy float on the lake, during which Otis leapt off after a duck, to no avail. Made a doozy of a splash, though. Then a little fishing, followed by corn dogs they got from a mobile vendor as they sat under a big pin oak tree. Otis declined the condiments.

With everyone worn out, they dropped Phil's dad off, then headed home, hit the showers, and settled in for a good night's sleep. Phil and Otis fell asleep on Willie's bed while reading him a story.

---

THE NEXT DAY was just as forecasted. Sun and blue sky. After some grass mowing and weed eating, during which Phil noticed Stanley doing the same next door, Phil and Willie headed over to Kara's house. Dinners with Kara were a welcome reprieve for Phil from his own cooking. Phil was a lousy cook. He was trying, but probably not as hard as he should be. He'd learned a few easy meals, which he cycled through quickly. He and Willie ate a lot of spaghetti. He'd come to consider his microwave to be a close, personal friend.

After dinner, the clear evening sky quickly gave way to some unexpected cloud cover, and then a light drizzle began to fall. The adolescent maple trees in Kara's back yard began to sway, showing the silver underside of their leaves in the breeze. With the kids settled in around the television, and the adults at the kitchen table trying to enjoy some after-dinner coffee, the volume of the kids' voices in the adjacent room began to elevate.

"Will you guys hold it down in there?" Kara barked. It was out of character for her. Phil and Gary exchanged glances at each other, sharing their puzzlement.

"What?" asked Kara, glaring at Gary.

"What's with you?" asked Gary.

"I've just got a headache all of a sudden. Can't you go in there and make them settle down?"

Gary went in to find his two kids struggling over the television remote, and Willie starting to sniffle.

"Quit it," Gary snapped, and yanked the remote away from them. This, in turn, caused Willie to start crying. The drizzle had turned into a light rain now.

"Watch it, Gary," Phil said, as he came in to inspect.

"Sorry. I think Kara gave me her headache."

Kara yelled from the kitchen, "That's right, it's all my fault." This was a scene Phil had never seen at his sister's home before. With everyone, including himself, on edge for some reason, he thought it best to go home. He picked up Willie, gave Kara a hug and thanked them both for dinner, then headed to the truck. The light rain was quickly turning into a steady rain.

As they drove home in the dusk, the intensity of the downpour picked up, and there were now a few flashes of lightning, accompanied by a whipping wind. Willie had never stopped crying, and it was becoming quite a distraction to Phil. He held back several urges to snap at Willie. A strange feeling was upon him. He, too, had a headache now, and everything seemed to enrage him: the glare off the wet road; the oncoming headlights; Willie's crying; even the rubbing noise of his worn-out windshield wipers smearing the rain all over the glass.

Strange sights abounded outside now, too, as he saw a woman next to her car, frantically waving her arms, ranting, and pointing in the face of a cop who had pulled her over. A few blocks further, a fistfight was in full bloom in the aftermath of a minor traffic accident. Several looters, in full view of anyone who cared to watch, were breaking storefront windows and walking right in.

Phil knew he had to get Willie home as soon as he could. He sped toward McHenry Street, encountering every sort of reckless driver, sometimes having to swerve to avoid being hit. Finally, he reached his driveway. Just in time, too, because now they were in a full-fledged thunderstorm.

He unbelted the still-bawling Willie and pulled him from his booster seat, carrying him as he trotted to the front door. After stepping in to the living room, he sat Willie down, turned around, and hung his coat on the hook on the back of the door. It felt oddly quiet in the house. When he turned back around, he found Otis eerily staring him down from across the room with a low, snarling growl.

This, of all things, confirmed to Phil that something was desperately wrong. In his seven years with Otis, he'd never heard him muster a growl at anyone. He even loved the mailman, for crying out loud. Otis had almost seemed to take a maternal role toward Willie, shadowing him night and day since his mother's incarceration.

Knowing things weren't as they should be, Phil couldn't afford to put his trust in a snarling dog that didn't appear in its right mind. So he quickly picked up Willie. Then, facing Otis, he stomped his right foot on the ground, yelling, "Git!"

Otis instantly turned and ran down the short hall into Phil's bedroom. Phil took Willie into the boy's bedroom and checked him over. He was still sobbing but didn't appear to have a fever or any physical problem. Not wanting to leave him alone, Phil carried him in to the kitchen to get him a drink. The storm continued outside, but seemed to be leveling off in intensity, not getting any worse. Phil's head was still splitting.

"Whaddya say we hit the sack, buddy?"

By the time Phil had Willie ready for bed, the storm had died down to just a light rain. They entered Willie's bedroom and closed the door behind them. Phil had already decided he was sleeping in Willie's room tonight, so he nestled in beside him and began to read him a story. The sound of rain outside was gone now. Willie was out fast. Phil's headache had subsided now, too.

Just then, there was a single, pitifully faint scratch at the bedroom door. Phil got off the bed and opened the door to find Otis in proper sitting position, with his big square head drooping down, as if to apologize.

"No problem, big guy. I know you weren't yourself. None of us were." Then they all settled in on Willie's big bed, worn out, falling fast asleep.

# CHAPTER NINE

A BLUE SKY was a welcome sight on any Monday morning, but especially after the bizarre happenings of the night before. Phil was running slightly ahead of schedule after dropping Willie off at Stephanie's house. The spring sun, in his eyes again, was heating up the cab of the little white truck quite nicely.

All around, however, the aftermath of Sunday night's storm was apparent. Signs of vandalism and debris scattered about the streets. If Phil hadn't witnessed it the night before, he would find it hard to imagine in friendly little Dover.

After a busy, but uneventful morning in the office, Phil and Gus were enjoying an outdoor lunch at the Outpost.

"Did anything weird happen to you during the storm last night?" Phil asked.

"Like what?"

"Just anything, I guess."

"Wasn't weird, but the TV went out during the game," Gus said.

"No, that's not weird. It was a storm, after all."

"Yeah, I guess," Gus said. "But here's a hoot. I got so irritated about it, I threw the remote at the TV, missed, and knocked a couple of books off the shelf."

"Yeah, that *is* weird," Phil said. "What are you doin' with books?"

"Shut up. I got smarts real good," Gus said.

"Seriously, that's what I'm getting at," Phil said as he leaned forward in his chair, "You're about the most easy-going guy I know. You don't do stuff like that."

"I guess I was just kind of cranky," Gus said. "I had a headache."

"I was at Kara's last night. You know my sister, Mother Teresa. Well, she was the biggest bitch you ever saw...for her, anyway. Everybody got kind of salty, so Willie and I left. He cried all the way home. Even Otis was growling at us."

"Kids cry and everybody gets crabby now and then, but Otis...that *is* weird," said Gus.

"Exactly," Phil said, "It's like, the worse the storm got, the more hectic and upset everything got. Then after it was over, everyone was better."

"You know, my headache did clear up right after the storm," Gus said, dipping his onion ring in ketchup. "But it must have been some sort of weather-related sinus thing."

"Well, evidently, the whole town went to hell last night. Crime everywhere," Phil said. "Saw some of it myself on the way home from Kara's."

When the meal was over, Phil went back to work, and Gus headed out to visit a client in Wilmington, about fifty miles away. When Phil sat down at his desk, he was greeted with yet another overdraft notice. Seems he hadn't considered the fees from his previous overdraft, and now those fees had caused him to overdraw again. And, as if on cue, Charlotte appeared in the door of her office.

"I've been waiting for you. Long lunch again?"

"No, Charlotte, just a normal lunch," he said in a defeated tone.

Like a march to the gallows, Phil slowly got up and trudged in to Charlotte's office. Upon his entrance, he again found her shadow, Russ Curry. Phil took a seat in front of Charlotte's desk, and she took her place upon her throne.

"Murphy, you are now officially on probation. Curry, here, is going to make a special project of monitoring your work output."

"I guess that'll give him *something* to do," Phil said. "But I thought this was about the overdrafts."

"It is. But it's about your volume of work, or lack of it, too. I just haven't seen the improvement I need to see."

"Come on, Charlotte, today's only Monday. It was just this past Friday that you gave me my reprimand. How much improvement could I have shown over the weekend?"

"You know," she said, "we've had a Saturday and a Sunday since then. You could've been in here."

Phil's gut began to burn, but he kept it buried. He hardly heard anything else that was said. Sensing Charlotte was done, he said nothing and left.

His stomach churning, he had to get out of there for a few minutes. So he headed straight toward the elevator, pressed both the up and down buttons, then waited. The longer it took, the more desperate he started to feel. There were four elevators, two across from two others. Surely, one would arrive soon. He placed himself in the center of the floor, equidistant to all four, so he could quickly enter any door as soon as it opened. Why gamble, he thought, by standing in front of one door, when it was a three out of four chance one of the other doors would open?

*Yeah, that's what's important now*, he thought. He was usually self-entertained by such overthought, but this time he was starting to feel anxious.

Finally, a door opened to reveal two passengers traveling down. He stepped inside of his sanctuary, finding a place on the back wall. Today's selection of music: instrumental jazz. Big surprise for elevator music. If he wasn't mistaken, this was a wordless horn and string version of "Shattered" by the Stones. As much of a crime as that was, whoever had come up with the idea was at least using their imagination.

When the ride stopped at the lobby, his co-riders exited. To his relief, no one was there waiting to board. The door shut. He pressed "7". Breathing wasn't such a chore now. He stood with his back in the rear corner, a shoulder blade leaning on each wall. Scooting his feet out from the wall ever so slightly, he was dead weight, with only the corner holding him up. He put his hands in his roomy khaki pockets, took a deep breath, and closed his eyes. It would only be for a moment, while the weight of his worries rinsed off him like soap under a shower. Momentary peace.

As his mind drifted, dandelion-yellow and sky-blue hues swirled about behind his closed eyes. He could hear the faint sound of something, but he wasn't sure what. It was starting to sound a little closer. Now he heard it clearly. It was the sound of sea gulls and the bells of distant fishing vessels. Soon, his mind's eye found him on a beautiful beach slathered with wind-swept dunes, looking up toward a vast green knoll, with an elegant, long, white house overlooking the ocean.

With the energy of a child, he ran from the sand up toward the home, onto the expansive grass that separated the beach from the house. There, he joined two children, a boy and a girl both older than him, playfully chasing each other under the warm summer sun while two loving parents watched from their lounge chairs in the distance. The feeling was blissful, yet somehow haunting. As quickly as the vision came, it vanished into shades of deep blue and emerald green.

Slowly, Phil opened his eyes. Upon doing so, he was aghast to find three people staring at him from the other side of the elevator. But he'd only closed his eyes for moment, no more, he thought. A glance at his watch revealed forty minutes had passed.

Little did Phil know, Jill had been dropping some papers off at the security office and had witnessed the staff having a roaring laugh at the expense of the "Rip Van Winkle" on the elevator. She paused to watch the monitor.

As the security staff was enjoying the show, Jill was starting to feel concerned for Phil. First, there was the episode she'd witnessed with his boss humiliating him as she walked by his desk. Then the anxious, slow-starting musical performance at the bar, where he stood silent before the crowd. Now this.

There was something in him that brought out a nurturing urge in her. In the last few days, she had taken the time to learn from a friend of Phil's custody predicament and the recent death of his mother.

Outwardly, he seemed concerned only with fun. But his responsible concern for his son and job belied his carefree exterior. Though she'd hardly spoken to him, she was beginning to feel a connection. His actions seemed a cry for help, somehow, and she found herself wanting to supply it.

Returning to his desk, Phil found Charlotte's door closed. Maybe she hadn't noticed he was gone, he thought. He slothfully went back to the drudgery of his number crunching. If the verbal bludgeoning Charlotte had given him was supposed to motivate him, it wasn't working. He might put in longer hours, but the berating only made him hate his job more, and that sure wouldn't result in more or better work.

Phil's attention was drawn to the opening of Charlotte's door and the emergence of Geneva, who was looking grim. But she always looked grim. She was followed out by Curry, who headed for his haven, the restroom.

As the end of the work day neared, Phil had a feeling that five o'clock wasn't going to satisfy Charlotte. He was right. Before he could sneak away, Charlotte came out of her office with another box of client financial records for Phil. Here at the turn of the century, more of the department's work was being done through personal computers, but paper files were still part of the picture, too.

"These have to be done tonight. I know they're not your clients. They belonged to Russ," Charlotte said, "but he's transitioning out of his position, and you're just going to have to take some of his old load." Carrying Russ Curry's weight as he moved up the ladder, while Phil struggled to cling to his job, was a bitter pill to swallow. Charlotte retreated to her office, got her coat, and left for the day.

Phil picked up the phone to call Kara's mobile. He'd have to ask her to pick up Willie again. He was thankful she had always been available. He felt like there was no one else he could ask, besides Gus, but he was still out of town for the day. Phil's rapidly aging father lived close by, but he didn't have the ability anymore to take care of a toddler, especially so soon after the passing of Phil's mother.

"What'll it be, Beavis?" was how Kara answered the phone.

"Man, there's no anonymity anymore," Phil laughed. "Any chance you can pick up Willie for me?"

"You don't hear a thing I say, do you?" Kara asked, sounding like a big sister.

"What did I miss?"

"We're all in Hershey right now. Gary and I took the day off, and we took the kids to the amusement park here. We won't be home until pretty late tonight."

"When did you tell me that?"

"When you came over for dinner yesterday."

"Oh, when you were so pleasant?" Phil asked with a chuckle.

"Yeah, I'm sorry. I don't know what the deal was. I really wigged out after you left. We all did, really," Kara said. "We eventually calmed down, though."

"Don't worry about it," Phil said. "I think something was going around. No problem about tonight," Phil said. "You guys have fun and be careful. I'll talk to you tomorrow."

Now, what to do? He couldn't ask Stephanie to keep Willie later than normal. She just wouldn't do it unless it were some type of emergency. He could go get him, then bring him back to the office, but he'd spend forty-five minutes in travel time and not get any work done with Willie there. He couldn't do the work at home, because he needed to be connected to the bank's computer mainframe. Maybe he could come into work a little early tomorrow and get a head start on it. Although, he really couldn't drop Willie off at Stephanie's early enough to make a real dent in the amount of work that needed done. The thought crossed his mind to ask Angela to pick him up, and she probably would, but he felt like he'd be taking advantage of her unreciprocated feelings for him.

*If only I weren't so damned honorable,* he thought, causing himself a muffled snort.

Seems the best of his lousy choices was to bring Willie to the office and prepare for a long, but most likely unproductive evening. He would do what he had to, but for now, he just felt too tired to get up out of his chair. So, he leaned back and propped his feet up, crossing them at the ankles on his desk, sleeves rolled up and hands behind his head.

Just then Phil noticed Jill coming through the Trust Department doors for her trek across the now mostly empty Credit Department floor toward the elevators. His lips parted slightly to feed his body some additional oxygen. He was careful not to seem too interested. For once, his genuine lack of energy was playing in his favor now. She was approaching his desk. Noting his feet crossed lazily on his desk, she smiled.

"You look like you could make me a deal on a one-owner SUV." Her voice was like a winter's day bowl of hot chicken soup—home-made, not the canned stuff.

"Well, you're just in time for our inventory clearance event." Lame, but it was the best his weary mind could muster.

"I think I want a job in *this* department," she said. "I like the laid-back vibe."

"Heh," Phil snickered lowly, "You don't want to work *here*."

She just smiled, a little sadly. "I'll take your word for it then. About done for the day?"

"I believe I am—for the moment, anyway."

"Even with all of that on your desk?" she asked, pointing at the box of files.

He smiled and said, "You sound like the Ice Queen in there," motioning with his thumb toward Charlotte's office.

"Oh no, I didn't mean it that way..." her voice trailing off.

"I know," he said quietly. "I need to stay and have actually been told that I *have* to stay. So, I'm going to go get my son in a minute and bring him back here."

"That doesn't sound like a recipe for getting much work done," she said.

"No, it doesn't, but I don't have any other options."

With his words still hanging in the air, Jill blurted, "I'll get him."

She gave her words no thought before saying them. She looked a little stunned, herself, as if even she was surprised.

Assuming she was kidding, Phil offered a low laugh. "That's a good one."

"Really, I can go get him, take him to my place, and you can stay here as long as you need. Just come by when you're done."

Phil was dumbfounded. She was too good to be true. A monsoon of thoughts rained through his mind in the span of a moment: He couldn't let her do that; Maybe he could; Why would she offer?

"I can't let you do that," he said, smiling, "I'll be really disappointed if you tell me you've got nothing more exciting to do tonight."

"Well I'm sorry to disappoint you, Mr. Murphy, but the idea of entertaining a little fellow for the evening is more excitement than I've had in a while."

"I feel your pain, Miss Wheaton," Phil said with a subdued grin.

For some reason, Phil didn't feel the doubts that he thought he should have. He trusted her, somehow. Although he didn't really know her well, he had known her family for years. He found himself wanting some sort of involvement with her, but not sure of what kind. Lord knows, he didn't need a steady girlfriend with all of the confusion in his life at the moment, but he was drawn to her on a cellular level. He just wanted to be around her.

"Okay. I'm in," he said. "You don't know how much I appreciate this."

"You know, I'm just doing this to have something to hold over you," she said with a wry smile. "You better get used to hearing, 'Remember that time...'"

So, Phil gave Jill the sitter's address. Jill gave Phil her address. They exchanged phone numbers. Phil called Stephanie and explained the situation. Stephanie told Phil that she would be asking Jill to show her ID when picking up Willie. Phil thought that was a great idea. Stephanie put Willie on the phone so Phil could tell him that his friend Jill was going to pick him up. Fortunately, Willie was a chip off the old block. He didn't say much but was comfortable around just about anyone.

Jill left, and Phil dug in. He couldn't remember working harder in his life. What a contrast to Charlotte's way to "motivate" him. They should find a way to put this into the management training manual, he thought. Hell, he could write it himself:

1) Dangle beautiful and charming co-worker in front of employee.

2) Promise employee time will be spent with said co-worker once his work is complete.

3) Stand back and watch result.

Over the next three hours, he churned out a half a week's work. He had mixed feelings: Resentful of Charlotte for making him eat shit, but victorious about chewing up and spitting out the work she'd dumped on him.

From now on, he decided, he would never let Charlotte see him miserable. If he had to eat shit, he'd put on a bib, grin, and have at it.

# CHAPTER TEN

IT WAS NEARLY 8:30 when Phil pulled into the parking lot of the condo complex where Jill lived in a secluded neighborhood on the north side of Dover. It had been a long day. Truck windows down, the scent of honeysuckle thick in the air. The speed bumps reminded him that his little truck still needed new shock absorbers. Shocks were an easy expense to put off, especially when everybody else had their hand in his pocket.

He located Jill's unit, parked his truck, and climbed the exterior stairs to her place on the second floor. After a tap on the door, it opened, and Phil was greeted with her wide, welcoming smile.

"Hey, there. Come in. You look like you could use a cold beer."

Out of her work clothes, and now in jeans and a dark green Dartmouth sweatshirt, she looked more appealing than ever. Some women look good in a dress but fail the jeans test. No such discrepancy here.

"Oh, no thanks," he said, "I'd probably fall right to sleep." He looked over to his right to find Willie sitting on the couch, legs straight out in front of him, looking at a magazine. "Hey, buddy." The little guy responded with a wave and a smile.

Turning back to Jill, Phil said, "I can't thank you enough. Was he any trouble?"

"None. We've had a great time, haven't we, Willie?"

The three-year old just grinned and nodded, keeping in character as the strong, silent type.

"He doesn't say much, does he?" Jill asked.

"Not much. He's learned at an early age that anything he says may be used against him."

"Now where would he learn such a thing?" she asked with a grin. "Have a seat. What can I get you?"

"Just anything, really. Whatever you're having."

Jill disappeared into the kitchen. Phil sat down on the couch beside Willie, and noticed he was looking at a *Glamour* magazine.

"*Glamour*?" Phil called out to Jill.

"Yeah," Jill replied as she came back into the living room with a glass of iced tea for Phil. "I'm afraid my subscription to *Truck and Tractor* just ran out. But he really seems to like that one... and my *Cosmo*. We were just getting ready to play with some of my old Barbies."

As she handed Phil his glass, he was swept up in a waft of the soft fragrance of her flaxen tresses. Even her voice was soothing. She didn't know it, but she was launching an all-out assault on Phil's senses. And the fact that she didn't appear to know how lovely she actually was, he thought, was one of her most endearing qualities.

She sat down in a chair, opposite Phil and Willie. "So, did you get that ugly cardboard box off your desk?" she asked.

"Yes, I did. It was a very productive evening."

Finally, a few moments of awkward silence had arrived.

"How's Thad? I haven't seen him in years."

"He's fine," she answered. "He settled in Piscataway after college, married to a girl he met at Rutgers. Their first baby is on the way. I'm going to be an aunt." Another pause. That subject seemed over. Phil took a sip from his glass, then Jill took a more direct path than Phil's meandering attempt at small talk.

"How hard is it being a single dad?"

In a moment before answering, Phil marveled about the fact that she was so unpretentious.

"Well, it can be pretty tiring." He paused. "But it's a lot easier than being a dad who's married to the wrong person."

With Willie eventually resting his head on the single dad's leg, the two adults talked about a little bit of everything. They gently poked at each other's history without being too invasive. He learned that she could have gone to college at nearby Johns Hopkins, but like many teenagers, wanted to get further away from her hometown. Admitting that she was fortunate to have such choices, she settled on Dartmouth. She adapted well enough, but for her MBA, she chose Princeton, staying in the northeast. Phil also learned that she'd had a boyfriend at Dartmouth who eventually proposed, but she realized she didn't have the same feelings for him and ended it.

Very quickly, 9:45 was upon them. With Willie fast asleep using Phil's thigh as a pillow, it was time to get him home. Phil picked up the sleeping sack of potatoes in one arm and headed toward the door. On his way, he took his empty tea glass into Jill's kitchen and put it in the sink.

"You didn't have to do that, but thanks," she said.

"I'd say that makes us even now," he said with a grin.

As he left the apartment and plodded down the stairs, carrying the still-slumbering Willie in one arm, he couldn't kick one nagging feeling. *She was out of his league.* Then why was she being so nice to him? Maybe she was just nice to everyone. He'd heard that about her.

Phil had always done well with women, good looking women, even. Jill, though, seemed flawless. Extremely smart. Funny. Kind-hearted. Beautiful. But she exuded such warmth that it almost didn't matter what she looked like. He'd felt an instant connection to her but wondered if that was a one-way street.

"Man," Phil whispered under his breath as he drove home in the dark. He'd better watch it, he thought. He had her up on some kind of pedestal already. Maybe the problem was that he just didn't know her well enough. That had to be it. She just hadn't had time to annoy him yet. As he knew her better, the faults would surely start to surface. But what if they didn't? What if she was one of those people who grew on you even more as you got to know her? Then things would get really complicated. But what a nice complication to have.

Worse, however, would be if she eventually learned of *his* flaws. Phil knew he had his share: occasional drunken idiocy; childish sense of humor; lack of career ambition. But the more urgent question he had to resolve, and what might scare Jill off entirely: what was happening to him lately? All-too-real visions in elevators and store front windows, and most creepy, the plane crash experience while blindly driving three hours home from the prison.

As he glanced over at his slumbering son, he knew for Willie's safety, he had to get to the bottom of what was happening. He had no clue how, but he now realized that he needed help, maybe *professional* help.

This much thinking would never allow him to sleep when he got home. He decided he would spring into action tomorrow. So, he turned the radio on low and enjoyed the rest of his ride home, bathing himself in Jill's aroma, which was still radiating from Willie's clothes.

# CHAPTER ELEVEN

THE NEXT DAY, when lunch time arrived, Phil met Gus on the patio of the Outpost. Gus had missed the previous day's events, having been out of the office all afternoon. Phil took a few minutes to fill Gus in. Probation. Jill offering to babysit. The short but incredible evening at her apartment. He also rehashed the vision incident on the elevator, and how he'd basically blacked out for forty minutes. The weirdness had now accumulated to a point that even Gus thought some kind of action was necessary.

"Well, that's it," Gus said, "we need to get you sized for a straitjacket."

"You think?" Phil asked sincerely.

"No, dumbass, but something sure as hell is going on, and I do think you need to talk to somebody. Not because you're crazy, but just to help you piece all of this stuff together."

The fact that Gus thought something was actually going on, and not that Phil was just a kook, was more proof of Gus's loyalty.

"I guess I need to do something," Phil said. "If not for my own sanity, then Willie's safety. I drove three hours the other night, and don't even remember it, all with my three-year-old son in the seat next to me."

"That *is* messed up," Gus conceded.

"Who do I talk to?"

"I don't know, a shrink maybe."

"That's what I was thinking, but I can't afford it. I checked the bank's benefits manual this morning, and our insurance does covers psychiatric treatment but I've got the biggest deductible that the plan offers—twenty-five hundred bucks. You know, the higher the deductible, the lower the premium."

"Maybe there's some help you can get on the internet."

"Somehow, I don't think the internet is the place to get psychiatric advice," Phil said.

"So, what *are* you gonna do?"

"I don't know. I've got a client meeting at the Donut Dinette after lunch today. I'll kick it around this afternoon and see if I can figure something out."

---

PHIL WRACKED his brain on the drive to the Donut Dinette, then did his best not to appear distracted to its proprietors during their time together. After leaving the meeting, he couldn't stand the thought of going back to the office, so he decided just to drive a little.

As the afternoon sun warmed, he let his arm dangle out the truck window and he began to relax a bit. Without even thinking, his little truck seemed to find itself homing in toward Delaware Bay College, his alma mater. If only all Tuesday afternoons could be like this. He hadn't been out of the office on a client call in quite a while, and revisiting his old college was icing on the cake.

He turned off the highway into the long, tree-lined driveway of the college's main entrance. The tall pines were so thick, they nearly formed a tunnel over his head. At the end of the driveway, it all opened up, with the cozy campus on display. *There's nothing like a spring day on a college campus*, Phil thought. DBC was in full splendor, complete with coeds sunning themselves, guitared wannabe balladeers under trees surrounded by fawning girls, and bicyclists everywhere.

He parked his truck in one of the visitor lots and made his way toward the quad. This was good medicine. He didn't know anyone at the school anymore. Not being the most conscientious of students, he hadn't really built relationships with any of his professors. The only faculty or staff who had actually engaged him were his baseball coaches, and they were all replaced two years after Phil graduated.

As he headed through the quad on its crisscrossed sidewalks toward the baseball field, a sign caught his eye: *Mullins Hall, Department of Psychology*. With no money for such extravagance, maybe there was a grad student or someone who could at least listen to his situation. After all, he was an alum; maybe that counted for something.

Upon entering the double doors of the long, three-story brick edifice, he found the building directory on the wall in front of him. Having no preference, he located the first name he came to on the alphabetically ordered directory and set out for the office of Dr. Virgil Abshire, in room 212.

He plodded up a nearby staircase, then down the hall toward room 212, acutely aware of the squeaking of his rubber-soled shoes on the tile floor of the empty hallway. The door to 212 was closed, and no answer was given to his knock. So he simply walked on down the hall until he found an open door at 218.

Popping his head around the corner of the open doorway, he spied the back of a woman with a short, disheveled mop of gray hair, looking out of a large window behind her desk. She was standing beside her chair, resting one arm on its back.

"Anybody home?" Phil asked quietly, so as not to startle her.

Turning around quickly, she smiled and said, "Why, yes, come in. What can I do for you?"

Phil was pleasantly surprised by her warm greeting. As a student, his visits to professors' offices were mostly unpleasant affairs, being that he was usually going there with the purpose of questioning a test score or to bargain unsuccessfully for a better grade.

"Well, I was hoping that I might bother someone with a few questions."

"Have a seat," she said, "I've got all kinds of answers. We'll just see if any of them belong to your questions. What's your name?"

"Phil Murphy," he said, holding out his hand to the cheerful lady, who appeared to be in her late sixties.

"Ann Culpepper," she replied, vigorously pumping Phil's hand. Slightly built, she had a pleasantly lined face. Her office had scads of books. Books everywhere. Books on her desk. Books on shelves. Books in boxes on the floor. No real surprise, considering this was a college professor's office, but Phil couldn't recall seeing so many books tossed about in such a haphazard way.

"Pardon the mess," she said. "I'm just moving in."

"New to the college?" Phil asked.

"Heavens, no. I'm just moving in to this *office*. I retired a few years ago and couldn't stand the monotony. So they've let me come back, in pretty much a pro bono capacity, slapping the old 'Emeritus' tag on me."

"That sure sounds impressive to me."

"Well," she said, "they don't have any classes for me to teach, but they said I could take this office, and 'consult' to my heart's content. I was a professor of psychology here for thirty-two years. Head of the department, the last twelve."

"It looks like I stumbled into the right doorway, then," Phil said. She sounded like a lonely person who needed a place to spend her days.

"So, about these questions of yours. Are you missing some marbles?" she asked with a laugh.

"Not really. I hope not anyway," he said, relieved to find that she had a sense of humor. "I'm not sure where to begin. You may have the urge to call security by the time I'm done."

"Try me," she said. "You'd be surprised at what I've encountered over the years. Have a seat."

Phil then eased into the events he'd recently gone through. The visions, the cryptic arrangement of the debris on the mall parking lot—he showed her the corresponding branding on his arm—and the violent storm with the cranky behavior of people during them. She seemed to be soaking it all up like a sponge, so Phil felt comfortable enough to go ahead and reveal the details of the wild ride home from Norfolk.

Ann sat quietly listening, even jotting down a few notes. Phil was fortunate enough to have found a knowledgeable person who was looking for something to do. He was getting her full attention.

When he finished, she said, "Now, you're not pulling my leg with any of this, are you? I admit that I've got some time to kill here, but I don't have time for a wild goose chase."

"Neither do I, Miss Culpepper—forgive me, *Doctor* Culpepper. I work long hours at a bank. I'm the single father of a three-year-old son and have a good bit on my plate. So I really don't have time for pulling your leg. And honestly, I don't think I've got the imagination to have made up something like this."

"Okay," she said. "But call me Ann. I haven't been a 'Miss' in generations. Technically, I'm still a 'Mrs.', since my husband passed away several years ago. And I've never liked that *Doctor* stuff. It irritated my colleagues to no end, but I've always felt that 'Doctor' should be reserved for medical types."

"All right, Ann. What do you think? Have I lost my marbles?"

"I don't think you have. The first question I have to ask, is what do you think all of this means?"

"Well," Phil started, "I have no clue what it means or why this is happening, but...." His voice trailed off.

"But?"

"I'm hesitant to say it out loud. It's just sounds so stupid."

"Give it a try."

"Okay," he said, looking down toward the floor. "Somehow, when I put all of these vision things together, I want to say that it has something to do with...the Kennedys."

Silence from Ann.

"You *do* think I'm crazy," Phil said.

"Not at all, dear. Tell me why you think what you do."

Phil continued, "This episode back on Thursday night was by far the most specific and detailed thing yet. I swear to you, I was on that plane. I could see, hear, smell, taste, and feel everything that this Davis fellow was experiencing. And while I never got a good, direct look at the pilot, I think I know who it was." He stopped, fearing it was just too ridiculous to say out loud.

"Who was it?"

Now there was silence from Phil.

"Come on," she coaxed.

"I think it was JFK, Junior." He looked her squarely in the eyes this time, with a bit of desperation in his voice. "And the strangest part of the whole thing was the bond I felt with him. He and Davis didn't speak to each other much at all, but the connection was incredible. I felt it as much as I've ever felt anything. I want to say it was almost...brotherly, like I was his kid brother."

"Well," Ann said, "I only know what was in the media last summer when his plane crashed. I've not studied the matter."

"Me either," Phil said. "I remember thinking at the time that it was very unfortunate, but I wasn't really upset or anything. Only thing is, if I remember right, there were only three people on the actual flight. In my...whatever it was...there were five of us."

"The mind is a beautifully odd, flawed entity, Phil, and I've come to believe over my lifetime of studying it that just about anything is possible when it involves the mind."

"You believe what I'm telling you?"

"I don't know what is happening to you. Could be you're just dreaming, but I do believe you're telling me the truth. I don't rule out anything when it comes to the human mind. And I don't know how the storm is related to everything, if at all. But I know the first thing we have to find out, though."

"*We* have to find out?" Phil asked. "You're interested in helping me?"

"Of course. A Nobel Prize will put a nice capstone on my career. You can be my lab rat," she said with a cackle.

"Deal," Phil said with a grin. "Now you were about to tell me what important piece of information we need."

"Why don't you tell me what that is, dear?"

He paused for a moment, then responded, "Kristen Minnows, the woman sitting beside me on the plane—she wasn't in the actual crash last summer." He paused again. "I have to find out if she's a real person."

"You're going to force me to share credit on my Nobel Prize, aren't you?" she asked with a chuckle.

"No, ma'am. I'd imagine my duties as lab rat will be all-consuming."

Before departing, since he couldn't leave his arm there, Phil scribbled down the formation he saw on the parking lot, identical to what was burned into his forearm, and gave it to Ann.

"It almost looks like Morse code or something like that," Phil said.

"I don't think so," she said, turning toward a credenza behind her desk and pulling out a camera.

"You don't mind if I get a photograph of your arm, do you?"

"Not at all."

Ann said she had an idea or two on where to start and would do some research. Through the college's main library, she had access to a huge online database of peer-reviewed academic articles. Between that, the internet, and the library's catalog of textbooks and other books about the history of psychiatry and psychology, she would be swimming in information. The two parted with a promise from Ann to contact Phil in the next few days to update him on her progress.

# CHAPTER TWELVE

WEDNESDAY MORNING FELT like a new beginning for Phil. He was hopeful and thankful about finding Ann Culpepper, and his visit to Jill's apartment two nights before seemed like a turning point. He was now armed with a new attitude about his job and boss. No more would he give Charlotte the pleasure of seeing him wilt under her tyranny.

The seventy-five minutes he spent with Jill on Monday night, strangely, had made him want to try a little harder—at everything. He felt a new motivation to step up his game. These feelings were not completely new to Phil. Many times in the past, he would "start over" and "clean the slate," but usually found himself back in his old habits pretty quickly. He had a hard time sticking to things and completing tasks he started. This time genuinely felt different, though.

He whipped his little truck off Loockerman and up the ramp of the parking garage. He thought he'd take the stairs down to the ground level, in lieu of the elevator. That's a pretty easy call to take the stairs at the beginning of the day when you're heading down. He'd see what kind of fortitude he had at the end of the day, when he had to go *up* the stairs.

After he'd passed through First Collateral's lobby and reached the bank elevator, he found that Russ Curry had already illuminated the

"Up" button. Time for some fun. Without saying a word, Phil approached the already lit button and rapidly pressed it several times.

"That doesn't make it get here any faster," Curry said.

"You know, Russ," Phil said, "an engineer friend of mine says that it does. He said most of the elevators manufactured in the last twenty years have a sensor that picks up on a rider's urgency after five successive deployments of the button. The system responds by not only increasing the speed that the elevator travels, but also decreasing the time that the doors stay open during the stops." Phil said it with such authority that Curry didn't know whether to recognize it as bullshit or not, so he didn't rebut Phil. Just then, the elevator doors opened.

"See?" Phil said with a manufactured smug grin.

The two entered, and just as the doors were closing, an arm reached into the elevator from the outside, stopping the doors. The appendage was attached to none other than Jill Wheaton. This was turning into a great morning.

She hurriedly entered the elevator, not yet noticing Phil. Perched on one leg, pulling her pump back over her heel after it had tried to escape as she crossed the bank's lobby. Even disheveled, Jill's beauty was undeniable. An April morning breeze through her naturally golden locks only added to her appeal. Lesser women would want to claw mother nature's eyes out for jostling their carefully constructed curls. But for Jill, the less she tried, the more beautiful she was.

After a moment, she looked up. Her big brown eyes met Phil's and she instantly smiled. Reflex caused him to smile back.

"That's a good way to lose an arm," Curry warned. "Those doors can be dangerous."

"I suppose they can," she said.

Phil and Jill each occupied opposite rear corners of the elevator, which had now started its ascent toward the third floor. Curry stood between them, slightly forward, facing the doors. Phil reached into his portfolio, pulling out a pen and a palm-sized sticky note pad. Only Jill noticed.

As he scribbled on the note pad, Phil asked, knowing the reaction he would get, "How's that car of yours, Russ? What is that, a Plymouth?"

"Good God, Murphy, it's an import."

"My mistake, Rusty. Mexican, right?"

"European," replied Curry, finally deducing that Phil was mocking him.

"That's right," Phil said, heartily slapping Curry on the back. When he pulled his hand away, a note was stuck to Curry's back, reading, "How about lunch?"

Jill's mouth gaped open momentarily in surprise, drawing in a gasp of air, then smiling. Her eyes met Phil's, and she nodded quickly.

Just then the elevator bell dinged, and Curry marched out hurriedly toward his desk. Phil and Jill stepped out, then paused outside the elevator doors.

"I hope you didn't misinterpret that note," Phil said.

"What do you mean?"

"Well, you do know it was meant for Rusty, right? I've been trying to get up the nerve to ask him to lunch for a quite a while now."

"You know, you probably should have signed your name to it. He may think it's from me," Jill replied. "And putting a couple of boxes for him to check 'Yes' or 'No' might have been a good idea."

"Oh, man. I knew I forgot something. I just get so flustered in these situations," Phil said. They started to slowly stroll away from the elevators toward their workplaces.

"Think about what you want for lunch, and we'll do it. Anywhere you want," Phil boasted, then adding meekly, "But my Taco Bell coupon expires tomorrow, so...."

"You're going to let Rusty walk around with that note on his back all day?"

"Figuring out how it got there will give him something to do today," Phil answered.

They parted ways, and each settled in to their workday. All morning, Phil hammered out his reports like a machine. His decision to not let Charlotte see him miserable was somehow conditioning his mind to actually *like* his work. Just before lunchtime, Geneva was called into

Charlotte's office, accompanied by Curry. The door closed. This had a familiar feel to Phil. Then Gus rolled over to Phil's desk in his chair.

"What do you think that's about?" Gus asked.

"This has the stench of 'reprimand' on it," answered Phil. "I know that dreaded march to the gallows all too well, I'm afraid."

"This is the second time," Gus said. "One day last week they did the same thing with her. You weren't here, I guess. Probably on the elevator, takin' a nap. Dip-shit."

"It's actually the third time for Geneva, ass-wipe, because I saw her coming out of there Monday while you were probably snoozing in some movie theater when you were supposed to be out of town working."

"Hey, I get some of my best sleep in movie theaters," he said.

"If that's Geneva's third time in there," Phil said, "then they're either promoting her or putting her on probation."

"She sure didn't have the look of somebody climbing the corporate ladder," Gus said.

A few minutes later, Charlotte's door opened, and out came Geneva, followed by Curry, with Charlotte stopping in the doorway. Gus took the occasion to roll in his chair back over to his desk and get back to work.

Charlotte cast a steely glare in Phil's direction, to which he responded with a shit-eatin' grin. Monday's Phil, still burdened with his old worried outlook, would have looked away and scurried back to work. He still had the same worries as Monday, chief among them hanging onto his job so he could maintain custody of Willie. But this was Wednesday, and he wouldn't give Charlotte the satisfaction of showing his trepidation.

Phil maintained eye contact with her, still wearing his crooked grin, while ten seconds or so went by—a long time to do nothing but stare someone in the eyes, especially for Phil. He had a bugaboo about eye contact. He'd always felt it was the most personal interaction two people could have, outside of sex. Even during a kiss, eyes are closed. But he kept staring her down. What started out as uncomfortable, was oddly turning into something amusing as he watched Charlotte's expression change to one of astonishment. He suddenly felt as if he could go on for days.

Charlotte, in a move of retreat, barked, "All right, break's over," and turned quickly back into her office, closing her door.

"What the hell was that?" asked Gus in half puzzlement and half awe.

"Nothin'. Her shit's just grown tiresome, that's all."

"When did you become such a gunslinger when it comes to Charlotte?"

"I'm not. I don't know what I'm doing. I'm just tired of seeing her get so much pleasure out of watching everybody around here crawl."

"So you looked directly into the beast's eyes? What did you see?" Gus chuckled.

"Eeeeevil," replied Phil, smiling. He was only half joking.

---

LUNCHTIME CAME, and Phil and Jill found themselves basking in the sun at a table near the sidewalk on the Outpost's terrace. After the waitress took their orders and walked away, Phil leaned in toward the table.

"Okay, Ms. Wheaton, my name is Mr. Murphy, and I'll be conducting this interview. Why don't you begin by telling me a little about yourself?"

Phil never had a problem with small talk. His casual way around women, in particular, had always served him well. In the night life of his college days, he'd often strike up a conversation with some of the best-looking women as they walked past his table. He'd get their attention with a quiet, "Hey," then ask something like, "What do think of my new glasses?" while not even wearing any. Soon, they had sat down with him. It didn't hurt that he wasn't a three-eyed troll.

The couple enjoyed a nice lunch, incrementally learning more and more about each other. After the meal, the waitress left the bill with Phil. In her final work toward the tip, she looked him in the eye, smiled at him, said "Thank you", then walked away. After a moment, Phil rolled his eyes.

"I'm really sorry about that."

"About what?"

"That waitress. It's uncalled for, really. I mean you're *right here.*"

Silence from Jill.

"Didn't you see the way she was throwing herself at me?" he asked. "At every place I eat, the waitresses do that. It just gets old after a while, that's all."

A smile slowly found its way to Jill's face.

"I mean, can't she see we're here together? I'm really sorry. Maybe I should call for the manager," he said.

"Maybe you should," Jill said, now openly smiling at Phil. "That has to be such a burden for you. Everywhere you go, being subjected to such advances. I would think you feel quite violated."

In his best martyr's voice, tilting his head and looking off into the distance, he said, "Sadly, I've grown accustomed to it." Pausing, he added, "But the real victims are those in my company, men and women alike. The women are traumatized by seeing me brazenly pursued right before them, while the men are emasculated by the enormous shadow I cast."

And at the end of the work day, Phil sprinted up parking garage steps, taking them two at a time.

# CHAPTER THIRTEEN

THE NEXT DAY of work passed uneventfully, with Phil hitting a productive streak. He teamed with Geneva to focus on clearing out a good bit of the department's backlog of overdue financial reporting. During their time together, they commiserated a little about their joint venture into probation. By actually listening to her, Phil also learned that a little cantankerocity is understandable when your back hurts most of the time. Maybe he'd give this listening thing some more effort. They got so much done, they were able call it a day at the customary time.

After dinner, Phil, Willie, and Otis spent a relaxing Thursday evening on their front porch. As April was nearing its end, the sun's surrender to the moon was taking a little longer each day, making the sidewalks and yards of McHenry Street come alive in the evenings. Tonight's entertainment: watching his snooty neighbor Stanley mow his grass for the third time since Saturday. Secretly fertilizing his yard at night was now paying dividends for Phil. Being able to hear him complain about it over the roar of his mower was icing on the cake. Sipping on a cold beer at the same time made the icing even sweeter.

Phil noticed Gus's car turning in off the street, pulling into his driveway. Otis lumbered down the porch steps, tail wagging, to greet him as he got out.

"Cold one?" asked Phil, holding up a cold beer he'd pulled from a chest of ice.

"Sure."

Before adjourning to the living room, they unwound on the porch a bit, wringing out the last remaining minutes of sunlight from the warm —by Delaware springtime standards—evening.

"I've got some news, my friend," Gus said, as he sat with his legs stretched out, feet crossed upon the porch railing.

"Is that so?" Phil said quietly, knowing how it would irritate Gus if he didn't ask what the news was. A pause ensued.

"Douchebag, don't you want to know?"

In a lord of the manor baritone, Phil moaned, "Unburden yourself, if you must."

"Well, if you ask me a little nicer, I'll tell you some good news."

"This isn't good news for *you*, is it?" asked Phil.

"No, no, good news for you," Gus answered. "Now, ask nice."

"Okay, how's this? Oh, please, please, will you tell me the good news?" Phil said with a mock whine.

"Not bad, but you didn't compliment me."

Laughing, Phil replied, "Do tell of the good news, oh, owner of all knowledge and goodness."

"Okay, but you forgot rule number one when dealing with someone as vain as myself: I prefer compliments that glorify my physical attributes, as opposed to those that celebrate any integrity I might have."

"Well, I guess we're done then," Phil said, "because there are no honest compliments that glorify your physical attributes."

"Well done, Murphy. That earned you the good news, which is..." Gus paused. "You aren't on probation!"

"Why do you say that?" asked Phil.

"Because I was up in Human Resources this afternoon, trying to look down Missy Henderson's blouse, and I mentioned you being on probation." More needling silence from ensued, this time from Gus.

"And?"

"Don't you want to know if I saw anything?"

"Down her shirt?" Phil asked impatiently. "What are you, twelve?"

"Well, don't you want to know?"

"Sure," Phil said with a tired smile.

"Just some cleavage. Fairly deep, but only cleavage."

"No nipple?"

"No," Gus sighed.

"Well that's disappointing. She's the redhead, right?" Phil asked.

"Yeah."

"You know the big question about redheads is the nipple," Phil said. "Pink or brown? You never know what you're gonna get. It's one of life's mysteries."

"Are you done?" Gus asked. "Anyway, I mentioned your probation to Missy, and she said she hadn't heard about it. She told me anytime an employee is placed on probation, a representative from HR has to be in the meeting with the supervisor and the employee. Your meeting was just you, Charlotte, and Curry, right?"

"Right, and Curry sure as hell isn't an HR rep," Phil said, his tone growing more heated. He took a swig from his beer bottle to the sound-track of Stanley's mower. "I don't know what the hell he does, but he's not in Human Resources."

Gus continued, "Charmer that I am, I was able to convince her to check your file, just to confirm it. And you aren't on probation. Not at all. No warning, no nothing."

"Holy shit!" Phil barked, but then turned down his volume after looking over at Willie trying to put a cowboy hat on Otis at the other end of the covered porch.

"Why the hell would Charlotte go through such a production?"

"My guess is to get more work out of you," answered Gus.

"I bet you anything Geneva's not on probation either," Phil said, "because there was no HR rep in her meeting. We saw who came out of Charlotte's office when they were done."

"Missy said it takes an act of congress to put somebody on proba-tion. Charlotte probably just didn't want to do the paperwork," Gus said, adding, "I told Missy to keep a lid on it, so she's not going to mention it to anyone."

Simmering now, Phil added, "And I bet if you have too many

people in your department on probation, it's probably a poor reflection on the manager. She's just trying to pressure Geneva and me into working more, probably to get rid of the backlog of work we have in the department. We did get rid of a lot of it this week."

Darkness was setting in, and Stanley shut down his lawn mower, thus ending the outdoor entertainment for the evening. So, the boys gathered up the toys and the beer then moved inside.

"If she'd just told me the department's in a bind, and asked me to spend some extra time, I would've done it," Phil said.

"Not me," Gus said. "I'd like to watch her twist in the wind for a while. You're too *good*, Murphy."

Once inside, Phil gave Willie his bath while Otis kept Gus company in the living room. After his bath, Willie gave Gus a hug, Phil tucked Willie in, and the fellows resumed their conversation during the Phillies game on the tube. Gus leaned back on the couch and plopped his feet up, crossing them out in front of him on the coffee table. Phil took the recliner by the window overlooking the front yard. Beer was quickly becoming a scarce commodity.

Otis was parked on the carpet in front of the TV, then took a notion to have a good long stare at Gus.

"Dad," Gus whined, "Otis is staring at me."

"Now Otis," Phil said, "leave your brother alone."

Upon hearing Phil say his name, Otis turned and looked at Phil. Directly in the eyes.

"You ever wonder how a dog knows to look you in the eye when you talk to it?" Phil asked.

"What do you mean?"

"Nothing, really, but why does he look me in the eye? How does he know to do that? I guess they all do it, but it's just a little weird, that's all. I guess the eyes are the portal to the soul, no matter what species."

"I guess," said Gus.

The evening rolled on, with more beer and junk food being consumed. Feeling the effects of the alcohol, they were soon good and relaxed. However, Phil couldn't let go of Charlotte's puppetry.

"She can't just get away with shit like that," Phil said, adding, "What kind of person does that?"

"An aging ice princess that's bumpin' her head on the glass ceiling, is my guess," Gus said, illustrating the concept that age is a relative thing. "How old do you think she is, anyway?"

"She's not old, really. I don't know, maybe forty," Phil said, as he got up to put Otis outside on his chain. Otis loved to lay in the cool grass at night, but Phil didn't trust him not to wander off. Otis's chain kept him tethered to a stake and allowed him to mosey around the front yard at will.

With the alcohol in their blood manifesting itself, Gus said, "It must be weird to watch yourself get old. Nothin' you can do about it. Time passing by, faster and faster. Time is always the same, so why should it go by quicker? I even notice it at our age. Why the hell is that?"

"It's gotta be all math," Phil answered, plopping back down in the recliner after letting Otis out. "Think about it. As time passes, each year, month, day, or whatever, becomes a smaller and smaller percentage of your life. I mean, a year to a five-year old kid is twenty percent of his life, a huge chunk. No wonder you tell a kid he's got to wait a year for something, it sounds like an eternity."

Phil swigged his beer and gazed at the television. "But to a fifty-year old, a year is only two percent of his life, and it would seem to pass much faster."

As he finished off the last of the Doritos, Phil concluded, "Betcha that's the whole explanation for patience. Older people aren't more patient than young people because they've accumulated wisdom or somethin'. It's only because older people are willing to wait the smaller percentage of their life on things."

"No shit?"

"No shit," Phil confirmed.

They drank all the beer in the house over the course of the baseball game. At its conclusion, both Phil and Gus were pretty much lit. Now, at 10:30, Phil was restless. Being manipulated by Charlotte was eating at him, and he was itching to do something about it. Gus was at the other end of the spectrum, sprawled out on the couch, drifting in and out of sleep.

From his recliner, out of the corner of his eye, Phil caught a glimpse of Otis doing his business in the front yard. With energy to burn and holding a grudge, Phil began to incubate a plan that he had yet to think through.

*Who says carrying a grudge isn't healthy?* Phil thought. *It's actually great exercise. Those things are heavy as hell.*

"You gonna sleep on the couch tonight?" He asked a half-asleep Gus. "You sure as hell can't drive,"

"Yeah," mumbled Gus.

"All right, I'm gonna go out for a little bit. Listen for Willie, will ya?"

"Okay."

With that, Phil grabbed a light jacket, then a sandwich-sized sealable plastic bag from the kitchen. He opened the front door, bringing Otis back into the house, then carefully maneuvered through the front yard until he came upon Otis's handiwork. Quite a trophy, it was.

"Good work, my friend," he said as he turned the bag inside-out, wearing it like a mitten, then grabbing Otis's product. Carefully, he turned the bag right-side-out and sealed the contents within. Otis was a big dog, so the bag was full.

Phil was flying high, but still in control enough to know he couldn't afford a DUI. Not with a custody battle on the horizon. So, he grabbed his bicycle from the back yard, and hit the street. Cruising through the April night air was exhilarating.

Charlotte's house was only about two or three miles away, and he could get there using mostly lightly traveled streets. A three-quarter moon in a clear, star-spangled sky lit his way.

His judgement was surely clouded, but he felt some sort of juvenile stunt was called for in this situation. Dog shit in the mail box. A classic. Even if Charlotte never knew it was Phil, he would garner some pleasure from her annoyance. He pedaled on, the cool night air in his face, encountering only a few cars along the way.

Upon his arrival to Charlotte's street, he hopped off his bike and pushed it over to a group of shrubs near the street, laying it on the ground behind them. His destination was a dozen or so houses away. Charlotte lived in a subdivision of mostly long brick ranches and split-level mid-entry houses. Charlotte's was the latter. Her house was located just about mid-way between two street lights, all the better to enhance Phil's secrecy.

No sidewalks on this street, nor many parked cars, as most were in their garages or driveways. He walked casually down the side of the street, toward Charlotte's house, now eight or nine houses away.

In the distance, maybe a quarter mile away, a set of headlights appeared. His mind sprung into over-action. What if it was a cop? Probably wasn't, but what if it was? How would he explain walking late at night in a neighborhood so far from his own?

He kept walking. The lights came nearer. Now maybe a hundred yards. Not wanting to risk an encounter with what might or might not be the police, he ran a few steps and knelt down behind one of the few parked cars on the street. He quickly realized if he was spotted crouching behind a car by a cop, or anyone for that matter, he would surely be in a bind.

The pace of his pulse had picked up significantly, and he was getting a bit of a tingle in his face. He spotted some hedges across the street. Nothing like that on his side of the street.

So, just before the head lights of the oncoming car could reveal him, he sprung from his crouch, darted across the street, and dove over a set of hedges four feet high. Landing on his stomach, pointing away from the street, he quickly did a slithering one-eighty. He remained on his belly, motionless, peering through the bottom of the hedges, as he lay in wait for the approaching car. He could feel his heart pound against the ground. Soon the headlights found the parked car, then passed it by. Not a cop.

An overreaction, sure, but Phil hadn't felt so alive in quite a while. He stayed put for a tick, making sure nothing else was coming. When his pulse normalized a bit, he arose, dusted himself off, and resumed his journey toward Charlotte's house.

In the half hour that had elapsed since Phil left his house, some clouds had started to emerge. A smattering of gusts arrived, pushing the clouds past the moon rather quickly, alternately illuminating and shadowing the earth below. Phil walked as casually as he could down the side of the street toward Charlotte's, now only three houses away.

He had no idea if Charlotte was home or not. No cars in her driveway, but she did have a garage. A couple of lights were on in the house, but no signs of life otherwise. He reached the house next door.

He glanced around as he continued walking. One last check for anyone who might see him. Nothing. He quickly scuttled from the street, across the neighbor's driveway, and concealed himself behind a large bush up against the front corner of Charlotte's house.

The run from the street to the bush required only a short burst of energy, but Phil was breathless, his jugular throbbing as blood was rapidly pushed through it. He knew it wasn't the physical exertion that had quickened his body's activity, but the anticipation of this moment. As he caught his breath, he cracked a smile and snickered quietly. The wind was picking up, and there was the sound of thunder in the distance. The moon had now disappeared.

From behind the bush, he peered up and down the street in preparation to approach the mailbox by Charlotte's front door. From his jacket pocket, he pulled the sealed sandwich bag. He paused, looking at the bag and its contents. He held his position behind the bush and pondered for a moment.

By this time, the effects of the beer had begun to wear off. While his activities up to this point could possibly be blamed on alcohol, he knew what he was doing now. He didn't much like that, either. He liked being able to say, "Well, I'd been drinking..." when he did something asinine. He knew he could stop now and go home if he wanted to.

Just then, he heard a muffled voice from the window directly above him. First a man's voice, then a woman's. He listened for a moment but heard nothing else. He moved ever so quietly along the side of the house toward the back yard. Phil's curiosity was now steering the ship.

A flickering glow shone through the windows above as shadows danced on the curtains. The windows on the upper level were just a few feet above Phil's head, since half of the lower level was underground.

As Phil approached the rear corner of the house, he maneuvered around two plastic garbage containers, the kind on wheels. This whole scene had a familiar feeling, but he couldn't put his finger on it. He'd only driven by the front of Charlotte's house on one other occasion, never seeing the back before.

Unconscious of the bag o' doody that he still carried in one hand, Phil came around the corner and into the back yard. There, he found an elevated wooden deck attached to the back of the house. From the ground, eight stairs led up to the deck, where a sliding glass door, lined on the inside by a thin drapery, led into the house.

Now with the moon fully obscured, Phil stood in the darkness of Charlotte's back yard, staring up at the light from behind the glass door. The gusting night breeze made the hair on the back of his thick neck stand up. He picked up on the slight movement of shadows in the room behind the sliding door. He cautiously made his way to the base of the deck stairs. Giving another glance around, he embarked on a cautious creep up the steps.

Finally, he made it to the top without incident. Wanting to get closer to the door, he was held back by concern of being visible to those inside. But he recalled something from his days as a middle-schooler, when he and his friends would peek at his thirty-something buxom neighbor through her window. If it was light inside and dark outside, no one who was inside could see who was outside. How about that? A deviant adolescent pursuit had actually borne fruit here in adulthood.

So, he crept closer to the glass door, still obscured by cloud-aided darkness. Finally, he parked himself about six feet from the door, leaning against the deck railing. Although thinly-veiled by the sheer drapery, Phil could now see who owned the dampened voices.

Sitting on the couch across the room, Phil found Charlotte and Russ Curry going at it like a couple of hormone-riddled teenagers. Curry was barefoot, but still in work clothes, while Charlotte was wearing only a sheer black robe. Russ appeared to be trying to floss Charlotte's teeth with his tongue. It was quite the spectacle.

The room was illuminated only by candles, but there must have been a couple of dozen of them, so it was fairly bright. Phil stood motionless, not more than twenty feet from them, as the wind whipped and the bellowing thunder grew closer. He felt the beginnings of some squeezing pressure on his temples.

As they continued, the sash at the waist of Charlotte's robe loosened due their impassioned kneading. In moments, the sash had fallen by the wayside. With her gown now open in the front and falling off one shoulder, she was in full view. Their adolescent make-out session was turning into something more now, with Curry making clumsy advances and Charlotte offering no defense to them. Outside, Phil was now in the midst of a full-blown storm, having to steady himself from the pushy, gusting wind. The deafening thunder only inflamed his now excruciating headache, as he watched the two on the couch grope each other in a most ungainly way, primarily due to Curry's apparent inexperience.

Just when their preliminary work was approaching the final act, lightning struck. Not the kind Charlotte and Curry had hoped for, but literal lightning, so close that Phil jumped out of his skin, losing his balance and falling backward over the deck railing. Down he fell, a good eight feet, helplessly landing on his back. Only the garbage containers broke his fall, causing them to burst open with a loud boom.

This brought Charlotte and Curry to their feet, struggling to gather themselves. Phil, meanwhile, lay stunned on the ground, surrounded by the rotten stench of garbage bags, some of which had burst open. Lying on his back, Phil turned his head to the side to come face to face with the bloody head of a large dog, protruding from a one of the bags.

In a period of two seconds, Phil's mind raced from tortured thought to tortured thought. His mind flashed to the silent video he'd seen on his television of bloodied gloves shoving a large bag of garbage in to a can. Seeing the dog's tongue hanging from the side of its mouth, flashed his mind to the suffering the poor animal must have endured.

And lastly, in the dog's face, he saw his own Otis, and he felt the punch in the gut it would be if this had happened to his own dog.

Gasping in horror, he scrambled to his feet and ran as fast as he could toward the street. Charlotte and Curry slid the door open, rushing out onto the deck. Curry's attention was drawn immediately to the garbage below, but Charlotte's eyes were locked on the shadowy figure running across her neighbor's front yard toward the street.

Before Curry could notice the dog carcass in the mess below, he cried out, "Ugh!" Looking down at his bare foot, he found a ruptured sandwich bag and Otis's masterpiece oozing out from between his toes.

Instantly, the wind died and the thunder quieted. Charlotte cast a knowing glare as she watched the trespasser run down the street and disappear in the night, beyond the streetlight's reach.

# CHAPTER FOURTEEN

THE NEXT MORNING, Phil slowly, stiffly, rose from his bed, feeling akin to Oz's Tin Man in need of his oil can. He hobbled down the hall to check on Willie, and found him out like a light with Otis at the bottom of his bed and tail thumping upon seeing Phil.

As he passed by the living room on his way to the bathroom, he noticed Gus had already left. Phil's face was stinging. Better have a look in the mirror.

He almost never looked in the mirror before leaving the house. He always lathered up and shaved in a steamy shower, rubbing his hand over his face until he could feel no more stubble. After his shower, the bathroom mirror was always steamed over. By the time he was dressed and out the door with Willie, he really had no idea what he looked like. To Phil, the purpose of clothing was just to spare his co-workers from having to see him naked.

This morning, though, he had a peek at his face before jumping in the shower. What he saw was a puffed-up, silver-dollar-sized abrasion on his left cheek, just under his eye. And he was sore—not the "good" sore he felt after a couple of hours of basketball. His neck and lower back were stiff. His left rib cage was sensitive to the touch. He couldn't ever recall falling eight or ten feet and landing on garbage cans before.

Phil's emotions were a mixed bag. He was mad at Charlotte. He was pissed at Curry. He was ashamed of his voyeuristic act. He was freaked out about discovering a dog carcass in a garbage bag and felt sure it was the same garbage bag he saw in the odd video on his television. And why did the storm and his headache stop when Charlotte and Curry were interrupted?

Most of all, he was mad at himself for drinking to the point that he felt it acceptable to risk losing Willie due to a childish and idiotic stunt. Worse yet, near the end, he'd been sober enough to stop it all, but hadn't. And the big worry: was he recognized at Charlotte's house?

As he gazed into the bathroom mirror, no longer really looking at his face, Jill crept into his thoughts. In Phil's mind, lunacy like last night was a result of the kind of a deal-breaking flaw that he wanted to conceal from her until he could get rid of it altogether. And that's what he would do. No more childish stunts.

After dropping Willie off at Stephanie's, Phil's mind started to wander, wondering what awaited him at work. Friday had come quickly after an eventful week, and he was looking forward to a relaxing weekend. Upon his arrival at the office, he found Charlotte's door closed. As he settled into his chair, Gus stepped off the elevator.

"I guess you made it back home okay this morning?" Phil asked.

"Yeah. What the hell's wrong with your face? It's even more messed up than usual."

Since Gus had been asleep on the couch when Phil had gotten back home the night before, he proceeded to quietly tell Gus the details of his adventure to Charlotte's house. Phil had a hard time keeping him quiet, quelling his outbursts as the story was told.

"I knew it," Gus said, adding, "That explains a hell of a lot about Curry's promotion."

"I would say so," Phil said.

"All right, now to the most important part of all of this," Gus said with a grin. "How'd she look?"

"You mean Charlotte?" Phil asked, looking over his shoulder toward her office.

"Yeah. I mean, was everything where it's supposed to be? She's not really a dude or anything, right?"

"Oh no, she's not a dude. Not at all. You know how we wonder about how good she must have looked ten or fifteen years ago? Well, she couldn't have looked much better back then. She just has to go and ruin it all by being Charlotte."

Just as Phil finished his sentence, Charlotte's door opened, and out she came.

"Good morning, boys," she said, taking a sip of coffee from her mug. Even a simple "Good morning" from Charlotte was an unusually warm greeting.

"Howdy, ma'am," said Gus playfully. Phil said nothing, just offering a forced smile.

"Had some trouble at my place last night," she said.

Still in cowboy mode, Gus said, "Some cattle get loose on the south forty?"

"No, just a prowler. Saw him running away, though. Got a pretty good look at the back of him."

"That *is* more interesting than wandering cattle," Gus said.

"What the hell happened to you, Murphy?" Charlotte asked, pointing at the scuff on Phil's face.

"Just some rough-housing with my son."

"Well, you know I'm always concerned with the well-being of my crew," she said with an undertone of sarcasm. She headed back toward her office, stopped at the door, then turned toward Phil and Gus. "I'm going to need you to work over this evening, and put in some time on Saturday and Sunday, too."

"Geez!" Gus moaned.

"Oh, not you, Austin. Just Mr. Murphy," she said with a smugly evil smile. She disappeared back into her office and closed the door.

"Well, that's it. I'm screwed," Phil said. "She knows it was me."

Quickly, all the things that could go wrong paraded through Phil's mind. At best, Charlotte would make his life at the bank miserable. And if he didn't obey her every command, she'd spill her guts about his lurid voyeuristic activities.

His mind was swirling, and he had to get away. So, he bolted from his desk to the familiar retreat of the elevator. Hurriedly, he strode to its doors, pushed the up and down buttons, and waited. If only the load of crap he'd told Curry about elevators were true. Finally, a door opened. No one on board.

He rode for ten minutes, up and down. People got on. People got off. Once he calmed down, he was slapped in the face by a realization. *He wasn't the only one out on a limb here.* Charlotte was screwing a subordinate. She might not be sure of what Phil had or hadn't seen, but she had to be sweating that bit of uncertainty. And Phil had completely forgotten about the staged probation ceremony that Charlotte and Curry conducted. He could put her in a real bind if he went to Human Resources with that nugget of info. It wasn't just his word against Charlotte's and Curry's, either. They had done the same thing to Geneva.

A wonderfully eerie calm beset him now. He pressed the "3" button and waited for the elevator door to open. When it did, he strode confidently off the elevator and straight to Charlotte's closed office door. He opened it without knocking. Charlotte gasped, unable to say anything momentarily, until she could muster, "What the hell do you want?"

Phil closed the door, sat down in the chair in front of her desk, leaned back, crossed an ankle over his knee, and smiled.

"I won't be working tonight, this weekend, or any night or weekend unless I think I need to."

Charlotte sat stunned, mouth agape.

"I know I'm not on probation, and neither is Geneva. You're going to tell Geneva she's off probation now, or I'll have a talk with HR." He was careful not to mention being at her house, as he wouldn't have been surprised if she recorded all the goings-on in her office.

Silence from Charlotte. Phil got up from his chair.

"While I'm thinking of it, Austin and I will probably take an occasional long lunch. Sometimes, a really long-ass lunch. I would imagine you'll have no problem with that, right?"

She said nothing.

"I'll take that as a 'no'," he said.

He headed for the door and opened it. Charlotte started to utter something, but Phil interrupted with, "Give my regards to Russ," cutting her off. "Oh, I'm sorry, I should've let you finish." After a short pause, he added, "That's probably Russ's go-to line, huh?"

With that, he closed her door, went to his desk, grabbed his jacket, and headed for the elevator to take the rest of the day off. He'd love to have shared the news with Gus, but he wasn't at his desk. As he neared the elevator, a thought struck him. He turned on one heel and marched back across the Credit Department floor, through the double doors into the Trust Department.

He hadn't been in that part of the bank for months, so he asked the receptionist to point him toward Jill's office. When he got to her open office door, he found her at her desk, shuffling some papers.

"Hey," Phil said.

A smile immediately came to her face. "Come in."

"No, this is a quick visit," he said. "Tomorrow night. Dinner?"

"Sure."

"I'll pick you up at seven."

"Okay." Her face told Phil she thought it was a great idea.

Phil grinned, then left. He picked up Willie, pleasantly surprising Stephanie with his lack of tardiness. Then it was off to home in the little white truck to get Otis, and then on to Phil's dad's house to pick him up.

A tight squeeze, but there were seatbelts for all three humans, and Otis fit nicely in the extended cab area behind the front seats. From there, the Murphy men went on to enjoy a beautiful Friday together at the lake.

# CHAPTER FIFTEEN

THE NEXT DAY was a busy Saturday of lawn mowing, errand running, and polishing up the little white truck for his date with Jill. After the chores were done, it was time for Phil to drop Willie off for the night at Kara and Gary's house. Phil never felt too guilty about leaving Willie with his aunt, uncle, and cousins. Willie always had fun and looked forward to going. With his mom gone, Willie could use the maternal affection that Kara showed him.

"So, what's on the agenda for the evening?" Kara asked, as Phil dropped Willie's night bag onto the couch.

"Food," Phil said in a stone age way.

"And?"

"I don't know. Should there be more?"

"Yes, there should be more. No movie? No..." she said, pausing, "Actually, what else is there to do around here?"

"I know," Phil said. "I don't know what else to do. A movie doesn't seem right, since we're trying to get to know each other. Just sitting there, all quiet for two hours. You know, Gus has a show tonight at the Stumble."

"You are *not* going to take her to that place on a first date."

"I'll figure something out," Phil said.

"I know you haven't done this in a long time, but you'll get the hang of it," she said. "You went out with Angela a while back, right? So you may not be as rusty as you think."

"Yeah, we had a meal together, but it didn't feel like a date. She's nice, but we were pretty much pushed together. I felt like we were just going out to get our friends off our backs. Tonight feels like a date, and I gotta say I'm feeling a bit nervous."

"You'll be fine. You're Phil Murphy!" Spoken like a sappy big sister.

"Don't remind me," he said with a laugh. "I mean, what if she's dressed up, and here I am putting her in my truck? I cleaned it up, but she's got be used to nicer things. She's got two Ivy League degrees, for cryin' out loud."

"If she wanted an Ivy Leaguer, she'd have one," Kara said. "I'd say she could have her pick of about anyone, and here she is with my brother."

Kara always had a way of making Phil feel like everything would be fine, and she'd done it again. So off he went in his gussied-up truck, toward the north side of town, windows down, the cool breeze soothing his scraped and swollen cheek. Looking out his driver's window, Phil saw the sun starting its descent. The afternoon had become a beautiful evening in the heart of spring.

Mother Nature was strutting her stuff. As the sun fell toward the horizon, its work was evident on the underside of the clouds. The western sky was flaunting a swirling cocktail of blues, whites, and pinks in varying depths. Out of the passenger side window, a nearly full moon was just on the rise, as if to chase the sun from the sky. Was it plucky persistence or only foolish optimism that inspired the moon in its relentless, fruitless pursuit of the sun every evening?

Phil wound through the maple-lined streets of the north side of town, finally entering the parking lot of Jill's apartment complex. He popped out of his truck and bounced up the outside stairs to the second floor, quickly arriving at her door. He cut loose with a buoyant drum roll of a knock with the ends of all five digits of his right hand, pinky to thumb in rapid succession, three times.

When the door swung inward, there stood what had occupied his mind all week.

"Right on time. How about that?"

"You look very nice. Hungry?" he asked.

"Sure," she said. "What's on the menu?"

"Well, since we didn't use my Taco Bell coupon during lunch the other day...."

"Perfect," she said. "I've had a craving for refried beans."

"Let's save the refried beans for a special night," Phil said. "How about The Cove Marker down at Bowers Beach? Best fresh seafood on Delaware Bay, if you can get past where it's at.

"You mean Murderkill River?"

"Yep," he said. "You know it worries me a little that you know about the Murderkill."

"That's right, mister. So you just watch yourself," she said. "because I also know that just down the road from there is Slaughter Beach."

"So, seafood sounds okay with you?"

"Sure, I love that place," she said, reaching up and placing her palm on his cheek, gently caressing the abrasion under his eye with her thumb. She did it without even thinking. "What did you do to yourself?"

"I'm just clumsy," he said with a smile.

She pulled the door closed behind her, and they made their way down the stairs to Phil's truck. They stood in front of their chariot and looked it over.

"I'm going to ask you something, and I want you to be honest," he said to her, as she looked intently at him with her big doe eyes. "Are you just going out with me for my truck?"

A smile came to her face.

"Guilty," she said. "It does buff up nicely, doesn't it?"

"Yep," he said. "Let's eat."

He grabbed her by the hand, led her to the passenger door, and delivered her into the waiting seat. He closed her door, walked around the back of the truck, popping in a Tic-Tac along the way, then reappeared, dropping himself into the cockpit.

After a relaxing dinner, they left the restaurant, made their way across the dimly lit parking lot, and got into Phil's truck. Darkness had set in. They sat for a moment.

"Well," Phil said, "this is as far as I've planned."

"Really?" she asked. "Oh, I get it. Dinner was an audition, and in case I didn't measure up, you could call it an early evening."

"Was it that transparent?" he asked with a grin. "I guess we're done, then. You understand, right?"

"That's a shame. I was having a good time," she said.

"Well, just for future reference, when you lifted your chowder bowl and slurped the last bit out, that was the straw that broke the camel's back for me," he said, as he held her hand in one of his palms and lazily made small circles on the top of it with the index finger of his other hand.

"So you didn't mind my shouting match with the waiter so much?" she asked.

"That, I liked," he said. "It almost got you a second date."

They quieted for a moment, and their eyes settled on each other's. The early rising moon that accompanied Phil on his way to Jill's apartment was flying solo now, and its beams lit the interior of the truck, dancing on Jill's golden, glistening hair.

Without any forethought, he gently placed the fingertips of his left hand on her cheek, eased forward, and their lips softly met. It felt completely like home to him. He was careful not to be too aggressive, not wanting to make a misstep. He found it a difficult thing to do, but after a dozen heartbeats, he slowly pulled away. As they parted, their eyes reopened, each to find a warm smile.

Again, she gently touched the scrape on his face.

"Really, what did you do to your face?"

"Just some rough-housing with Willie," he answered. Quickly changing the subject, he asked, "So what do you think of the Phil Murphy experience, so far? I mean, come on, a make-out session in a parking lot?

It may be a mistake for me to spoil you this way on a first date. I'm afraid I'm setting the bar way too high. You need to know that it's possible not all of our time together will be this cultured. Can you handle that?"

"I'll try."

"You know, I actually wasn't kidding about not having made any plans after this," Phil said. "We could probably still make a late movie if you like."

"I'm afraid a movie would just seem so dull now after all this parking lot affair," she said with a grin. "I mean, look, there's even a dumpster over there."

"I hesitate to mention another option that we have, but Gus has a show at the Stumble tonight. Have you ever seen him do what he does?"

"No. What does he do? Sing?"

"Sort of. Not really. You just have to see it."

"That sounds fun," she said.

With that, Phil started the truck, and they headed downtown to the Stumble On Inn. Once in, Phil spotted Gus at his usual table by the wall. He was accompanied by a male and female acquaintance. Phil was a little relieved not to see Angela there. Not that he feared any sort of scene. Angela was too thoughtful for such nonsense. Rather, he was afraid of hurting her feelings.

"Murf! Come here and sit down," Gus called out loudly, as his two friends scooted their chairs closer together to allow room for Phil and Jill.

"We're not too late, are we?" Phil asked.

"No, I go on in about a half hour."

"You know Jill, don't you?" Phil asked.

"Sure," Gus said. Although Gus had never actually spoken to Jill, he had known of her for years. After introducing the newcomers to the others at the table, Gus pulled two beers out of the icy bucket at the center of the table and handed them to Phil and Jill.

"Maybe one," he said as he twisted the cap off Jill's bottle for her.

"Would you like something else? You don't have to have beer," Phil said to Jill.

"No, this will hit the spot," she said.

They all relaxed and chatted for a while. After a bit, Gus's friends saw another friend at a table across the room, and stepped over to say hello, leaving Gus, Jill, and Phil alone.

"All right Jill, here's your chance to find out whatever you want to know about this guy," Gus said, motioning toward Phil with his thumb in a hitch-hiking gesture.

"I already know it all," she answered. "All he did at dinner was yammer on about himself. He's awfully chatty," she said, smiling at Phil, who sat quietly nursing his beer.

"What did he tell you? Probably a bunch of stuff about serving soup to blind orphans or some crap like that," Gus said, grinning from ear to ear. "Well, I'll tell you all the things that he never would."

"Do tell, then," she said.

Phil said to Gus, "Are you sure you want to start down this street? Traffic flows in both directions, you know."

"I'm not worried about that," Gus said, "She could care less about the skeletons in *my* closet." Jill looked over at Phil, mildly raising her eyebrows as if to say, "He's got a point."

"Okay, then," Gus started, "Did you know this wonderful guy sitting next to you secretly fertilizes his neighbor's yard under the cover of darkness, just to watch said neighbor grudgingly mow his grass three times a week?"

She glanced at Phil, and he merely grinned his crooked grin and took a sip from his beer bottle.

"Oh!" she said with a toothy smile, slapping Phil on the arm.

"What else?" she asked Gus with a big grin.

"So that wasn't a deal-breaker for you?" Gus asked. Not waiting for an answer, he went right in to number two, literally.

"Okay, have you been to his house yet?"

"No."

"When you get there, in the living room, you'll notice a disposable plastic grocery bag on the little table by the front door."

Phil let out a weary sigh, albeit with a little smile.

Gus, grinning widely, continued on.

"The bag is always there. Its contents: a pine cone and a paper towel."

Jill, saying nothing, turned toward Phil and gave him a puzzled look. Phil only raised his eyebrows and took another sip of his beer.

"So, what's that for?" she asked Gus.

"I'm having second thoughts now," Gus said. "He's my best friend, and I can't do this to him. It would be too damaging."

Phil casually took the last sip from his bottle.

"Well, you can't stop now," Jill said, smiling. "I need to know whether I should find another ride home."

"Okay then," Gus told her, "He takes the mysterious bag with him at night when he walks the dog around the neighborhood. When Otis drops a deuce in someone's yard, Phil pulls out the paper towel, bends over, and uses it to rip out a handful of grass immediately next to the canine steamer."

Gus continued his tale, ever increasing the dramatic tone.

"While still bent over, he drops the grass from the paper towel, covering up Otis's calling card, then returns the paper towel to the bag to reside with the pine cone, which is masquerading as the deuce. To any observer, particularly at night, our friend here just looks like a responsible pet owner."

Jill turned to Phil with a quizzical look. He grinned, let out a snicker, and said, "Shall I call you a cab?"

"You *do* have a mischievous streak, don't you?" Jill said.

From the stage, the MC started Gus's introduction. He hopped up from the table and made his way toward the stage. The driving drum beat began, and Gus launched into his act. Jill found great delight in Gus's show, laughing openly.

"Oh, is it ok to laugh?" she asked Phil.

"Sure. There's no wrong reaction."

After a moment, Jill quietly said, "You know, I was here the night you sang."

Phil dropped his forehead onto the table.

Lifting it partially back up, but still looking down at the table, he said, "When you said you hadn't seen Gus's act before, I just assumed you'd never been here. Do you come here a lot?"

"No, that was my only time."

"Were you with friends?" Phil asked.

"No. Just some guy."

After a moment's pause, Phil asked with a grin, "What kind of loser brings a woman to a place like this?"

"It was the highlight of the evening," she said, grabbing his hand and squeezing it.

They watched Gus preen and strut around the stage, and when his show was done, they told him goodnight and left. The pair enjoyed a slow, moonlit drive back to Jill's condo.

As they climbed the stairs toward the second floor, Phil was glad he'd already broken the ice with the kiss in the truck earlier. He wondered what would happen at the door. Would she invite him in? Should he go in? How far might things progress? Did Gus's playful tattling sour her just a little?

As well as the night had gone, Phil was still unsure of himself. Not only was he rusty after being married for four years, but this was not the caliber of woman he had been used to dating. He was outside of his comfort zone but loving every minute of it.

They arrived at Jill's door. Facing each other, no words were spoken. With her back to the door, she reached up and placed a wrist on each of his broad shoulders, allowing her fingers to stroke the back of his neck.

With their eyes fixed upon each other's, he placed his hands on her waist, leaned down, and their lips met. He slid his arms around her lower back and pulled her close to him. They started gently, softly. Soon though, they'd pressed themselves closer together, until there was nothing between them but the clothes they wore. They continued their kiss, occasionally pulling apart for a moment, then letting their lips find each other again.

Jill was just as hungry as Phil was. Since coming back to Dover, she'd had a smattering of dates, but with no one that impassioned her.

Their kiss continued as they leaned heavily upon her door. Finally, they slowed, and gradually pulled away. He gently brushed her hair from her forehead.

"This was a very nice evening, Mr. Murphy."

"I'd argue if I could, Miss Wheaton."

Sensing there would be more of such evenings, there was an unspoken satisfaction between them to end things at the door. So, Phil was the first to say "goodnight," and she replied likewise. She went inside, and he moseyed down the stairs and got back into his truck, looking up to the light in her window as he pulled away.

On his drive home, he was accompanied by Jill's fragrant aroma again. This time it wasn't coming from Willie's clothes, but rather, his own. He liked it a lot.

# CHAPTER SIXTEEN

WITH THE WEEKEND DONE, and most of Monday under his belt, Phil stopped to take a breather from the productive day he'd put in at the bank. Ever since he'd decided to brainwash himself into enjoying his work, that's exactly what was happening. He'd kept his nose to the grindstone so successfully, that he hadn't seen Jill all day. Phil was never a game player, and to make sure Jill knew he wasn't, he decided to pay a visit to her office.

He popped up from his desk, passed through the double wooden doors into the Trust Department, down the hall to the fourth door on the right, and there was the pot of gold at the end of the rainbow. He found her sitting at her desk, pecking at the computer, her thick blonde locks glimmering in the sun shining through her downtown-view window.

"You've made looking busy an art form," Phil said.

Looking up from her screen, she flashed a smile. "Well, you never know who may be watching. Thankfully, it wasn't anyone important this time."

"Ouch. You know, these barbs of yours roll off the tongue just a bit too easily. If I weren't so sure I had you right here, I might be concerned," he said, wiggling his pinky finger.

"You just go ahead and get good and relaxed with thoughts like that," she said. "Then I'll have you right where I want you."

"Just stopping by to tell you what a nice time I had Saturday. I spent half a day in the card shop looking for a way to express myself," he said, "but the closest thing I could find was a sympathy card."

"What are you doing this evening?" Jill asked.

"Not a thing," he said, "Damn, I answered that too fast, didn't I? You probably want me to help you move or something."

"Well, you're not far off, actually. Come with me to Wilmington, to my aunt's for dinner. I need a big strong man to help me move some boxes up to her attic."

"Big strong man, huh? I'm not sure I know any."

"Fortunately, I do," she said with a smile. "My aunt Gwennie's in her eighties now, all alone, and her mind's slipping. Someone new might stimulate her."

"Ok."

"Pick me up at 5:30? It'll take us about an hour to get there."

"I do have Willie, you know."

"Even better," she said. "He'll light up that dark old house of hers."

---

MUCH TO THE delight of Stephanie, Phil left work early enough to pick up Willie and swing by his house to feed Otis. The truck time allowed him to soak in a little more of his "Spanish For Dummies" CD, which had become a fixture in his player. He made it to Jill's stoop by 5:30, and with Willie in his left arm, he deployed his fingertip drumroll knock on her door.

The door swung open to reveal the welcome sight of Jill in an Orioles jersey, perfectly fitting jeans, and sneakers. Give Phil a woman who looked comfortable, as opposed to one overdressed and overly made-up, and he was a happy man.

"Are we ready to go, Mr. Willie?" Jill asked. Even the little guy couldn't resist her, flashing a big grin, then shyly turning his head back into his dad's shoulder.

An hour north on DE-1 brought them to Wilmington, Delaware, just a stone's throw from both the Pennsylvania and New Jersey state lines. Jill's Aunt Gwennie lived in perhaps the most opulent part of Wilmington, in an area where most of the homes were a hundred years old and nestled far off the streets among mature trees. They turned off a shady street into a long, brick-paved driveway lined with a wall of tall shrubbery on each side. Eventually the shrubbery gave way to a view of a massive three-story Tudor.

Upon seeing the home, Phil had a sense memory of the insecurity he'd felt as the turd in his prep school's social punch bowl. Many of his classmates had lived in homes like this, and being the school's charity case, Phil had always felt out of place when he'd occasionally visited them.

As they approached the front door, Jill said, "Aunt Gwennie's got the beginnings of Alzheimer's. My parents seem to find it a chore to visit her now that her mind is going, but I just can't stand the thought of her all alone. She was so good to me, growing up."

"She lives in this huge place all by herself?" Phil asked.

"No, she has a full-time caregiver who lives here, too. My Uncle Scott died years ago, and they never had children."

Even the doorbell rang in a stately manner, and it was soon answered by a middle-aged woman who led the couple and Willie toward the main staircase.

"She's not having a very good day today," the woman said quietly as they began their ascent of the wide stairway. "She's awake but has been incoherent most of the day. She's in bed now. We won't be having dinner tonight."

"That's okay," Jill said. "We'll just visit a bit with her, and then take care of any chores she has."

At the top of the stairs, the group proceeded down a wide hallway, their footsteps muted by an ornate, flowery rug runner that ran its entire length. Aunt Gwennie's bedroom was the last door on the left at the end of the long hall. Aside from his reminiscent class-disparate discomfort, Phil had another feeling as they walked down the seemingly endless hallway—an eerie feeling. Maybe it was just the setting, or perhaps the fact that an old, demented woman awaited them in a lonely bedroom at the end of the corridor. Regardless, he paid the feeling no heed, just chalking it up to unfamiliar surroundings.

Finally, the group reached the open doorway of Aunt Gwennie's bedroom, the caregiver leading the way and Jill next in line. Phil, carrying Willie, thought it best to wait outside the door until Jill told Aunt Gwennie she'd brought company.

"Hi, Aunt Gwennie," Jill said cheerfully, as she and the caregiver entered the bedroom. Phil and Willie stayed in the hall.

There was no answer from the unseen aunt.

"How are you doing today?" Jill asked, to which there was again no reply. Jill and the caregiver exchanged a sad look.

"I've brought a friend to help me move your boxes to the attic," Jill said, simultaneously motioning for Phil and Willie to come into the bedroom. Only silence came from Aunt Gwennie.

When Phil stepped through the bedroom door, he saw a gaunt, white-headed woman sitting upright, covered from the waist down, in a bed that dwarfed her. She sat motionless, staring straight ahead.

"Meet my friend, Aunt Gwennie," Jill said.

Slowly, Aunt Gwennie turned her head toward the doorway, her eyes widening as they locked on Phil's, and she called out to him.

"*Davis?*"

Phil's lips parted to gasp, as that one word and her penetrating stare caused the hair on his arms to stand erect.

"Actually," Jill said, "his name is Phil, Aunt Gwennie. And this is Willie." She placed her hand gently on top of Willie's head.

The next few seconds of silence seemed an eternity to Phil. But then Aunt Gwennie let exhaust from her pale lips a grim warning.

"*They're closing in on you, Davis.*"

Phil's mind raced, too confused to formulate a question for her.

"She's getting worse," Jill whispered to the caregiver. "We'd probably better go."

"I think you're right," replied the woman. "She doesn't even seem to recognize you."

"We're going to do a few chores, Aunt Gwennie, then get out of your way. I'll see you in a few days." Jill went over to the bed and kissed her forehead. There was no response from Aunt Gwennie, who still had her eyes fixed upon Phil.

Phil, Jill, and Willie exited the bedroom, leaving the caregiver to tend to Aunt Gwennie. After moving the boxes into the attic, they had returned to Phil's truck within twenty minutes, and were heading back down the long brick driveway, between the tall hedges, toward the street.

"I'm sorry she wasn't doing well today," Phil said, trying to comfort Jill. "I'm sure she was a lovely woman in her day. And it's such a great house." It took all of Phil's concentration to muster up some small talk with Jill as the multitude of possible explanations for what had just happened swirled through his head.

"If you don't mind me asking, what did she and her husband do for a living?" Phil asked.

"Uncle Scott was a very successful businessman, involved in a lot of different things," Jill replied. "Aunt Gwennie was always so bright and beautiful. I hate to see her wither this way, especially after having such an interesting life."

"What did she used to do?"

"Among other things," Jill said, "she was an aide in the Kennedy White House."

# CHAPTER SEVENTEEN

THAT NIGHT, after getting Willie to bed, Phil found himself in front of his computer at the small desk in the corner of his living room. Maybe now he could find out if his alt-world girlfriend from the plane crash, Kristen Minnows, was a real person or just part of an all-too-realistic dream.

With Otis curled up on the carpet at his feet, Phil clicked the "Connect" button for his internet provider, America Online. It was nice having access to so much information right in his own home here in the new millennium.

After the familiar quiet screeching of his dial-up phone service signaled that he was connected, he was ready to get busy. He input the name "Kristen Minnows" into the search field on Yahoo.

"Glad we're not lookin' for Mary Smith, eh, Otis?" Phil's question was interesting enough to Otis for him to open his eyes, but not so much that he might raise his chin from the carpet.

A list of websites slowly appeared on the results page, the first few of which, predictably, were advertisements for people-finding sites. *Find Kristen Minnows; Reconnect with Kristen Minnows*, and the like.

As he scrolled down the page, a chill struck him, and his eyes lit up at the sight of the heading, *George Magazine—Assistant to the*

*Director of Circulation, Kristen Minnows*. Phil felt his pulse quicken, and he hurriedly clicked on the link, which took him to the website of *George* magazine, on a page listing its prominent employees.

"Bingo, my friend," he said, sharing his excitement with Otis.

He'd struck double gold. Not only had he found a Kristen Minnows who worked in Manhattan, but also, *George* magazine had been created and run by John F. Kennedy, Junior.

Again, the hair on his forearms stood as he plowed through the site. Phil, like a lot of people, casually knew that JFK, Jr. had started a magazine. He was a little surprised that it was still in business nine months after his passing.

Unfortunately, while there were several photos of JFK, Jr., there were none of the Assistant to the Director of Circulation. No other information about her specifically was on the site, only the address of their offices in Manhattan.

He returned to the Yahoo results page for his Kristen Minnows search. The further he scrolled down the page, the more he waded into irrelevant fishing web sites, thanks to her surname's similarity to the creatures that get their oxygen through gills. While he hadn't been able to see a photograph of her, the discovery that she was also connected to JFK, Jr., albeit indirectly, solidified in Phil's mind that he wasn't crazy after all.

"Maybe I'd rather be a kook, buddy," Phil said, wondering aloud to Otis if losing his mind might be preferable to what was actually happening.

The search hadn't taken long. Since he had some time to kill, he thought he'd research something else that had been looming in his mind. Why was the voice of the air traffic controller Charlotte's?

So, he entered "Charlotte Timpkin" into the Yahoo search field. Nothing. Only the people-finding site advertisements. For the halibut, he searched "Providence Rhode Island Air Traffic Controllers". This yielded only a myriad of information about the Providence airport and information on how to become an air traffic controller. Disappointing, but Phil was at least thankful, again, that her name wasn't so common he'd be led on a wild goose chase.

Charlotte had supposedly come from a bank in New Jersey. Phil thought he might give Gus the assignment of coaxing a peek at Charlotte's personnel file out of Missy in HR. The bank generated and stored its personnel documents on a computer but kept hard copy backups in fireproof file cabinets for each employee.

"That might be out of bounds, eh, buddy?" Phil asked Otis, who responded by thumping his tail on the floor. Any words in a pleasant tone to Otis yielded such a reply. In the right tone, Phil could tell Otis, "I'm taking you to the pound," and he'd still wag his tail.

"How 'bout a can of tuna?" Phil said, as he shut down his computer and headed toward the kitchen. The two split a small can of Chicken of Sea, and after checking on the sleeping Willie, headed off to bed, with Otis curling up in his familiar spot at the foot of Phil's mattress.

The next morning, Phil found himself at his desk, enveloped in the mundane drone of office noise and savoring his life-giving coffee. With Charlotte tucked away behind her closed office door, Gus rolled his chair over to Phil's desk.

Phil took the opportunity to fill Gus in on the previous evening's further weirdness with Jill's senile aunt Gwennie and finding a Kennedy-connected Kristen Minnows on the internet.

"My God, you *are* screwed up, aren't you?"

"I wish I was screwed in the head, but I'm starting to think there's something very real about all of this. Anyway, I need your help. I've got a secret mission for you. Do you think you could..."

"Hell yeah, I can," Gus interrupted.

"You don't even know what I'm going to say."

"I don't care. You had me at 'Secret Mission'."

"All right. I need you to go to the police station, dressed in drag, and..." Phil began.

"Okay, what do you really need?"

"I've got to find out more about Charlotte. I want you to help me get a look at her HR file."

"I bet Missy would let us look at it," Gus said.

"I don't know. I wish there was a way we could do it without implicating her. I'd hate to see her get in trouble. This is my battle, not hers." Phil said.

"Yeah, I know what you mean," Gus said. "She's so cool that she'd probably help. But I'd rather try to distract her or something, and let you look at it. That way, she'd stay innocent."

So the two hastily threw together a plot to temporarily swipe Charlotte's file, then return it. At the standard lunch hour, Phil and Gus went up to the seventh floor and entered the Human Resources department.

It was a small operation. First Collateral Bank was pretty much a stand-alone entity headquartered in downtown Dover, with only a few branches sprinkled throughout Delaware. Missy served as the receptionist and clerical liaison with the department's three HR reps, whose offices were offshoots of the lobby that Missy solely occupied.

Since she had to stay and man the lobby desk while the reps were out to lunch, Phil and Gus knew she would be alone. The file cabinets were located in the lobby with Missy, so they had a chance to pull off the feat, albeit slim.

"Here comes trouble," a smiling Missy said as Gus and Phil popped through the door. Phil could see that her wry tone was music to Gus's ears.

"Trouble tucks its tail and runs whenever it sees us," Gus said.

"Did you say you're having trouble with the runs?" she coyly asked, going toe to toe with him. Phil saw why Gus was enamored with Missy. Not only was she tall and full-figured with a round, cheeky face, she was also the owner of a stinging wit, perhaps born of her flowing red hair. She had a bit of a Mae West quality about her.

"What brings you boys to my neck of the woods?"

"We know where the action is in this building," Gus said. "We're having a hard time staying awake down on Three, and just thought we'd see what was cookin' up here in the nerve center."

"Phil," she said with a grin, "don't you know that time spent with this chump is just thrown away?"

"I'm a slow learner, Missy."

With that, Gus sat down on the front corner of Missy's desk, one leg on the ground and one dangling. Phil moved toward the file cabinets behind Missy's desk. As Gus clowned and flirted with Missy, Phil scanned the labels on each drawer of the cabinets.

There were a dozen cabinets lining the wall, each with four drawers. He quickly came upon a cabinet with the top drawer labeled "Shields A-F", the bank's term for employee files.

So that he wouldn't draw attention to himself by being too quiet, Phil said, "Not a bad view from the Penthouse here, Missy," as he appeared to be looking through the doorway of one of the HR reps' offices, out the window.

"Yeah, it'll do," she answered without turning around, adding, "Too bad my back is to it all day."

With that, Phil located the "S-Z" drawer, and quietly slid it open. Gus's natural speaking voice was so loud that that he easily drowned out any noise the sliding drawer may have made. Using his index finger, he hastily rifled through the files until he landed on "Timpkin, Charlotte", pulled it out, rolled it up, and stuck it partially down the back of his pants so that his jacket would cover it up. Gus, chatting all the while with Missy, saw that Phil had completed his mission.

"Well, I'm starvin'," Gus said. "How 'bout you, Philly?"

"Yep. Let's get some grub."

"What are you two, on a cattle drive?" Missy asked.

"Nope, little woman," Phil said as he backed toward the door, "Just, when it's time for grub, it's time for grub."

When they got to the elevator doors, the two grinned at each other and Phil pushed the down button.

"Holy shit, that was fun," Gus said.

"I just hope to hell that there's no video surveillance in that office," Phil said.

"You worry too much," Gus said, "Besides, anybody looking at a video of that would be mesmerized by the trance I put on Missy."

"Man, you really live in a dream world, don't you?"

"More like, livin' the dream, that's all," Gus said with a smile.

The elevator's ding signaled the pair to step toward the door. As the

doors began to move open, they stepped even closer. Upon full opening, they found themselves face to face with Charlotte.

"Jesus, how about giving me a chance to get off the damn
elevator?"

"Sorry, Charlotte," Gus said as he stepped aside for her. Phil didn't
move, and said nothing, only casting a steely glare down at her.

"What are you two doing up here?" she asked as she stepped
around Phil.

"Just visiting," answered Gus. "How about you?"

"Just taking care of a couple of HR items," she said.

Then, with a shit-eating grin, Phil said, "Well, I *guess* that's all
right. But no long lunches, now." And then he winked at her, knowing
it would eat her alive. Having her personnel file shoved down the back
of his pants while he mocked her face to face was about as good as it
could get.

She said nothing and strode toward the HR office. Phil and Gus
entered the elevator. Knowing the elevators had video monitors, Phil made
sure to keep the file hidden in place. There was no audio monitor anymore,
as a lawsuit a few years back had determined that was a step too far.

"Geez, you're full of yourself, huh?" Gus said.

"Let's just get this file copied and back in the cabinet. Your duties
are done. You can go on to lunch if you want."

"No, no, this is too much fun," Gus said. "Besides, you'll need me
to distract Missy again when you're putting it back."

"Let's do this quick," Phil said. "I'd like to get back up there before
the HR reps get back from lunch."

As the elevator doors opened on the third floor, Phil wondered if
Charlotte's business in HR pertained to an employee or something of
her own; health insurance or the like. What if Missy needed Charlotte's
file, and it wasn't there?

"You know, I don't want to be standing at the copier here with her
file if Charlotte comes back," Phil said. "I'm going take this over to the
Trust Department and use one of their copiers." Phil didn't mind the
thought of popping in on Jill, either.

"All right," Gus said, "I'll just hang at my desk until you get done, then we'll go back up. I'll dream up some shit we can tell Missy to explain."

In the Trust Department's small lobby, Phil gave a nod and a smile to the receptionist and kept walking into the hallway toward Jill's office. Down the hall, he approached Jill's door, on his right. Upon arrival, he found the door closed. All the better, he thought, as this was no time for chit-chat anyway.

A few feet past her door was an alcove housing the copier, a water cooler, and a shelving unit holding office supplies. A quick glance around revealed no one, so he reached back and removed the tightly rolled folder, pulled out a stack of paper half an inch thick, and plopped them into feeder on the copier. He punched the start button, then waited patiently to the rhythmic cadence of the copier as it stacked up page after page. Even though the copier made fast work of the file, it seemed more like ninety minutes than ninety seconds.

Finally, it was done, and Phil scooped up the warm copies, rolled them up tightly, secured them with a nearby rubber band, and slid them as far as they would go into the pocket inside his sport coat. He placed the originals back in the folder, rolled it up, and shoved it down the back of his pants again. He couldn't risk Charlotte or the all-seeing elevator camera catching him with the file.

As he began to walk away from the copier, he paused to consider knocking on Jill's door. As he raised his hand to knock, he heard a muffled version of Jill's laugh. He paused, hand still raised. Immediately, he heard a man's voice, also muffled by the door, and then more laughter from Jill. Those sounded like the same laughs that escaped her pouty lips when they were together.

Phil waited silently at the door for another few seconds, unable to recognize any words due to the dense wooden door. Knowing it was probably just some sort of business and that his window of opportunity was fast closing to get the file back to HR before the reps returned from lunch, he left.

Back down the hall, past the Trust receptionist, through the double doors, and toward the elevator, Phil went. The awaiting Gus arose from his desk and joined Phil in stride, like a car merging on to the interstate from the entrance ramp. They said nothing as the elevator doors opened, revealing an exiting Russ Curry.

"What it be like, Russ?" Gus asked, half hoping to provoke him in to some sort of ridiculous comment.

"Doing okay, I guess," Curry said. The lack of usual coldness in his voice was almost shocking to Phil and Gus.

"Soundin' kind of down, there, Russ," Phil said. "You all right?"

"Yes, I'm fine."

Tempting as it was to probe into Curry's behavior, they had no time. They entered the elevator and headed for the top floor.

"We'll just tell Missy we came back to ask her to come to lunch with us," Phil said. He pushed the door to HR open with a manufactured smile on his face, only to find Missy's desk vacant. They looked at each other in mild surprise. Not saying a word, they dispersed, each checking the offices of the HR reps for occupants. Empty.

Phil hurriedly found the correct cabinet drawer and replaced Charlotte's file, purposely placing it close to its original location, but slightly out of alphabetical order. He didn't want the file to have mysteriously reappeared if Missy had just looked for it during Charlotte's visit. This way, the file's absence could be blamed on misfiling.

"Let's get out of here," Phil said.

"Yeah, I'm gettin' hungry."

"No," Phil said, "I'm mean, let's get the hell out of here. We're done for the day."

# CHAPTER EIGHTEEN

IN A HALF HOUR, Phil and Gus found themselves at a little-used park just outside the city, poring over Charlotte's file at a picnic table under a tall pin oak tree. Each had taken his own vehicle, so they wouldn't have to go back to the bank.

"You think it looks funny that we're sittin' on the same side of this table, so close to each other?" Gus asked.

"What, are you not ready for the world to know about us?" Phil said with a grin.

"I just think it looks funny."

"Then sit on the other side."

"Then I'd have to see all the papers upside-down."

"Holy shit, I'll hand you each sheet after I've looked at it," said Phil, temporarily misplacing his patience.

"Okay."

The first several pages of her file were run-of-the-mill personnel forms—resume, insurance, and the like. As he promised, Phil handed the papers to Gus one at a time. Phil paused.

"Here's a filing for criminal charges in Essex County, New Jersey."

"For what?" Gus asked.

"Petty Larceny."

"What did she do?"

"Looks like her neighbor's *dog* came up missing," Phil said, as he continued on down the page. "The charge was eventually dismissed. Charlotte claimed the whole thing was a misunderstanding."

"Poor Charlotte. So misunderstood," Gus said.

"The investigating officer wasn't buying it, according to his write up. He said the neighbor had observed Charlotte trying to lure her dog to her, and that there was a small amount of dried blood on Charlotte's garage floor."

"Holy shit."

"Holy shit is right," Phil said, his eyes still fixed to the page. "But looks like it all fell apart when the prosecutor's office didn't want to spring for DNA testing on the blood for only a misdemeanor."

"Killing somebody's dog is only a misdemeanor?"

"Well, without a carcass, I guess they couldn't prove she killed it." Phil said. "Animal cruelty would be more than a misdemeanor, but I don't think theft would be. It's weird, but I think the law just looks at pets as property, even though they're much more to most people.

Phil pondered silently for a moment, then wondered aloud, "I wonder if that dog met the same fate as the one I saw in Charlotte's garbage can?"

He continued to leaf through the pages, one by one, then hand them over to Gus.

"Huh," Phil exhaled. "She was born in Cuba and came here in 1980."

"Exactly how old is she, anyway?"

"Born in August of '61 and this is 2000, so she'll be 39 in August. Two Thousand, that still sounds weird to me."

"So, what's with her last name...Timpkin?" Gus asked. "That doesn't sound very Cuban."

"I don't know, maybe she was married and divorced. Or maybe that's just a Hispanic name. Does every Cuban have to be named Castro?", Phil asked with a grin. "I gotta say, though, she's done a good job of losing whatever accent she had. I don't pick up on one at all now."

As the two sat silently parsing the contents of the file, the only sounds in the park were those of shuffling paper and the wind through the new springtime leaves of the overhanging oak trees.

"Here we go," Phil said, causing Gus to lift his head from his page.

"Whaddya got?"

"I hold in my hands a copy of the FAA paperwork showing Charlotte's *pilot's license*," Phil answered.

"So?"

"So?" Phil said, "I'm convinced it was Charlotte's voice I heard on the cockpit radio in that episode I had on the plane."

"Yeah, but you said she was the air traffic controller," Gus said. "Is there anything in there about that?"

"I don't see anything," Phil said dejectedly, "But this is at least something related to planes, and shows that she's been around them plenty. Wonder if there's any way to take control of another plane's radio?"

The question went unanswered as they sat silently for a moment.

"So what else you got?" Gus asked.

"Well, I can say the bank is thorough. They did a background check on her. I wonder if they do that to all of us."

"Probably," Gus answered. "We all sign a blanket authorization that allows them to do everything short of a proctoscopy."

"Looks like her father was a Cuban soldier, and died April 17, 1961," Phil said. "Man, that was right in Castro's heyday. There was a bunch of shit going on about that time. That date has a familiar ring to it."

"I know what it is!" Gus said. "That's the date Charlotte's dad died."

"You're a lot of help," Phil said with a grin, as he kept his eyes on the paper. "Listen to this. Her mother drowned in the Florida Straits in the summer of 1980 when she was lost from a makeshift boat trying to come to the Keys. Good God."

"Shit, Charlotte was only about nineteen when her mom died," Gus said.

"And her mom was pregnant with her when her father died in '61," Phil added.

"Almost makes you understand why she's such a heartless bitch."

"Almost," Phil said, "but it doesn't explain why she keeps dog corpses in her garbage, or why she tells her employees they're on probation when they're not, or why a storm seems to build while she's having sex and then abruptly stops when she's interrupted, or...."

"Shitballs, I get it," Gus said. "But what's all this about the weather?"

"Just a dumb hunch, I guess," Phil said. "Let's shoot some ball."

The two adjourned to the adjacent basketball court with the ball Phil kept in the extended cab of the little white truck.

"So, what's the deal with Jill?" Gus asked. "How long 'til you find out if she can touch her knees to her ears?"

"Come on, now," Phil answered.

"What's this? Did I step on an ingrown toenail?"

"I doubt I'd be at liberty to report to you on such a matter," Phil said, as he flicked a shot up and in from the foul line.

"Oh, no," Gus said in a disgusted tone, as he gathered Phil's foul shot and bounce-passed it back to him. "I can tell...you've got too much respect for her, don't you?"

"No... I don't know. Maybe," Phil said, as he stood at the foul line with the ball under one arm. "I just don't want to go too fast and mess things up. It's weird. I can't keep my hands off her, but at the same time, I've got this feeling that I've got all the time in the world. I'm enjoying looking forward to what's ahead. It's kind of like how the anticipation of going on vacation is better than the actual vacation sometimes, you know?"

"I get it," Gus said, "but the next step with Jill sure ain't gonna be like a day on a crowded beach, littered with hypodermic needles and screaming kids."

"Yeah, you're right about that," Phil said. "And you're a little right about the too much respect thing. I thought by now I'd find something about her that annoys me. It ain't happenin'."

Phil stood at the foul line, lazily dribbling the ball shoulder high at his side. "You know, she's not like any woman I've ever gone out with before. For lack of a better comparison, she's like this perfect thoroughbred racehorse, with her championship bloodlines and Ivy League education." He zipped a behind-the-back pass to Gus at the baseline.

"I realize they aspire for a diverse student body," Gus quipped in a snooty register, "but I didn't know they let the equine into Dartmouth."

"You know what I mean."

"Yeah, I gotcha," Gus said. "And you feel like you're the slow-witted, inbred stable boy, just lucky to be shoveling her manure, and dreading the moment she finds out who you really are."

"Damn. That's not far off," Phil confessed.

Gus flipped up a left-handed hook shot from the baseline, only to have it miss the rim entirely, sending the ball off the court, into the grass.

"Always heard you had a problem findin' the hole," Phil said.

"Now, that's just hurtful."

At that moment, Phil's phone rang. He pulled it from his pocket and looked at the incoming number, which he didn't recognize.

"Hello?"

"Phillip, this is Ann Culpepper at the college."

"Hey there. Since you're going to be so formal, calling me Phillip, I'm going to go the other way and call you Doc."

"Well, I've been called much worse than that, dear."

"That's hard to imagine. What's going on?"

"I've been researching your situation and have found some very interesting information. It's a bit too involved for the phone. Do you think you could come by my office?"

"Absolutely. I can be there in twenty minutes."

# CHAPTER NINETEEN

On his way over to the college, questions were ping-ponging off the walls of Phil's mind like a lottery drawing. Why was the voice of the air traffic controller Charlotte's? Did she really move from New Jersey to Delaware just for a banking job? Was there any significance to the date of her father's death?

After emerging from the long tree-tunnel driveway of the college's entrance, Phil guided his truck toward the visitor lot, parked it, then hoofed it toward the heart of the campus. When he arrived at the concrete stairs leading to the entrance of the psychology building, he heard a familiar voice.

"Over here, Phillip."

Twenty yards to his right, on a shade-enveloped bench, sat Professor Ann Culpepper, taking in the students who passed back and forth on the sidewalk in front of her. Her welcoming smile drew Phil to her like a moth to a bug zapper, only nicer, without the horrific ending. In twenty paces, he found himself standing in front of her.

"It's much too nice today to sit in a stuffy office," she said. "Let's take a stroll, shall we?"

Phil extended his broad palm to her, by which she pulled herself to her feet. They began a saunter down the wide, maple-lined sidewalk.

"I didn't expect to hear from you so soon," Phil said.

"Well, I haven't figured out everything by any means, but I believe at my age, I should report any progress immediately. Otherwise, I may be taking secrets to my grave," she said with a mischievous snicker. "Since you're my entire clientele at the moment, I don't find myself distracted. I was so enthralled with my research that I only got four hours of sleep last night."

"So what have you found out?"

"Like I said on the phone, this is rather complex," she answered, "and actually a little 'out there'."

"Well, you've got my attention. If a psych professor thinks something is 'out there', then it must be weird," Phil said, as the two continued their leisurely walk amid the bustling campus.

"Okay. There was a *very* theoretical psychiatrist from Austria in the 1930s named Klaus Clavos, who spent most of his career developing a theory called *Vorstellung Wiederanweisung*."

"Wow, that's a mouthful."

"Well, it translates to *Conception Reassignment*," Ann said. "It's very involved, and the results of Dr. Clavos's experiments were, at best, inconclusive."

"That's encouraging," Phil said.

"Dr. Clavos was working to prove that at the moment a human sperm implants itself inside of a female's egg, an explosion of sorts occurs."

"Okay..." Phil said, waiting for more.

"He believed the moment the little swimmer claimed the egg, and they became one being, a flash forward, if you will, occurred."

"Flash forward?"

"Yes. Everything that basic little life form will ever see, hear, feel, smell, taste, and touch—everything it would ever experience in its entire life—was shown to it right then, at the moment of conception."

"How in the world could he know that?"

"He was a relentless researcher and conducted hundreds of interviews. But let me again say, his work was very theoretical."

"What does his work have to do with my mess?"

"His term, Conception Reassignment, basically theorizes this: If a human embryo is terminated in any way prior to delivery, it's essence is reassigned to another mother."

"That *does* sound pretty 'out there', Doc."

"It does, I agree," she said, as they took a left turn on an intersecting sidewalk, taking them toward the quad. "He believed his theory of Conception Reassignment provided explanations for such vast ideas as Deja vu and fate."

"How so?"

"Through hundreds of interviews and case studies, his work indicated that Deja vu was nothing more than a person recalling scenes and feelings from the flash forward they experienced at conception. If, for example, right now, I had a Deja vu moment, feeling that you and I had taken this walk and had this conversation before, the reason it would feel so familiar is because it was already shown to me in the flash forward of my entire life that I had at conception."

"Lordy."

"Indeed, Phillip."

"I'm still not clear on how this pertains to me."

"I haven't gotten to that part yet," Ann said. "For almost everyone, Deja vu is just when a person *recognizes* a moment in his current life that was previously seen in the flash forward he had at conception."

"Okay," Phil inserted, just to confirm that he was following her.

"But for a person who was terminated after conception—sometime during the pregnancy—then reassigned to another mother, here's how the whole process would go: the victorious little sperm who beat out the other fifty million, gets in to plant his flag and claim the egg."

"You paint quite a picture, Doc."

"At that moment, he has his flash forward, seeing everything that will ever happen to him throughout his life as if the event that terminates the pregnancy never happened. But, some time passes, then something happens and the pregnancy is terminated; miscarriage, abortion, what have you."

"All right..." Phil said as he bent over to retrieve an errant Frisbee, then sail it back to its owner.

"The essence of the miscarried embryo then finds itself in a new mother, is born, and begins living its life. That person can *never* have Deja vu. Never. Tell me why, Phillip."

Phil paused, stooped to tie his shoe, and while doing so, looked up at Ann.

"Because he isn't living the life that he saw in the flash forward?"

"Oh, I bet you did very well in school!" Ann said.

"Unfortunately, my lessons were never so artfully delivered, Doc."

"You flatter me," she said. "There's another way I like to look at Conception Reassignment. I think a better name would be Soul Reassignment."

"Why's that?"

"Well, the author C.S. Lewis is sometimes credited with a quote that says, 'You don't *have* a soul. You *are* a soul. You have a body."

"Yeah, I've heard that one," Phil said.

"I believe, as Dr. Clavos did, that we are a soul and our bodies are just a shell we occupy while we're here," Ann said. "So then, an embryo would just be a vehicle for getting us into the world."

"I think I believe that, too," Phil said.

"And no matter what, a child will be born, one way or another," Ann said. "If an unborn child is miscarried or terminated, it will find another way to get into the world."

"So," Phil said, "what you and Klaus Clavos are saying, pretty much, is that we are all souls that just use a body, any body, to get into the world."

"Yes."

"So one way or another, I was going to be born, and if something went wrong, I'd just be put in any other body to get myself born," Phil said. "I mean, I could have this body or one of a blonde-headed woman on the other side of the world, and I'd still be the same soul."

"That's what Dr. Clavos theorized, yes," Ann confirmed.

"So let me see if I can tell where you're going with this. Do you think that I'm one of these people who was the victim of a terminated pregnancy, and was then reassigned?"

"Yes."

"I can't believe I'm about to say this out loud, but do you also think that my original parents were John F. and Jacqueline Kennedy, and the visions I've been having are recollections of my flash forward at conception?"

"Also, yes," Ann said.

"Weird stuff, Doc."

"Think about this, Phillip," she said. "In the plane crash vision, you described what seemed to be a 'kid brother' feeling you had in relation to the pilot. So that would seem to make you younger than John Jr."

"Okay."

"And Mrs. Kennedy, sadly, gave birth and lost a child in the spring of 1963, named Patrick. Patrick was a delivered child, so you wouldn't be seeing his flash forward. No, I believe your conception occurred later."

"Why not earlier?" Phil asked.

"Well, the experience you had in the store window in the alley, with the voices, the three loud bangs, the sudden shifting, would seem to point toward the assassination, in my opinion."

"How many shots were fired during the assassination?" Phil asked.

"Three."

"Good God."

"Indeed," Ann said.

"Well, it was definitely a moment of extreme stress for her," Phil said, "and from the pictures I've seen, didn't she kind of lunge from the back seat onto the trunk lid?"

"Yes, she did, the poor thing. That combination of stress and physical exertion could absolutely cause a miscarriage," Ann added.

"So, you think I was miscarried during the assassination," Phil said. "But if the flash forward shows my life as if the event that ended the pregnancy never happened, how would I see that event in the flash forward—which I did, you know, in the vision in the store window?"

"Dr. Klavos's work indicated his patients often saw in the flash forward *both* the life they would have lived if the termination event never happened—and the termination event itself," Ann said.

"So that's how I've been able to recall visions of the pregnancy termination during the assassination, and still had another vision where JFK was alive, where he and Jackie sat in chairs up in the yard watching us kids play on the beach?"

"Yes," Ann answered. "In your flash forward, JFK is alive because the event that terminated your pregnancy—the assassination— never happened."

"You know, one of the things that John Junior mentioned on the plane was that 'Mom and Dad' were going to be at the wedding. So, JFK was alive."

"My goodness," Ann said.

"This is a lot to take in," Phil said. "I don't remember reading about her being pregnant at the time of the assassination, though."

"Well," Ann said, "this leads me to the *second* reason I believe the assassination is when you were lost. She probably didn't even know she was pregnant when the miscarriage occurred."

"What makes you think that?"

"Remember the drawing you gave me of what you saw in the parking lot, and the burn on your arm?"

"Yeah."

"Those dots and dashes are clear and organized in a very specific way. The way they are lined up, I'm sure that they are Mayan numerals. The Mayans stacked their numbers in columns."

"Mayan? You mean, like the ancient people from Mexico?"

"The very ones," she said. "but I didn't know exactly what numbers they were until I researched it a bit. Now, I know."

"And?"

She pulled the drawing from her purse.

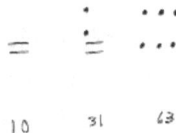

"10, 31, 63?" Phil asked.

"Yes."

"You don't mean, the *date*, October 31, 1963?"

"They're just numbers. All by themselves and out of context, I would have no idea if they refer to a date," Ann said. "But within the context of everything that's happening to you, I believe this is the date you were conceived, about three weeks before the assassination. I did some research and learned that President Kennedy was in DC that day, and not out of the country. So, he and his wife would have been together."

"One question, Doc," Phil started. "I, Phil Murphy, wasn't born until May 5, *1970*. Why the seven-year delay?"

"The research of Doctor Clavos found that to be common. Evidently, destiny owns no calendar, Phillip."

"You know, Doc, I lost my mom a couple of weeks ago. Right before she passed away, she came out of a coma and called me her little Halloween baby."

"Oh, my."

"She couldn't have known about this, *could* she?"

"Not while she was alive and well, I'm sure," Ann said. "But with a mind that had been altered by a coma...well, we'll just never know."

Before they knew it, Phil and Ann found themselves back at the bench in front of the Psychology building. They sat down. Phil propped his right ankle up over his left knee and lifted an arm to rest on the back of the bench.

"Doc, what you're saying seems to piece together," he said, "but how is it that my would-be parents just happen to be two of the most famous people of the twentieth century? It's just a little hard to swallow."

"You are fortunate, Phillip."

"Fortunate?"

"Well," she started, "perhaps not so fortunate that this is happening to you. But fortunate in that most of the adult life of the parents who conceived you is very well documented, and their lives are rather easily identifiable."

"What's so good about that?" Phil asked, as he lifted his chin to catch a slight breeze with his neck.

"It's good," she answered, "because almost everybody else in your shoes would have been conceived by ordinary parents, would have no way to ever know who their conception parents were, and most likely wouldn't have a clue what was even happening to them," she said.

"I guess you're right," Phil said. "I've been recalling flash forward moments of JFK's assassination, playing at the Kennedy Compound, and John Junior's plane crash."

"Right," Ann said, "You've been able to recall some of the most exciting and traumatic moments in the life you missed. Other reassigned conceptions might see exciting moments, too, but with unrecognizable family members, they'd have no way of knowing who their parents were."

"I wonder if there's anyone else out there that this has happened to," Phil mused. "I mean, who had prominent conception parents."

They left that thought hanging in the air and started a slow stroll back to the parking lot, during which Phil updated Ann on the existence of Kristen Minnows, and the fact that she had worked for JFK, Jr. He also told Ann about how Jill's Aunt Gwennie had worked in the Kennedy White House and had called Phil "Davis".

"That is particularly interesting, Phil. We're just now learning about how Alzheimer's causes the brain to work differently, and how it may perceive things a healthy brain can't."

As Phil put the key in the door to unlock his truck, he turned to Ann, who was heading back to her office.

"Oh, I almost forgot. Is there anything special about April 17, 1961? In history, I mean."

She paused for a moment, then replied, "That's when the Bay of Pigs invasion occurred in Cuba."

"Lord, didn't Kennedy order that?" Phil asked.

"You learned more in school than you admit, Phillip. Why do you ask?"

"That's the day Charlotte's father died, and he was a member of the Cuban military."

"Oh, my," Ann said, her voice trailing off. "I'll talk to you soon."

WITH HIS MIND preoccupied by recollections of his meeting with Ann, Phil was in downtown Dover before he knew it. Stopped at a red light, still several blocks from the bank, he caught a glimpse of something troubling.

Through his passenger side window, he saw Jill exiting the front door of the Esquire, one of Dover's most upper-crust restaurants. She was accompanied by a tall, handsome man in an expensive suit, who appeared to be in his mid- to late forties. Phil watched intently as the two walked slowly down the sidewalk ahead of him, unaware of their audience. Although side by side, she occasionally turned toward the tall man, walking sideways, her feet slowly crossing over each other, while smiling up at him.

Phil's eyes were glued on the pair as they smiled and chatted. While there was no physical contact between the two, Phil's imagination was getting the best of him, and he seemed to see a captivated look on Jill's face. Although envy of physical traits had always been a stranger to Phil, memories of being a working-class kid in an upper-class high school caused his blue eyes to turn green.

Abruptly, a car horn blew loudly behind Phil, alerting him that his traffic light had changed. The horn had also caused Jill to turn toward it, resulting in her recognizing Phil and his truck. Their eyes locked for instant. Then, the same little white chariot which had carried them on their magical evening together sped away, desperately searching for a place to hide.

# CHAPTER TWENTY

PHIL SPED down Loockerman and out of Jill's sight. The discoveries of the last forty-eight hours had him down and confused. Once he was a sufficient distance away, he whipped his truck over to the right, into a metered parking spot by the sidewalk.

He needed to collect himself. What the hell was happening to him? Visions that took him over; an old, demented woman calling him by a name of a person who had never been born; an esteemed professor who believed him to be the unborn son of Camelot; his vengeful boss appearing to be some sort of weather-controlling temptress; and now, he'd found the girl of his dreams walking on a cloud next to a worldly looking man who could probably buy and sell him a thousand times over. He was probably the same guy who Jill was laughing with behind the closed door of her office earlier that day.

He pulled his phone from his pocket, dialed, and awaited an answer to the ring.

"Kara. Am I interrupting?"

"Of course you are, Beavis. Aren't you always?"

Her voice soothed Phil like one of those babbling brook white noise sleep machines.

"You doin' okay, sis?"

"Yeah. Are you?" she asked. "Don't answer. I can hear it in your voice. What's wrong?"

"I'm having a weird couple of days. Everything's inside out. I might be losing my marbles."

"What can I do to help?"

"Nothing. Just knowing you're there helps," he said. "I just feel like I need to bury my head in the sand for a while."

"Can you fill me in on what's happening? Sometimes it helps just to tell someone."

"There are too many things, they're too weird, and not enough time now," he said. "Maybe later, if you have time."

"Okay. But listen, we're going to our cabin for a few days," she said. "Why don't I go get Willie from the sitter and take him with us? He'll love it, and you can use the time to get your head on straight."

"You don't have to do that," Phil said.

"Not only do I not mind," she said, "but the little guy is so quiet, easy, and entertaining to my kids, it actually makes things easier for me when he's here."

"Okay." And he let out a cleansing sigh. "Thank you."

"Don't sweat it. We'll stay in touch, and I'll see you in a few days."

"Love you, sis."

With that, Phil got out of the little white truck and headed down Loockerman on foot. He needed a place to think. He could use a drink, some time, and a place to lay low. The Stumble On Inn was calling him. In a minute, he had reached the tall, wooden double doors of the Stumble. The bright sun of late afternoon rendered him nearly blind when he entered the darkened saloon. Not one window in the place.

After his pupils dilated, he found the Stumble to be quite barren. No great surprise, really, at five o'clock on a Tuesday. He was pulled toward a stool at the empty bar like he was the last bit of water being sucked down a bathtub drain.

Behind the bar, a middle-aged woman with her back turned was organizing the stock. In his dealings with the Stumble during the course of his job, Phil had become acquainted with most of the staff. He didn't know this one.

"Boy, you don't waste any time, eh?" She glanced at her watch.

Phil looked at his, noting the minute hand was slightly on the declining side of 5:00.

"That's right. You open at five, don't you?"

"What can I get you, handsome?"

"Just gimme a shot," Phil said coldly.

She handed it over, and he threw it down, set his empty glass on the bar, and silently pointed at it. She obliged, and he repeated the ritual, this time ending it by tapping his index finger on the rim of the glass, rather than pointing. Again, she obliged.

"How long are we gonna do this?" she asked.

Phil said nothing and poured the third one down his throat. It burned. Phil was a beer drinker but was not a complete stranger to the sour mash. This stuff tasted like discount store generic compared to the top-shelf scotch Davis had sipped on the plane.

He sat quietly while the matronly bar maid yammered on. Suddenly the front doors opened, blinding his now dark-adapted eyes with the glare of the sun. Another patron. Moments later, even more. The sullen tranquility that Phil sought was becoming an elusive commodity.

"How 'bout a Stroh's?" Phil said, as he arose from his stool, pulled some cash out of his pocket, and laid it on the bar, making sure to take care of the bar maid. He took the frosty beer bottle from her extended hand and headed toward the large back section of the Stumble, where booths lined the walls, and tables filled the rest of the large room. He chose a booth in the back corner and nestled in, facing the stage on the other end of the room.

Over the course of the next four hours, the Stumble filled up, and Phil filled his gut with beer after beer, alone in his dark corner booth. He was singlehandedly keeping Stroh's Brewery afloat. In the excitement of Charlotte's file heist during lunch time, he had failed to eat. A proper dinner had eluded him, too, and he'd only snacked on shelled peanuts, washing them down with barley and hops. With his stomach empty, his consumption was hitting him hard.

Rather than acting as a salve for Phil wounds, the vast amount of alcohol he'd consumed was grinding salt into them. Why hadn't Jill tried to call him? Shouldn't she be calling him to explain? His attention was drawn to a table full of boisterous drunks having too much fun, in Phil's opinion. Didn't they know some people were here to drown their sorrows?

As the drunks momentarily quieted, Phil began to transition from his sullen state to something more predatory. The Stumble's Master of Ceremonies had now struck up the house band, stirring Phil to some semblance of life. On stage, the MC made the announcement he typically made every night at the Stumble.

"Okay, you guys know the routine," he said over the playing band. "We invite you to come up on the stage and let us hear your pipes."

With that, Phil brought himself to his feet, leaning heavily on the booth's table with one hand. He'd hardly been visible, slouched down in the corner booth. But now that he'd stood up, he heard a call from a table near the stage.

"Phil! Phil! Over here."

It was sweet little Angela from the bank. She had stood up from her table of friends to wave him over. Good old Angela, he thought. *She* wanted him. *She* didn't need some rich guy. And she was looking pretty good tonight, especially through the eyes of inebriation.

Like a crutch, Phil leaned on the back of every chair between him and Angela, on one occasion inducing a yelp from a seated woman whose hair he'd accidently pulled.

"I'm sorry, I'm sorry," Phil slurred to the woman. "I'm just going to see my friend."

He continued on, finally arriving at Angela's table, dropping down heavily into a seat next to her, courtesy of her friends sliding around. He immediately placed his left arm on the top of Angela's chairback, and began to twirl his index finger in her short raven locks.

"I didn't know you were here, Phil," she said, as a nervous grin appeared on her cute face. "How are you?" she asked.

In response to her timid attempt to make chit-chat, Phil leaned into her ear and more loudly than he knew, whispered, "How 'bout you and me head out to my truck, and you find out how I am?"

Angela's friends looked on in shock. This was not the Phil they knew.

"Phil, maybe you've had too much to drink," Angela said. Not only his behavior gave him away, but also the stench of alcohol.

"I know what I'm doin'. Do you?" he said loudly. "This is your big chance."

With that, one of Angela's male friends stood up as if to quell Phil's abhorrent behavior. Phil rose immediately, facing him eye to eye, and sternly said, "You'd better sit down, junior." And he did.

"I think you should go, Phil," Angela said with quiet disappointment.

By this time the band had finished their intro tune, and no one had yet taken the stage. Phil took this as his cue to give the gift of song to the packed house of the Stumble On Inn. Saying nothing to Angela, he made his way over to the four steps at the side of the stage and trudged his way up like a three-toed sloth.

"Looks like we got one, people," the MC announced. "You're up, Phil."

As Phil wobbled across the stage, he turned to the band.

"What are we gonna play, boys?"

"Your choice, Phil," the drummer said.

"How 'bout—"

"Hey, I wanna sing!" came a loud voice from the table of boisterous drunks who had previously drawn Phil's attention. "Hey, buddy, I wanna sing." The man directed his slurred words at Phil.

"You can have your turn after I'm through playin'," Phil said in a labored, but measured, tone into the microphone.

"You can play with yourself anytime!" blurted the drunk, a burly lout who was sitting with two other mouth-breathers, all three of whom appeared to have parents who were cousins. They were laughing hysterically now and were the center of attention.

Phil's blood began to boil, but he held it in. Shading his eyes from the spotlight, he gazed toward the table, swaying a bit, and said, "Hey, I know you. Can't remember your name, though."

"Eddie! My name's Eddie, but you're a lying sack o' shit, 'cause you'd remember my name if we'd met before," shouted the lout as his buddies slapped him on the back.

"No, no," Phil assured him. "Eddie's an old friend of mine," he told the audience through the microphone. "I've known him a long time. He even told me about the first time he ever had sex."

A quiet came over the crowd as they collectively wondered where this was going.

"Eddie's a studly mother, too," Phil continued as he leaned on the microphone stand, "cause he was only eighteen."

Phil took a swig of the beer he'd brought on stage with him, and then went on with his story.

"Ya see, when Eddie was in high school, he came home late one Friday night and his dad was sittin' at the kitchen table. He said, 'Hey Dad, guess what. I got laid tonight!'"

There was silence from Eddie's table, as they didn't know what to make of the situation. So far, Phil's story was massaging drunken Eddie's ego, so he didn't interrupt.

"Eddie's dad was so proud," Phil continued, "the next day he bragged to all his buddies about what a stud his son was."

Phil took another drink from his bottle.

"So, the next night, Eddie's dad waited up for him in the kitchen. When Eddie got home, his dad asked him, 'Well, son, did you get laid again tonight?'"

Phil took the last drink of his beer, then finished his story.

"Eddie told him, 'Not tonight, Dad. My asshole's still sore from yesterday."

The dead silence partially relented to a few drunken cackles that escaped from the crowd like air bubbles from an empty bottle held underwater.

Then from Eddie's table, Phil's radar picked up on an incoming beer bottle hurtling at him end over end like a tomahawk, whistling by his ear and crashing into one of the drummer's cymbals, knocking it over.

Everything that Phil had been holding down for months churned deep in his gut: a deceitful ex-wife; a villainous boss who used his precarious custody situation to her benefit at work; his questionable heredity; the idea of losing Jill to a well-to-do stranger—if not this one, maybe some other; and now a mouthy drunk who'd just launched a beer bottle at his head.

Phil Murphy couldn't hold it down any longer, and Eddie the Drunk had awakened a sleeping junkyard dog. Phil's thick neck bowed as his eyes shot laser beams at his prey. Acting purely on instinct, he leapt off the front of the stage, landing feet-first on a table, violently flipping it and knocking its chaired occupants to the floor. Phil hit the floor face-first, but immediately sprang to his feet and waded through the tables, pushing them and the people they contained aside, making a beeline to Eddie.

As he closed within a few feet, Phil dove across the table at the lout with both hands extended, simultaneously knocking his two friends on either side to the ground, all three falling like bowling pins for a 1, 2, 3 spare. Phil felt a surge of energy bolt through his forearms down to his powerful hands as they locked around Eddie's massive throat, driving the big man into the beer-soaked wooden floor of the Stumble. Years of squeezing baseball bats had turned Phil's hands into vises, and his sporadic work on his pullup bar at home kept them that way.

Women screamed and bystanders scrambled to get out of the way while Eddie struggled to free himself, but Phil was now sitting on his chest with both hands closing off his air channel.

One of Eddie's friends had now made it to his feet, and with two hands tugged fruitlessly on Phil's left arm in an attempt to free Eddie, who was now gasping for air. Still perched on Eddie's chest, Phil let loose of Eddie's throat with his right hand long enough to violently turn his upper body and plant his flat, knuckled fist squarely on the mouth of the arm-tugger, sending him flying straight backwards and on top of an adjacent table. The quick, powerful twisting of his torso was the same motion that Phil had employed during the thousands of swings he had taken with a baseball bat throughout his life. The muscle memory was still there, mere reflex.

Shedding the arm-grabber had cost Phil his balance, giving Eddie some much needed air and wiggle room. Just as Phil turned his attention back to Eddie, he felt a blinding pain in the right side of his body, accompanied by an audible cracking sound, administered by the recently risen second friend who had delivered an NFL-worthy punt to Phil's rib cage.

As Phil fell off Eddie's chest to the floor, the Stumble's two bouncers infiltrated the ruckus and were now policing the incident. They swiftly acted as judge and jury, pulling Eddie and his bloody-mouthed friend up off the floor, forcing the arm of the punter behind his back, and quickly ushering all three of them out the back door of the Stumble, leaving them in the moonlit alley.

When they got back to Phil, they found him raising himself from the floor, bent over in pain. Phil was a friend of the bar. Being a well-liked regular and having been the bank's liaison with the Stumble's owner, Phil was deemed the victim by the bouncers. In fact, they had been among the few cacklers at Phil's off-color joke made at Eddie's expense. They'd witnessed Eddie's initial provocation when Phil took the stage, then his assault with the weaponized beer bottle he'd thrown.

"I'm sorry," Phil said to the bouncers in just above a whisper. "I didn't mean to tear things up."

Rather than throw Phil out, the pair decided to help him back to his booth in the corner, where he could sit alone in the dark and lick his wounds.

"We're going to leave you here, Phil," said one. "But just don't start any shit with anybody."

The most Phil could manage in response was a tortured attempt at a smile to show his appreciation. In a matter of seconds, order was restored, tables were up-righted, and soon the comfortable drone of the crowd resumed, as well as the house band's music. Phil leaned back into the corner of his booth, facing the stage. It was dark, and he was glad of it. He didn't want to be seen. Even though he was drunk, he was aware enough to know that he'd disgraced himself.

He was pretty sure the noise he'd heard when he was kicked in the ribs was the sound of some fracturing. A dangerous level of alcohol coursing through Phil's veins was currently providing a partial anesthesia. With his torso throbbing, Phil laid his head back and closed his eyes. The low rumble of the crowd, combined with the thumping of the house band and liquor saturation, had eased him into a state of sedation. As his mind drifted, dim shades of crimson and emerald swept into view behind his closed eyes. As he got more comfortable in his darkened corner, all the sounds of the room melded into a soft hum. Phil's once aching body was now tingling in an alcohol-drenched massage of his senses.

He had slowly become aware, however, of a soft, warm, and ever-so-mild moist sensation on the left side of his neck. The lids of his closed eyes felt like bags of wet sand, keeping the blinds pulled down on his window to the Stumble's confines. He was completely drained of all energy. Meanwhile, the tender sensation that was enhancing his relaxed state of tingle had now found his ear.

He felt the sensation sliding down the side of his neck, though all he could still see were swirling clouds of fervent color behind his closed eyes. Still devoid of energy, Phil's head remained resting against the corner of the booth and the wall, a passive object to the will of whatever was having its way with him.

It had now made its way to his face, darting and probing between his lips. Phil felt simultaneous pleasure and powerlessness. Not that he wanted to, but he couldn't fight what was happening to him.

Another sensation had now crept in to this happening. A gentle pressure was massaging Phil's khakis beneath the table. Evidently, he did have some energy somewhere inside, because it was manifesting itself down below.

Oddly, Phil picked up on what sounded like distant thunder. His mind still swirling in a kaleidoscopic haze, he felt the warmth on his lips descend to his chin, then downward, pausing to frolic at the top of his chest. From there, it sank toward his belt. At that moment, Phil's temples began to ache.

The array of murky, dark colors quickly began to clear like a morning fog being burned off by the sun. He heard again the sound of thunder, closer now than before. While he'd been immersed in pleasure, Phil Murphy knew deep beneath his liquored shell that something was wrong.

*Boom!* A loud crack of thunder, as if on top of the Stumble, suddenly opened his eyes. There were accompanying shrieks from startled patrons. In the moments after his eyes opened, all he could see in the darkness of his corner booth was the back of a head sinking toward his lap, and its owner's body sitting beside him in the booth, bent over at the waist. As the visitor's head neared its intended prey, Phil reached down, grabbed the owner by the back of the neck, and pull upward, bringing them eye to eye.

"Don't stop now, Phil boy. The damage is done."

To Phil's horror, he'd come face to face with Charlotte.

It was the most sobering moment of his twenty-nine years. In an instant, a thousand thoughts collided in his mind, worked themselves to a boil, and pushed outward on his skull, making his head want to explode.

Saying nothing, he moved forcefully away from the wall, sliding on the booth's bench, spilling Charlotte out onto the floor. Phil stepped over her and did his best to run toward the door, slumped over in the pain supplied by his freshly fractured ribs. At last, he made it to the wooden double doors of the Stumble On Inn, burst through them onto the sidewalk, and hobbled as fast as his damaged frame would allow, into the rain that had seemed to come out of nowhere.

# CHAPTER TWENTY-ONE

THE EARLY MORNING sun made its way between two office buildings on Loockerman Street, finding the windshield of the little white truck and creating a wall of reddish-orange murk behind Phil's closed eyelids, finally causing them to open. As he stirred from his horizontal position across the bench seat of the truck, he momentarily struggled to recall where he was, and even more so the events of the night before. The sharp pain in his rib cage jogged his memory.

As he tried to upright himself, he let out a low groan of agony. Without the anesthetic river of alcohol coursing through his veins, each painful breath was like reliving the kick that had cracked his ribs. Short, shallow breaths would appear to be in order.

He turned the key on the steering column, and his dependable friend started up. The clock also appeared in the dashboard, telling him it was 6:12 AM. He wearily maneuvered his way home, traveling the opposite way of the early morning commuters. Otis met him at his front door, and Phil could barely muster the air necessary to greet him.

"Hey, buddy," he let out quietly. In situations like this, Phil was glad Otis had a dog door and a bowl of dry dog food that Phil kept perpetually filled.

After getting Otis a proper meal, Phil headed straight for the bathroom to get a hot shower, shake off the cobwebs, and soothe his aching torso. The belt buckle in his khakis echoed as it hit the tile floor. Easy enough. The boxer briefs that followed required only a mild bend forward. No big deal. Next was his oxford work shirt. Unbuttoning it offered no more pain than what he endured by just breathing. Now, pulling his undershirt off over his head would be another matter. After a couple of gasps and a groan, it was a no-go. Couldn't get his arms over his head. So, he opened the medicine cabinet, pulled out a pair of scissors, and cut his undershirt from the bottom, up the middle over his stomach, and up to the neck. Once he slid it off, Phil stood naked on the cold tile. The right side of his body was quite the spectacle. Black, green, and yellow.

"How 'bout that, boy?" he said to Otis in just above a whisper. "Looks like the devil's rainbow."

Phil's budget was tight, as were the hours in his day. Knowing it was possibly ill-advised, he acted as his own physician. He'd coughed a couple of times on his drive home, and while the pain nearly caused him to swerve into the guardrail, there was no blood in his mouth. So, he deduced, his lung must not be punctured by a protruding piece of rib. Also, he neither saw nor felt any deformity. He recalled from high school, a teammate who'd been drilled with a fastball, fracturing a rib. Phil knew the only treatment for a non-displaced fractured rib was pain management. He figured he'd swallow a large dose of Tylenol and stay on them, waiting for the cracked bones to heal.

After his shower, he eased himself down on his couch. Otis, who usually was at Phil's feet, had now sheepishly crept up onto the couch beside Phil. Sensing his owner's distress, the big boy sat on the couch and gently waved his left paw twice in succession at Phil, as if reaching out to comfort him.

"Glad I've got you, buddy," Phil said quietly, as he scratched the big guy under his chin. "It'll be good to get Willie back home, won't it?"

From his sitting position, the weight of Otis's body slowly caused his front legs to slide forward, and he laid himself down, head resting on Phil's thigh.

"First thing we're gonna do is go straight to the source of the problem," Phil said aloud to his counselor. "I'd imagine she thinks she's got some sort of upper hand on me now." He paused for a few moments, all the while resting his right hand on top of Otis's head.

"All this just to get more work out of me?" Phil wondered aloud. "That just doesn't seem likely."

With that, he pushed himself up off the couch, eased himself into the little white truck, and drove toward the office. Along the way, questions shot through his mind. Phil recalled the jolting thunder that had snapped him to consciousness as Charlotte was preying on him in the booth at the bar. Twice now he'd seen Charlotte involved in a sexual act, and twice violent weather accompanied it, then subsided when she was interrupted.

He also wondered how her connection, albeit indirect, to the Bay of Pigs invasion might relate to the recent discovery of his possible Kennedy heredity.

What had faded from Phil's mind was the idiotic jealous notion that Jill was enamored with a rich older man. He realized it was likely just business, and fortunately, all that Jill really knew was that Phil happened to be driving by as she exited the restaurant. That seemed unimportant now, and Charlotte was going to be the outlet for the wrath that was mounting as he got closer to the office.

Into the parking garage, guardedly out of the truck, slowly down the garage stairs, across the bank lobby, and into the elevator he went, pulled toward Charlotte's office. The ride up to the third floor seemed an eternity, as he ignored the other riders and the throbbing in his ribs, focusing only on confronting Charlotte.

Finally, the bell rang, the doors opened, and Phil stepped as forcefully as he was able toward Charlotte's office. As he approached her door, Gus called out in a hushed tone to Phil from his desk, attempting to flag Phil down before he entered Charlotte's office. With only a glance in Gus's direction, Phil waved him off and marched to Charlotte's open office door. He stopped in the doorway, staring down at Charlotte, who sat behind her desk.

"You and I are going to talk right now," Phil said with as much command as his shallow breathing would allow.

"Well, come on in, Phil, and we'll talk about anything you want to talk about," Charlotte replied in a sickeningly sweet voice. "Join us," she said, extending her hand toward a chair.

Phil looked quickly to his right to find that Charlotte had a visitor.

It was Jill.

There she sat, in one of two chairs against the wall, across from Charlotte's desk. She sent an uncomfortable smile in Phil's direction. Phil was momentarily speechless.

"What brings you here?" he asked Jill, covering his anxiety the best he could.

"Well, Charlotte was just extolling the virtues of her team here in Commercial Credit."

With a smile, Charlotte chimed in. "I'm trying to steal her away from those know-nothings in Trust who don't know how to utilize her talents."

"Now, Phil," Charlotte said, "what's so important that it brought you storming into my office this morning?"

"It'll wait," he answered.

Jill saw this welcome interruption as a chance to exit. She stood and said, "They're going to wonder where I am this morning. I'd better get moving."

"We'll talk more later," Charlotte said, addressing Jill, but looking directly at Phil when she said it.

As Phil escorted Jill toward the Trust Department, they passed Gus at his desk, who gave Phil an "I tried to warn you" look. They approached the double doors leading into the Trust Department.

"Thanks for saving me in there," Jill said.

"What was that all about, anyway?"

"I had just got off the elevator and she asked me to come into her office. She said she wanted me to consider coming to her department," she said and then paused. "There's something very strange about her. I get a bad feeling around her."

"Your intuition is right," he said.

"So, what was your big hurry yesterday?"

"What do you mean?"

"You zipped right past me in your truck without even waving."

"Well," he said, scrambling to come up with something that didn't make him look like the insecure goof that he felt like, "it looked like you were on business. I saw you look my direction, but I didn't know if you knew it was me or not, you know, with the glare on the truck windshield and all. So, I didn't wave or anything."

He felt he'd made the best of a bad situation with his on-the-fly sun glare notion, but it still felt lame.

Wiggling her pinky finger, Jill said, "If I wasn't so sure I had you right here, my feelings might be hurt for being snubbed."

Phil gently enveloped her pinky in the palm of his fisted hand. "How can I be right there," he said, wiggling his own pinky, "when I've got you right here?"

She smiled, and Phil felt as though he'd dodged a bullet.

"I'll see you later," he said.

Turning from Jill, relieved that yesterday's event with her was a non-issue, he refocused his attention on Charlotte. Passing by Gus, who was now on the phone, he went straight through Charlotte's office door without stopping this time, closed it, then turned back to face Charlotte.

"What brings you back, big boy?"

"Shut the hell up," Phil answered. "I don't know what you're trying to do, but it's not going to get more work out of me."

Charlotte sat quietly for a moment, then sighed, "Phil Boy, you think I really just want more work out of you?"

"I don't know what you want, but whatever it is, you aren't going to get it."

"It's not more work from you that I want," she said. "It's you."

"Me?" He didn't believe her.

"That's right. And after getting a grip on what was under that table, I believe I just won't be taking 'No' for an answer."

Phil stood still and quiet, dumbstruck.

"I can make your life a lot easier, Phil. Just ask Russ. He knows to play ball with me, although he's about to be benched for my new star player," she said with a wicked grin.

Phil felt his upper lip curl, a gut reaction to her sickening proposal. She immediately picked up on it.

"Oh, Phil Boy, that's not the reaction I'd hoped for. Why don't you just think about it a little?"

"I don't have to think about anything, except about finding a new place to work."

"I hate to hear that, Phil. We would miss you around here. I wonder how understanding that sweet little girlfriend of yours would be if she knew about you and me?"

"There is no you and me."

"But we have a history now, Phil. Last night was magical."

"You mean, you molesting a near-corpse in a barroom booth?"

"You were enjoying yourself, Phil Boy."

Then, grasping at straws, he said the first thing that came to his mind that felt like ammunition.

"Tell me, how does one make the transition from air traffic controller to banking?"

His comment was met with complete silence. In an instant, Phil regretted his question. It was a knee-jerk reaction to battle back. He might have said too much, revealing he'd looked in Charlotte's personnel file. The expression on her face was one of surprise.

It took a moment, but her look of astonishment was supplanted by one of purely evil elation. Not until then did Phil remember that it was not from her personnel file that he'd thought her to be an air traffic controller; it was from his on-board crash experience.

"Well, well..." she said. "Only one person—one person—would ever imagine me to be an air traffic controller. So that person is *you*, Phil Murphy?"

Phil said nothing as he stood in front of the closed office door, silently facing her. He now wondered just what he was up against. Suddenly this seemed something much bigger than working extra hours, keeping his job, or even his relationship with Jill.

"I knew I'd be in the ballpark when I moved here to Dover," she said, "but I wasn't sure exactly which player I was looking for."

"What are you talking about?"

"All bets are off now," she said in a chilling and resolute tone. "All that rubbish I just said about *wanting* you was a lie. Last night in the bar was about tipping the balance of power back toward me. I couldn't have you running around here all cocky and smirking at me with that smug grin of yours."

Phil stood still and quiet.

"You had your chance to make it easy on yourself here. That chance is gone. Stay, go, get a new job, I don't care. I've been working on the project of all projects, Phil Boy, and I've got one step left. After that, I'm quite sure you and I will be seeing each other again, and you won't be wearing your smug little grin. You'll be desperately pondering the things in this life that matter to you most."

Her words brought a frost to Phil's spine. He turned his back to her and left the office, closing the door behind him.

# CHAPTER TWENTY-TWO

As much as Phil would've liked to get a new job, any job, or at least get out of the office temporarily, he felt it better to stay put, where he could keep an eye on Charlotte. Keep your enemies close, and all that. So he found his way to his desk and sat down.

"I tried to stop you, douchebag," Gus chided.

"I know. An army wasn't going to stop me from going in there, though."

"Why was Jill in there?"

Charlotte's door remained closed, so Phil proceeded to fill Gus in on the rumble at the Stumble the night before, as well as Charlotte's advances on him in the corner booth. Predictably, he had to quell Gus's outbursts as he recounted the events. He also gave him the condensed version of Ann Culpepper's theory about his heredity. Getting everything out was good therapy for Phil. Like the trusted friend he was, Gus soaked up Phil's words like a sponge.

"So what are you gonna do now?"

"Not sure, but I know I've got to find out what she's up to. Somehow...."

"Hell, we don't know anything about her, not really," Gus said, "Even after looking through her personnel file."

"We know more than we did."

"What else do you want to know?"

"I think it's turned into *needing* to know. Her whole tone changed in her office just now. She's gone from just a hard-ass boss to something worse," he said, pausing. "I think...to something dangerous. If she can be responsible, like I think she is, for JFK, Jr.'s plane crash, then she's capable of anything."

As Phil's words were reverberating, Charlotte's door opened, and she exited with a leather portfolio under her arm.

"I've got a meeting down on Two," she informed Curry, whose desk was just outside of Charlotte's office. She headed toward the elevator and disappeared into it when the doors opened. As soon as the elevator doors closed, Curry arose from his chair and headed across the floor toward the break room.

"I'm goin' in," Phil said quietly to Gus, still short of breath from his rib damage. He slowly got up, then walked as casually as he could toward Charlotte's open office door.

"What now?" Gus asked as Phil walked away.

Saying nothing, Phil continued in to Charlotte's door, then stepped to his right two paces, so as to be out of the view of his co-workers. His eyes darted about like hot popcorn kernels, scanning the office for something, anything. He could feel his pulse in the front of his neck, and it was quickening. He didn't even know what he was looking for, but then he found it. Her purse lay on the floor beside her chair.

Still not knowing exactly what he sought, Phil closed the door, went over to Charlotte's desk, painfully dropped to one knee, and with his back to the door, began to rummage through the purse. Then he heard it. The sound of someone at the door.

Without turning around, he bent over further and looked under Charlotte's desk, mumbling, "Where the hell is my phone?"

"Is that all you've got, the old lost phone routine?"

It was Gus, doing all he could to keep from laughing out loud.

"Funny stuff," Phil said.

"Relax," Gus said, "I'll be your lookout. Keep going."

With that, Phil turned his attention back to the purse. All he found at first was some makeup, a couple of envelopes, and her wallet. Then he noticed a key chain hanging from a loop. Only four keys. One was obviously a car key. Another was the same key that Phil and every employee on the third floor possessed—the key to the third-floor conference room. The third key was very small and would appear to open a proportionally sized lock of some sort. The last key looked like a house key.

"Still clear?" Phil asked Gus without turning around.

"Yeah," Gus said. "Now shut up and get busy. Charlotte's gonna be gone a good while, but Curry could be back any second."

Phil's mind raced but settled quickly on what he knew he needed do. He was skipping over *how* to do it, but he'd decided: he was going into the devil's lair.

"Hurry up," Gus urged.

Phil's thick fingers worked fruitlessly to get the house key off the ring. The faster he worked, the more he fumbled. Turned out his mom was right all those years ago. Haste really does make waste.

"Great, here he comes," Gus said.

"Now, are you shittin' me, or is he really coming?"

"No shit, he's really coming," Gus said with an ever-widening grin, finding the whole situation oddly amusing.

"Well, go stop him."

"What am I supposed to do?"

"Jesus, use your imagination. Get goin'," Phil said.

At Phil's urging, Gus disappeared from Charlotte's doorway, and Phil grabbed the whole set of keys, put the purse back in place, and crept toward the door, dropping the keys into his pocket.

A few feet away from the door, and still obscured by the wall, Phil slowly moved his head sideways until his right eye could see out over the credit department floor. What his right eye witnessed was Gus walking briskly toward his desk, picking up his half-empty cup of coffee without stopping, continuing to stride toward the fast-approaching Curry, then Gus stumbling, falling, and launching his tepid coffee, cup and all, directly into Curry's chest.

"You idiot!" Curry yelled, his mouth agape and arms out to his side, looking down at his sopping shirt.

"My fault, Rusty," Gus said as he picked himself up off the floor.

As all eyes in the office were fixed on Curry brushing coffee off his clothes, Phil slipped out of Charlotte's office and headed into the elevator. He emerged from its open doors on the ground level, and strode through the lobby as briskly as his tender ribs would let him. On his way out to the street, he was simultaneously awed and amused by Gus's dedication and lack of concern about playing the part of the fool.

Phil didn't know how long Charlotte would be in her meeting, so he had to act fast. He walked as quickly as he could, without drawing attention to himself, four blocks down Loockerman, then left for two more on South State Street to arrive at Merritt's Hardware. Dover's downtown was bustling with pedestrian traffic on a mild April morning.

Upon arrival at the store front, Phil paused to remove the house key. While he was at it, he may as well have the car key copied, too, so he removed it. This tedious exercise confirmed to Phil that he was not suited for a career as a surgeon, never mind the tortuous years of study.

What the heck, he'd just go ahead and get the little mystery key copied as well. Removal of the small key proved particularly frustrating. With a final twist, it was freed from the ring but slipped from his fingers, bouncing off his shoe out into the street, striking the fender of a passing car, and ricocheting back toward the curb and into a storm drain.

"Well, shit."

He stepped into the store and made his way to the section where keys could be copied.

"I need these two copied," Phil said to the man near the machine.

As he waited, his eye was caught by the vast number of blank keys hanging on hooks, awaiting a life as a duplicate key.

"While you're at it, I'd like one of these, too," Phil said, pointing toward a row of small keys that looked similar to the one he lost in the street.

"Okay, just give me the original," the man said.

"Not a copy, just one of those blanks," Phil said.

"Okay," said the man. "The customer's always right, I guess."

Even if the key wouldn't work, at least Charlotte wouldn't notice it missing. He paid with cash to assure no electronic trail.

Upon leaving the store, he made his way back to the bank entrance and crossed the lobby toward the elevator. As he faced the doors, waiting, Angela appeared at his side. Although he couldn't remember some of the details from the night before at the Stumble, he remembered enough to know he'd been way out of line.

"Hi, Angela."

She said nothing and continued looking straight ahead. A good thirty seconds of awkward silence ensued before the ding of the opening elevator doors broke it. Phil mutely extended his hand toward the door in a "ladies first" gesture, and Angela proceeded inside. More silence as the doors closed.

"Angela, I'm really sorry...."

The ding of the elevator bell interrupted him, stopping on the second floor. The elevator doors opened, and there stood Charlotte. Looked like Phil hadn't made it back quite quickly enough.

"Angela," Charlotte said with a nod.

No such greeting for Phil. Fine with him.

"Hi, Charlotte," Angela replied. "Meeting over?"

"Just a break until after lunch. Will you be joining us?" Charlotte asked. Any other clerical in the bank wouldn't get so much as a grunt out of Charlotte. But Angela, the President's assistant, caused Charlotte to gush sap like a Vermont maple.

Phil's mind raced to figure out how to get the keys back in to Charlotte's purse. She was surely going to her office to get it before heading out to lunch.

"No, Mr. Adams has me getting some notes ready for the directors' meeting next week," Angela said.

The elevator bell chimed, sounding their arrival at the third floor. At the ding of the bell, Phil blurted out the first thing he could think of as he stepped toward the still-closed door.

"Curry said Mr. Adams needed to talk to you two up on Seven as soon as you were out of your meeting."

"Me and Curry? What about?"

The elevator doors opened. Phil felt his pulse in his jugular again, but somehow mustered a calm demeanor, turning back toward Charlotte.

"I don't know, but Russ was pretty excited about it," he said as he backed out the elevator door.

Charlotte took a step toward the open door.

"I'll talk to Russ first."

"He's gone up there already," Phil said, while he could clearly see Curry sitting at his desk. From her vantage point inside the elevator, Curry was out of Charlotte's view.

"Good God, I'd better get up there before he says something idiotic," Charlotte said. "Did Mr. Adams say anything to you, Angela?"

"No, but I'm going there now. You can come with me."

The door closed.

Phil had bought himself two or three minutes at most. He needed only a few seconds in her office this time. Just enough to deposit the key chain with the little dummy replacement back into her purse. How would he get past Curry, her office sentry? Phil moseyed casually toward his desk.

"Russ, Charlotte needs you up on Seven with her in Adams' office. Now."

Adorned in a clean shirt that he must have kept in his desk, Curry was up and gone toward the elevator. No questions asked. There was schmoozing to be done. As soon as he disappeared inside the elevator, Phil headed into Charlotte's office. There was no Gus around this time to act as a lookout, so no dallying. He made the deposit, then hit the stairwell so as not to risk meeting up with his marionettes on the elevator. Charlotte would be tied up in her meeting for a while after lunch, so he knew now was the time to infiltrate her lair.

# CHAPTER TWENTY-THREE

THEY SAY character is what one does when nobody's looking. As he slid a copied key into the lock of his boss's front door, Phil Murphy was pushing that saying out of his mind in favor of one his dad taught him as a kid: in a real fight, there are no rules.

He'd parked half a mile away and had taken what appeared to be a leisurely stroll to Charlotte's house. Leisurely, for the purpose of not attracting attention, and also because he was still feeling the effects of his injured ribs from the night before. As he had hoped, her suburban subdivision was pretty much dormant in the early afternoon of an April school day. No one had seen him approach the front door—as far as he knew.

Crime was new to Phil, and he hadn't thought to bring gloves, so he untucked the front of his oxford shirt and used it to turn the knob. He was appreciative that there was no barking dog to challenge him. Then again, any dog of Charlotte's would probably already have met its maker.

Once inside, he paused at the entry of the split level. Six steps up, six down. He chose down. The idea of invading Charlotte's home having occurred to him only this morning, he'd not put much thought into what he was looking for.

On the lower level, half-submerged belowground, he found a laundry room, a den, and the entrance to the garage. A cursory tour around revealed nothing obvious. He turned and headed up the stairs, bypassing the garage for now. He needed to get to the nerve center of the house—Charlotte's personal home computer. That's where he would have the best chance of striking gold, if there was any to be mined.

Upstairs, he found the living room, scene of the spectacle between Charlotte and Curry that he'd witnessed some days earlier from the deck, just outside of the sliding glass door. No computer in there. Down the hall, he passed two bedrooms before arriving at the master at the end of the hall.

He stood in the doorway. It was a big room, as far as bedroom's go. King-sized bed on the right end with the door to the master bath beside it. On the other end of the room, a large closet with four sets of louvered doors. Against the wall opposite the door, there it sat—a small desk with a computer and printer.

Still concerned with fingerprints, he pressed the power button to the computer and monitor with his knuckle. As the screen began to glow, he was glad to see her desktop screen boot up by default, with no password. Placing his untucked shirttail over the mouse, he clicked on the Internet Explorer icon and listened as the soft screech of the phone line connected to the internet.

First stop—Yahoo, to check her search history. Upon first glance, he noted some typical names that might interest a well-dressed woman: Coach Purse, Nine West, Saks. There were also searches for banking and finance companies.

Phil then noticed some unfamiliar names for searches: *CATOA* and *Bokor Manhattan*. He clicked on CATOA to reveal the results of the search: The Central American Tribunal of Occult Activities, an organization devoted to the study of voodoo.

"Shoulda figured," he whispered to himself.

He then input Bokor Manhattan into the search box, which yielded mostly people with the last name of Bokor, located in Manhattan. Not sure what to make of that.

His curiosity pushed him to take one more step. He checked her browser history of web sites visited. A dropdown box appeared, listing the sites in alphabetic order. Near the top of the list, he again saw the word Bokor in the name of one of the sites, causing him to click on the link. He watched as the page slowly loaded onto the screen.

"Holy shit," he uttered.

His eyes strained to make sense of the images he was viewing. Definitely some sort of voodoo sorcery site, and it gave him a chill. He ventured through a few pages, but then moved on, as he'd gotten the gist. No time for an in-depth study now. He could always look these sites up back at his house.

Down the list of sites on the browser history, another caught his eye: the site for the Essex County, New Jersey Airport, with a forward slash adding the maintenance department. Another connection to aviation. Her personnel file at work had revealed she held a pilot's license, and now Phil had learned she'd had an interest in a little airport in New Jersey.

Playing on a hunch, Phil typed a phrase into the Yahoo search box: *JFK Jr plane crash airport*. He had to use his fingertips to type this one in; otherwise he'd be hunting and pecking all day with his knuckle. He'd just wipe the keyboard when he was done. The results page populated as quickly as the phone line would allow. At the top of the page, the confirmation of Phil's hunch was revealed.

"CDW - Essex County Airport".

He turned the printer on and started printing the list of sites in her browser history. As the printer chugged, Phil tried to put all of the pieces together in his head. His vision, re-experience, or whatever it was, of the plane crash was having manifestations in his real life now.

He pulled the page off the printer, folded it, and shoved it into his back pocket. After shutting down the computer and scrubbing the keyboard with his shirttail, he peered around the room. Benign enough. Candles everywhere. Some women like candles, he figured, but this was an inordinate amount of them, all over the room.

He headed out the bedroom door, noticing in the hallway ceiling a pull-down door to the attic. His interest piqued, he pulled the door down and unfolded the steps.

At the top of the attic stairs, he found a light switch that illuminated the whole attic. Fortunately, the roof had a moderate pitch to it, providing enough head room to crawl, but there was no floor, only pink insulation laid between exposed joists. He'd have to crawl around on his hands and knees, with cracked ribs and bruised knuckles, carefully placing his weight on the joists; otherwise, he'd knock a hole in the drywall below. A good distance away, Phil noticed a wooden chest, old and worn. As he crawled toward it, he wondered what the hell he was doing. Thoughts of Willie playing innocently on the living room floor at Kara's cabin swam through his mind. It was about his nap time now. Images of his little guy sleeping made him start to yearn.

Why was Phil in his boss's attic in the middle of the afternoon, risking jail, when he had a son depending on him? What would become of Willie, or even Otis for that matter, if both of their parents were in prison? Would Jill have anything to do with someone who did the things Phil was doing?

Perhaps the reason Phil was more relaxed than he probably should be, was that he knew the answers to those questions. Because he had so much to lose, he had to take drastic measures to protect it. Charlotte had an air about her that had turned from merely annoying to treacherous. Phil was becoming more sure that she had crashed a plane, killing its occupants, and now she'd turned her focus on him. He had to learn what she was up to in order to protect himself and his family.

He found himself kneeling in front of the chest. Opening the lid, he found a cornucopia of artifacts related to witchcraft and voodoo, the difference between them being lost on Phil: emblems, knives, bird feathers, an old map of the Caribbean, and several dust-covered books, all written in Spanish. There was, however, one book written in English—a biography of John F. Kennedy.

Phil suddenly heard a rumble below him. It was the opening of the garage door. From his bent-over position, he rose quickly. He felt a sharp, burning pain on the back of his head. Stunned and disoriented, it took Phil a good ten seconds to realize he'd hit a rafter.

*What the hell is she doing here already?*

Still a hair groggy, Phil righted himself, and started to crawl as quickly as he could back toward the attic door, thirty feet away.

"Will you get in here and quit fooling with that?" Charlotte said as she entered the house from the garage on the lower level. Phil knew he was running out of time.

He had to temper his near-frenzied pace in order to keep quiet. Having to control his crawling over the attic joists was doing no favors for his fragile ribs. He wondered who Charlotte was talking to, although from the tone of what he'd heard her say, he had an idea. During his scramble back to the attic door, his thoughts turned from getting out of the house, to getting out of the attic and hidden somewhere on the upper level. As he got to the attic door, he heard Charlotte's voice growing closer.

"Yes, the pink bag. Bring it," she curtly instructed her company.

Phil now heard the clip clop of her heels on the wooden stairs. His Plan B of getting out of the attic was sinking like a bottomless boat.

The attic stairs were still down. Lying on his stomach, he placed his left hand on the attic opening, spread his legs wide for balance, and lowered his torso out of the opening in the ceiling, reaching for the folding point of the stairs with his right hand. The clip clopping of the shoes neared.

In a last desperate lunge, and with blinding pain in his rib cage, he grasped a rung far enough down to allow him to pull up the stairs, folding them as he tugged. Although he performed the procedure as quietly as he could, there was still a muffled *thud* as the attic door closed flush into the hallway ceiling. Fortunately for Phil, Charlotte's incessant barking at her company had drowned it out.

Phil could only hope Charlotte and her guest would be spending their time on the lower level, so he could eventually get out of the attic, then exit through the upstairs sliding glass door onto the deck and down into the back yard.

No such luck thus far, as he could hear her voice and commotion in her kitchen, which was on the upper level. The sound of a second voice was also present now. Phil knew the voice. As he suspected, it was Russ Curry.

# CHAPTER TWENTY-FOUR

THE TWO SPENT a few minutes in the kitchen, mostly with Curry babbling on about the office, and Charlotte remaining silent as she opened and closed cabinet doors and the refrigerator. As Phil listened from the attic, he began to pity Curry just a bit. How sad it must be, Phil thought, to have only the mundane drudgery of the bank's affairs as the focus of his interest—no family, no friends.

"I'm telling you, I did not even see Mr. Adams, much less tell Murphy that Adams wanted to see us in his office," Curry said.

"He was up to something," Charlotte said, finally breaking her silence. "Not only did he get me up to Adams' office, but he got you up there, too. That was quite an impromptu orchestration. Couldn't you tell he was lying to you?" Her clear lack of respect for Curry was ever present.

"Couldn't *you*?" he retorted in a rare display of backbone, which brought only icy silence from Charlotte.

Curry's spine quickly dissolved, however.

"Sorry," he whimpered.

"Just shut up and get over here."

This was followed with a minute of rustling and muted voices, which Phil interpreted as an afternoon make-out session in the kitchen.

If she had so little respect for Curry, why did she spend time with him? Phil assumed it was because she was domineering, and Curry was born to be domineered. In a moment, he heard the television come on in the living room, obscuring Charlotte and Curry's voices.

There was only one way out of the attic, and that was through the folding steps which came out of the ceiling in the hallway. There were fixed gable vents on each end of the attic, but they were part of the structure and couldn't be opened or removed. If he could manage to get out of the attic quietly enough, he couldn't get out of the hallway without going through the living room unless, he'd try to exit through an upstairs bedroom window. Even if his ribcage could withstand a jump from the upper level, he couldn't attempt it during the daylight hours for concern of being spotted by a neighbor. He'd come to grips with the fact that as long as Curry and Charlotte were on the upper level of the house, he couldn't get out without being seen.

He then had the bright idea that he could call Charlotte and get her out of the house somehow. A jolt of searing pain shot through his rib cage as he reached for the pants pocket where he kept his phone. Only then did he remember leaving it in the console of the little white truck.

So Phil Murphy settled in for the duration. He'd just listen for his opportunity and hope for his chance to get out. Thank goodness Willie was with Kara at their cabin, and not at the sitter's. He decided to carefully crawl back and explore the wooden chest, being sure to place his hands and shins on the joists, keeping off the itchy pink fiberglass insulation.

He lifted the dusty arched lid. Inside, under the books, he came upon a single yellowed, unlined piece of paper filled with words written in Spanish.

Phil had taken Spanish in middle school, high school, and even two semesters in college, but had let it seep from his mind as soon as each course was over. He never used it but decided a few months earlier to make a new year's resolution to do so. He'd been recovering a bit of it recently, soaking some in with the "Spanish For Dummies" CDs in his truck. Still, he knew just enough to be dangerous.

"To call the teacher," was the best Phil could do in trying to translate what appeared to be the title at the top of the page. Under the title were bullet points, outlining steps in a procedure. On each of the bullet points, he was only able to pick out a phrase.

Line 1: "gift of rabbit"

Line 2: "gift of hound"

Line 3: "congress with a simple man" and then, "gift of his body"

Below the list, near the bottom of the page, he could again decipher "call the teacher", and "reward with vision."

Phil didn't know what it all meant, but folded the delicate page as best he could, and slipped it into the back pocket of his pants. He'd try to figure it out later. He placed everything else back in the chest the way it was then closed it. Then he waited.

Two and a half hours passed, with nothing but the drone of the television and some occasional muffled conversation over top of it. Finally, Phil heard footsteps and both voices coming nearer, traveling under him, down the hallway and into Charlotte's bedroom.

"Get your clothes off," he heard her say.

"Sure, but don't you want to fool around a little first?"

"You just do what I tell you, and this will be a night to remember," she said. This was most assuredly not a romantic relationship. Just as Phil glanced at his watch to see that it was now 7:15, he began to hear the beat of drums from below. No music, only the soft rhythmic pounding of an army of drums, evidently pulsating through the stereo speakers he'd seen in Charlotte's room earlier.

He considered the idea of getting out of the attic now that they were in the bedroom, but the attic door was in the hallway ceiling right in front of Charlotte's bedroom door. He didn't know if her door was open or closed. He couldn't risk being seen, so he decided on staying in the attic for now.

With the drumbeat piquing his curiosity, Phil executed a furtive battlefield crawl across the insulation and joists toward Charlotte's room, muffling the painful breaths being shot out of him like a bellows each time he reached forward and quietly landed on his forearm. Once there, he found himself next to a section of flexible ductwork that connected to a register in the ceiling of the bedroom.

"Yes! Plastic sheets," he heard Curry say. "We're going to slither around like snakes, aren't we?"

No response from Charlotte.

The drums coming through the speakers, while not overbearing, did allow Phil to get away with a little noise. So, he slowly removed the tape attaching the duct line to the register boot. He slipped the light-weight, flexible duct line off the register, which allowed him an eight-by-twelve-inch view through the louvers of the register. He felt it safe to peer through because he was in the darkness of the attic, behind the louvers, and his performers were in the light of the room, making him virtually imperceptible.

The first thing he saw, looking down on Charlotte's bed, was her standing beside it, fully clothed and squirting lubricant from a bottle onto the plastic sheets. There were no covers now, only a comforter folded at the foot of the bed. Curry, fully naked, cautiously sat down on the edge and reclined, positioning himself on his back in the center of the king-sized bed. He was already very obviously excited and ready to go.

"Come on," he said, patting the bed beside him. "I can't believe we're finally going to do it."

"Not just yet," came Charlotte's voice. She was outside of Phil's view from the ceiling register.

Phil saw Curry's face light up, and Charlotte emerged into the frame with a set of handcuffs dangling from each index finger. The drums continued to pound from the stereo.

"Now, you just keep quiet, and relax," she said as she attached the cuffs to Curry's wrist, and then to a post on the headboard. "I want our first time to be special," she said. She moved around the bed to repeat the process with his other wrist.

Phil had a hard time imagining that this was their first time. Espe-cially since he was witnessing something so replete with kinkularity. He'd seen with his own eyes that they had done some mutual explo-ration the night he fell off the deck. Maybe, Phil thought, Curry would have gotten lucky that night if he hadn't interrupted them.

"I don't know about the handcuffs, Charlotte," Curry said, his back against the headboard, his arms stretched up to its corners.

"Nothing to worry about," she said with a sultry growl. "See, I can unlock them anytime." She held up her keychain by the same little key Phil had bought to replace the one he lost that very day.

Phil began to feel the recently all-too-familiar throb of his pulse in his jugular again. But, the thought of Curry handcuffed naked to the bed without a working key did tickle his funny bone just a tad.

"I don't know," Curry said.

"Just trust me," she said, giving him a light caress with the back of her hand just where he wanted it most.

"Okay," he relented.

With that, Charlotte began a slow parade around the room, lighting every candle in it. She spent the next few minutes igniting dozens of candles. The vent register acted as a chimney for the room, with the burning of so many candles forcing Phil to suppress the urge to cough, doing his aching rib cage no favors.

With the candle-lighting done, Charlotte stood at the foot of the bed, slowly loosened her skirt, and let it slide over her hips and down to the floor. Next was her slip, which fell to the ground in much the same way. There were no panties to remove. Above him, Phil now heard the gentle patter of rain on the roof.

Never taking her eyes off Curry, Charlotte simultaneously unbuttoned her silk blouse and pushed the skirt and slip off to the side with her foot. The army of drums continued to pound through the speakers.

"Oh, yeah," Curry started.

"*Tranquilo!*" she barked.

She began to pace like a caged panther, back and forth at the foot of the bed, all the while unbuttoning her blouse and never taking her eyes off Curry's. After the last button gave way, she paused, gently shrugged her shoulders, and the silken garment slid down to the small of her back, over her round backside, and finally to the floor.

The wind outside was picking up now, and Phil could feel it tearing through the attic from one gable vent to the other, across the length of the house.

Charlotte now stood still at the end of the bed, facing Curry, who was losing his lustful mind. With a black scarf in one hand, she reached back between her shoulder blades with the other to undo her bra. In spectacular fashion, the bra sprung forward, abruptly freeing her suffocating breasts, causing them to bounce recklessly off one another until they came to rest, perched magnificently atop her hourglass figure. The spectacle brought to mind the words of a crusty uncle who once told an adolescent Phil, "Titties are always bigger when they don't have a bra chokin' em."

While he usually got a silent chuckle from his uncle's words, he could feel his mood souring. His temples felt as if they were in a closing vise. He'd felt this way before.

The dropping of Curry's jaw was synced perfectly with a sudden crack of thunder, close enough that it vibrated the rafters in the attic. The wind raged now as Charlotte crawled up onto the foot of the bed, over the comforter, and crept slowly on all fours toward Curry.

Hanging down, her breasts swayed ever so gently side to side as she moved forward, grazing Curry's shins, then his thighs. As she passed over his pelvis, they drug over his stiffy like the heavy cloth straps of an automated car wash.

The rain was now pounding on the roof above Phil, while down below him, the drums continued to thump as Charlotte resumed her slow creep up Curry's body.

"*Convoco al maestro*," she uttered, lowering herself until she lay flat on top of Curry. She slid ever closer to his dumbfounded face.

"I didn't know you were bilingual."

"*Silencio!*"

Phil picked up on the "*maestro*"—teacher—reminding him of the paper in his back pocket.

"*Preparaos para recibir mi regalo*," she said in a sultry timbre.

She spoke quickly. Between the wind and rain's orgy outside, and the pounding drums below, Phil couldn't understand much at all. However, he did pull out of her words, "*regalo*"—gift.

Still lying prone on top of Curry, she slowly laid the scarf over his eyes, then tied its ends together behind his head. With Curry blindfolded, Charlotte sat up so that she now straddled him. Leaning forward ever so slightly, she reached back behind her until she found what she wanted, and then they were adjoined. At the exact moment of their union, came the loudest crack of thunder to ever rattle Phil's eardrums.

Phil was now seething with bitterness, much like the night he'd been caught in the storm, driving Willie home from Kara's, only worse. He had a sinking feeling that he was watching something more than a live peep show. Dread and urgency tightened Phil's muscles and roiled in the pit of his stomach. Something bad was going on.

"*Preparaos para recibir mi regalo!*" she shrieked, as their pace picked up.

Then it hit Phil like a Monty Python sixteen-ton weight. As the wind ripped the shingles off the roof above him, he put it together. Like the instructions he had in his back pocket, Charlotte had already made a "gift"—sacrifice—of the dog he'd found in her trash the night he fell off her deck. She'd already "called the teacher" tonight, and now she was right in the middle of having "congress with a simple man" and making a "gift of his body."

Phil had glossed over a bit during the five seconds it took him to process that info, and now refocused on the two below him. While Charlotte continued to grind away on the blindfolded Curry, Phil saw her right hand reach behind her and slide under the comforter folded at the bottom of the bed.

Phil now found himself in the midst of chaos: torrential storm outside; animalistic sex to the pounding of drums below; and a runaway locomotive of pain inside his head that had jumped the tracks and was speeding over a cliff.

Charlotte's right hand had found what it was seeking. It emerged from the comforter with a knife sporting a wide blade, at least a foot long. All the while, she never ceased her "congress" with the unsuspecting Curry.

"*Pongo mi regalo a tus pies!*"

And with that, she put two hands on the knife's handle and slowly began to raise it over her head.

Instinct took over, and without thinking, Phil quickly sprang up to a "push up" position, turned his body sideways, and threw his left shoulder down through the sixteen-inch space between the joists. He felt a burning sensation on his forehead and shoulder blade as he broke through the insulation and drywall ceiling, falling headfirst on top of Charlotte, pounding her skull with his own.

The collision sent an unconscious Charlotte crashing into the night-stand beside her bed, launching lit candles in every direction.

Phil had bounced off the bed and now found himself dazed and lying prone on the floor. Cracking noggins with Charlotte only worsened his headache, and he opened his eyes to find the room swirling. While he couldn't make heads or tails of the room, he could hear the blindfolded Curry yelling.

"Charlotte, what the hell!...Charlotte! Charlotte!"

In a few seconds, Phil's vision improved enough to see flames crawling up the curtains of both windows. Still on the floor, he turned his head to see the comforter on fire at the foot of the bed.

In desperation, he lifted himself to his hands and knees. The curtains were now completely engulfed in flames and toasting the ceiling. In trying to raise himself up from all fours to a standing position, it was like he'd been blindfolded, mercilessly spun around over and over, then released. His body helplessly followed his head as it went sideways across the room, crashing into the dresser, sending even more candles plummeting into the carpet.

With the drums and Curry's repeated cries for Charlotte providing the soundtrack, Phil once again tried to right himself. His sense of direction ever-improving, he managed to stand up and quickly take account of the situation. The room was now ablaze, and there would be no putting out the fire. Oxygen was becoming harder and harder to find in the smoke-filled room. Every cough felt like a body shot to his fractured ribs. Every incoming breath felt like gasoline poured down his esophagus.

Phil found his way over to the motionless Charlotte on the floor by the bed. He bent down, scooped her up like a baby in his arms, and carried her out to the living room, laying her on the couch.

He ran back down the hallway and into the dense smoke of the bedroom to find the still-handcuffed and blindfolded Curry now lying motionless on the bed, his head slumping off to the side, most likely due to smoke inhalation. Phil knew there would be no unlocking of the handcuffs, since he had lost the key earlier. Time was short. There was no air in the room to breathe.

He moved quickly to the side of the bed. In karate fashion, he turned his body sideways and delivered a crushing kick to the center of the headboard, just inches from Curry's cranium. He heard it crack, but it was still intact. He regained his balance and again turned to deliver a second kick. That one snapped the headboard in half. Two more quick kicks freed the legs of the headboard from the bed's metal frame.

"Don't read more into this than it is," Phil said to his unconscious co-worker as he threw Curry's naked body over his shoulder. "I think we should just be friends." Then he carried him, with the broken head-board pieces dragging behind, out of the room, down the hall, and into the living room.

The furious storm that raged outside had now completely stopped. Phil quickly studied his two unconscious co-workers, and found both of their chests were rising and falling. They were still alive. He knew getting them to the living room wasn't enough. Soon the whole house would be engulfed.

As intimately as Phil had been involved in this episode, his identity was still unknown to Charlotte and Curry. However, he couldn't let the house continue to burn, endangering the homes on either side. He also knew Charlotte and Curry needed medical attention.

Even though Charlotte had been about to mutilate Curry in some sort of ritualistic sacrifice, and the world would be better off without her, all life must surely have some value, Phil thought, even hers. He couldn't let *anyone* just die, not even Charlotte.

The flames were now in the hallway, and Phil heard the ceiling crash down in Charlotte's bedroom. He had to get them out of the house fast, but first he picked up her house phone, using his shirttail as a makeshift glove, and punched 911 with the knuckle of his index finger.

"911. What's your emergency?" the dispatcher asked.

Summoning the highest pitch his voice could reach, Phil said, "Fire. Two people injured. We'll be under the gazebo in the back yard."

He hung up, knowing he didn't need to provide an address or repeat anything, as the landline would identify the location and all calls were recorded automatically.

Darkness had recently fallen, allowing him some cover. He grabbed a blanket off the back of the couch, wrapped it around Charlotte's nakedness, carried her out the sliding glass door onto the elevated deck, and down the stairs. He took her as far from the house in the back yard as possible, laying her down under the small gazebo near the property line. Running back into the house, he repeated the process with Curry, who was still tethered by handcuffs to the broken headboard fragments. They would be safe from the fire, and their blankets would shield them from the cool spring night air, as well as the embarrassment of being found naked. Nothing Phil could do about the embarrassment of being found handcuffed to a headboard. Where for art though, little lost key?

Phil sat with the two in the darkness under the gazebo. As he did, he wondered how things had gotten so out of hand. He wondered what kind of father he was. With his custody of Willie so iffy, any involvement in something like this would certainly do him in at a custody hearing. Look at the destruction he'd caused.

He had to stop to remind himself that Curry would not be alive if he hadn't been there. He also had to tell himself that he'd been threatened by Charlotte. Her words were tantamount to an attack on him. And in his mind, as Willie's sole provider and protector, any attack on Phil was an attack on Willie. After witnessing her capabilities this evening, maybe he should've let her burn, he wondered in a fleeting thought. Now, though, every cell in his body began to ache for Willie.

Flames were now breaching the roof line and reaching for the night sky, evaporating Phil's cover of darkness. He could hear the wail of sirens now. Knowing Charlotte and Curry would be in helping hands in mere minutes, he raised his stiff body off the ground, took one last look at the hellish inferno, and then hurriedly slipped away through the darkened back yards of suburban Dover.

# CHAPTER TWENTY-FIVE

PHIL'S EYES opened slowly to see the swirling ceiling fan blades in his bedroom. Even his eyelids were sore. Lately, it seemed every morning he'd awakened stiffer than the one before. For just an instant, he thought it was Saturday, and could sleep in a little. Nothing like starting your Thursday out with that kind of disappointment. The morning sun poured through the window and flooded his room. Otis lay at the bottom of the bed, tail thumping.

"Mornin', buddy,"

The dog responded by crawling up the bed and laying his chin on Phil's chest.

"It'll be good to get Willie back today, won't it?"

As he began his morning ritual, Phil's mind was immediately overtaken by worry over the health of Curry and Charlotte. More Curry than Charlotte. As far as he knew, no one was aware of his presence at Charlotte's the night before, not even the two he saved from the fire.

---

PHIL LET out an audible groan as he landed in his desk chair at the bank.

"So what did you get into last night?" a familiar voice said from Phil's periphery. Here came Gus from the kitchen with a cup of coffee. It seemed like days since Phil had seen him, when in fact, it had been less than twenty-four hours. Still, he was a sight for sore eyes.

"Come here, and let me tell you," Phil said without hesitation. His trust in Gus was complete. Gus pulled his chair over to Phil's desk.

"Damn, this already sounds good," Gus said.

"Where's Charlotte and Curry?"

"Don't know. Haven't seen 'em yet."

"Well, I left here yesterday," Phil started, but then halted when, to his left, he saw two Kent County Deputy Sheriffs step out of the elevator and stop the first passerby, saying something. The lady turned and pointed in Phil's direction.

"Oh, shit," Phil mumbled to Gus.

"What?"

"I can't say now, but if I'm not around, will you be sure to ask Kara to hang onto Willie? They're coming home from her cabin this afternoon."

"Yeah, sure," Gus said.

The deputies turned and strode forcefully toward Phil's desk. His face began to flush. In the subsequent ten seconds, the worries in his head rattled like the muffler on the little white truck. A neighbor must have seen him last night. Maybe Curry had been able to see him somehow. How would he explain being in Charlotte's attic? What would Jill think of him? Was this the final blow that would cause him to lose Willie to his soon-to-be-paroled mother?

They finally arrived at Phil's desk. The familiar throb of his pulse in the jugular was back. He felt like he'd hit rock bottom.

"Gus Austin?"

"Yeah?" Gus answered.

"You're under arrest for Breaking and Entering, Battery, and Arson."

Phil was dumbfounded.

"What?" Gus said.

"Did you not understand what I said?" the deputy asked.

"Yeah, I speak English, but who did I assault and burn?"

"That will all be explained," said the deputy, as he put Gus's hands behind his back and applied handcuffs.

"You have the right to remain silent—"

"Wait a minute," Phil said, getting up from his chair. "He didn't do anything."

"That will all have to be sorted out," said the deputy.

"Officer," Gus said, "can I have a quick word with my friend, just make some arrangement for my car, and what to tell my parents and stuff?"

"Make it fast."

Phil and Gus separated themselves a few feet away from the troopers.

Leaning into Phil's ear, Gus said calmly, "I bet this has something to do with what you were about to tell me."

"Yes," Phil whispered in a desperate tone. "I'm not going to let them take you to jail."

"The hell you aren't," Gus said under his breath. "You can't afford any trouble, not with Belinda wanting Willie back."

"This isn't your problem," Phil said.

"I'm not worried. Remember, I didn't do anything wrong, and I don't know nothin' about nothin'. So, don't tell me now."

"So, you're all right with this?"

"Sure. I'm innocent. Let them run off in the wrong direction for a while."

"Want me to get you a lawyer or come to the station with you?"

"Nah, I don't need a lawyer, and you should stay the hell away from the cops. If this is about something last night, I'll be out fast. All kinds of people saw me at my show last night up in New Jersey. I was with my manager, for crying out loud."

"I owe you."

"I didn't feel like workin' today, anyway," Gus said with a grin.

"All right, come on," said the deputy, who then finished his recitation of the Miranda Rights and led Gus off to the elevator and out of the building.

Phil had no idea why the police wanted Gus and not him, but he was in no position to bring the error to their attention. Phil had the urge to get out of the office, but he might be able to learn about Charlotte and Curry's condition if he stayed put. After all, he couldn't just go the hospital and ask about them. There would be no legitimate reason for him to know they'd be there.

The elevator doors opened, and Angela got off.

"Phil, did you hear about Charlotte?"

"No."

Evidently, she was speaking to him now, albeit with a chill in her timbre.

"Her house burned down last night, and she's in Kent Memorial. Russ Curry's there, too. Evidently, they were working together at her house last night when somebody broke in, attacked them, and set the place on fire."

"My God," Phil said with all the earnestness he could muster. "Are they okay?"

"They'll be okay. Just some smoke inhalation, and Charlotte had a pretty bad concussion."

"Geez," Phil said in a subdued tone, making sure not to overact. He wasn't going to say anything to Angela about Gus, so as not to damage his friend's reputation.

"Have they already taken Gus away?" she asked.

"You know about that?"

"The police came to tell Mr. Adams first."

"Yeah, they took him away a few minutes ago. He was in New Jersey last night. Why do they think it's him?"

"The police said that Charlotte told them it was Gus."

"So says the woman with a concussion," Phil said. "Does Curry think it was Gus, too?"

"They said Russ didn't get a good look at him."

# CHAPTER TWENTY-SIX

WHEN LUNCH CAME AROUND, Phil went to the police station to check on Gus. Upon his arrival, he found his friend had already been released. He went out on the courthouse steps and called Gus.

"So you're out?"

"About fifteen minutes ago. Told ya."

"Did they tell you anything?" Phil asked.

"Only that Charlotte positively identified me at her house last night. I told them I was 75 miles away, my manager's name, and what club I was singing at."

"And that was it?"

"They made a few phone calls, I guess, then let me go. So, what the hell did you do, anyway?"

"It's probably better if I don't tell you for a while," Phil said, "Just in case they want to re-question you. Then you don't have to lie when you say you don't know anything."

"Ah, ignorance really is bliss, isn't it?"

"Want some lunch?" Phil asked.

"Nah, I'm going home. Maybe catch a nap."

After ending the call, Phil acted on an urge he'd had all morning. He called Jill's work number.

"Jill Wheaton," she answered.

"In ten minutes," he said in his best deadpan, "there'll be an unmarked, white compact pickup truck waiting in front of the bank. You will enter the truck, shower the driver with affection, then proceed to have a pleasant lunch."

"But what if I find the driver repulsive?"

"Just do it," he said. "And no cops."

With that, he hung up. Her voice was like a salve for all that ailed him. He didn't feel like he could completely unburden himself of all of his troubles, but just seeing her would help.

In ten minutes, he was parked at a meter in front of the bank and was watching her walk across the plaza toward him. The sun glistened off her breeze-blown hair as it bounced off her shoulders. The passenger door opened; she entered and closed the door. As instructed, and without a word, she leaned toward him, placing her left hand on the back of his muscular neck, and brought her lips softly to his. Gently, yet passionately, she pulled at his lower lip with her teeth, then dragged the inside of her upper lip across his. Phil passively absorbed its healing effect. After a half minute, she slowly pulled away, the pupils in her big round brown eyes fully dilated.

Phil hadn't the energy or ability to speak. All he could do was look into the vacuum of her eyes and breathe. He was tired. Tired and sore, physically and emotionally. He could see the concern on her face, and was amazed at how well she already knew him. In the total absence of words, she could feel him ache, instinctively knowing he was struggling.

She quietly placed her palm on his cheek and caressed his temple with her thumb. With an accompanying look of sadness, she moved her finger to his forehead to gently nurse a scrape. Every time she saw him, he had some new injury. Even though Phil's rib cage still stabbed at him with every slight movement, being in her presence made it easier for him to breathe, somehow. A minute had passed, and they hadn't spoken.

"Is there any way I can help you?" she asked him with all sincerity.

"You already have."

"You know," she said, "you can cut a problem in half just by sharing it."

She didn't know the extent of his troubles, and he wanted to spare her any details. Even though he felt justified in his struggle, the details, he thought, would put him in an unsavory light. Phil was learning that sometimes you've got to get down in the mud to keep what you love. Deep down, he still felt unworthy of her.

"Let's just have some lunch," Phil said.

"I'd love to, but I've got a meeting starting soon. You hung up so fast after your silly instructions, I didn't have time to tell you."

"Okay, then," he said, doing his best to conceal his disappointment.

"I'll make it up to you," Jill said, as she placed a hand on each cheek and softly kissed him.

Phil drove away from the bank feeling better. Not good, but better. Like steam from a boiling kettle, he let a few thoughts verbally escape his head as he sat a stoplight.

"Let's see, my ex-wife will be out of prison soon and wants her son back. I'm failing at a job that I need to keep in order to hang onto my son. My boss, who acts like she knows something about me that I don't know myself, has fondled me under a table in a seedy bar. Then I watched her screw a co-worker from her attic, and I burned the house down stopping her from killing him. And best of all, I can't tell anybody about any of it because I'd go straight to jail."

As the light turned green and he pulled forward, he added, "Oh yeah, it appears I may be the unborn son of the first couple of American Camelot."

This recitation, while therapeutic, confirmed in Phil's mind that he had made the right decision not to share his problems with Jill. Next stop was Kara's house to retrieve Willie. When he got there, he found everyone on the backyard patio in the afternoon sun.

"How's my buddy?" Phil called to Willie, who came running to his dad. "Did you have fun?"

"Yeah!" Willie answered with his usual conservation of words.

As the kids continued to play in the back yard, Phil and Kara sat down at the patio table.

"I've got a problem," Phil said as he squinted into the sun.

"Well," Kara said, "I didn't think you'd need it at twenty-nine, but they do make a pill for men who have blood flow issues."

Phil let out a low snicker.

"No clever retort?" she asked.

"I'm too drained."

"So, what's bugging you?"

Not wanting to implicate her or put her in a position to have to lie on his behalf, he was vague.

"I've got several pretty weird things going on, and I may be keeping some irregular hours in the next few days."

"Then why doesn't your little pal camp here with us for a while?"

"I'm not going to even bother with the little dance we do," Phil said, "where I ask, 'Are you sure it's not too much trouble?' and you assure me it's not."

"Good," she said with a smile. "That's so played." A pause ensued.

"Am I a lousy father?"

"How can you even ask that?"

"It just seems like Willie has spent more time with you than me lately."

"Listen to me," she said. Then turning to her husband, she said with a grin, "Gary, cover your ears." Turning back to Phil, she continued, "You're the best father I know. Look at your circumstances. You two are all alone. If it's better for Willie to be with me for a while, then that makes you an even better dad for recognizing it."

"I hope you'll let me tell you that you're the best, and how much I love you," Phil said.

"You may."

He gave her a firm hug.

"Well?" she said, "are you going to?"

"Going to what?"

"Tell me how much you love me?" she asked with a big grin.

"Asking if I can tell you is as close as you're gonna get," he said with a chuckle.

"Men...."

# CHAPTER TWENTY-SEVEN

AFTER LEAVING WILLIE WITH KARA, Phil found himself in his favorite chair on his front porch, plotting his next move. Dusk was setting in. By way of a phone call to Angela at work, he learned Charlotte would be in the hospital another couple of days. She was polite enough, but something in her voice wasn't quite right. She likely still had lingering feelings about his brutish behavior two nights earlier at the Stumble.

"Which way do we go, boy?" Phil asked Otis, who lay on the porch at his feet.

He had done some more internet research on the information he'd obtained from Charlotte's computer. He'd learned that CDW, the Essex County Airport in New Jersey, was the location from which JFK, Jr. took off on the night of his crash. He'd also found out that a Bokor is a voodoo sorceress, and Charlotte's computer had revealed that she had done a search for one in Manhattan.

Phil had a lot to figure out. Charlotte's words to him in her office the day before made it sound as though he was the prize at the end of some sort of quest. The info he'd found on her computer about the Essex County Airport, coupled with his experience "in" the plane, and her reaction to him saying she was an air traffic controller, led Phil to believe she definitely had something to do with the crash.

"Somehow, she was feeding John Junior some bad information," Phil said to his four-legged friend.

"Was she really an air traffic controller?" he asked his silent partner. "Or is there a way she could overtake his cockpit radio, and just pose as a controller?"

Otis was mum on the issue.

Phil felt like he was grabbing at notions as they swirled about his noggin. With Charlotte in the hospital, there didn't seem to be anything productive he could do in Dover.

His mobile phone rang.

"Hello?"

"Phillip, this is Ann Culpepper."

"Hey, Doc."

"I've just got a minute, but I want to tell you about something I've learned."

"Okay."

"I've found someone else like you."

"What do you mean?"

"In my research, I've come across a man in a federal prison in New London, Connecticut—for murder."

"How is that like me?"

"I'll give you the details when I've got more time, but I really think we should go talk to him."

"We?" Phil asked.

"Sure, Phillip. This new area of study has been quite invigorating for me."

"Don't get me wrong," Phil said. "I would love your company. I just don't want you to have to go to the time and expense."

"Money is not an issue, and I can't think of a better use of my time. I can go anytime you want."

"Okay, thanks."

"Just let me know. I'll speak with you later," she said before ending the call.

Phil's attention was then brought to a car pulling into his driveway behind the little white truck. It was Jill. Otis raised himself up and lumbered out to greet her at her car door.

"Well, hello," Phil said, as he joined Otis in welcoming her.

She wasn't smiling.

"I'm glad to see you," he said.

"We need to talk."

He didn't know what was on her mind, but Phil was getting a bad feeling in his stomach.

"You haven't known me very long, but you should know that I'm a very honest person," she said.

"I know that."

"I never play games," she added.

"I wouldn't expect you to," he said. "What do we need to talk about?"

"I'm going to ask you a question, and I want you to look me in the eyes and tell me the truth," she said.

Her words brought his pulse into his neck again.

"Okay."

"Are you involved with Charlotte Timpkin?"

He let out a puff of air through a relieved smile.

"No," he said in the most definitive tone he could produce. "Why would you ask that?"

"I spoke to her at the hospital this afternoon."

"Why in the world would you go to talk to her?"

"Her secretary contacted me and said she wanted to see me at the hospital."

The relief Phil had felt moments before was turning back into worry.

"What about?"

"She said that the two of you were involved, and that she was going to help you advance your career at the bank."

"That's a complete lie!"

"That's what I told her," Jill said, "but she said the other night at the Stumble On Inn, you two got 'physical' in a corner booth."

Phil's stomach was churning.

"She said," Jill continued, letting out a deep breath, "that if I haven't...gotten into your pants yet..." her face showed her level of discomfort, "that I have a pleasant surprise coming my way."

"Let me—" Phil started, but Jill interrupted.

"She told me to ask you, yourself, because you were so 'damned honorable', you would admit to it," Jill said, tears welling up in her eyes. "So, like I said when I got here, I want you to look me in the eyes and tell me the truth."

Phil reached for her to pull her toward him, but she stepped back, leaning against her car.

"There is nothing between Charlotte and me. Nothing. I've never had such hatred toward another human being, to be honest."

"What about the Stumble?"

He looked into her round brown eyes, glossed over with tears, and said, "Okay. I was at the Stumble and had way too much to drink," he started.

"So, then it's true?"

"No. Let me finish. I was passed out in a booth, and she basically molested me. I didn't even know anybody else was in the booth with me. When I figured out what was happening, I knocked her out of the booth onto the floor and ran out of there."

Phil knew...even though he had been Charlotte's victim at the Stumble, he could feel Jill slipping away from him.

"I know it sounds awful, but that's the truth," he said.

Phil again stepped toward Jill in an attempt to bring her into his arms.

"No. Just get away," she said as she turned from him, scrambling to get in her car.

"Wait," Phil urged. "That's all that happened, I swear to you."

"That's all?" she said through tears as she started her car. "That's all?"

Then the car backed out into the street and sped off into the dusk. Phil was beside himself. He couldn't let her get away. He didn't know what he would say to her, but he'd just have to figure that out when he saw her.

He jumped into the little white truck, fumbling with his keys. What if she wasn't going home? Where would he find her? Finally getting the key in the ignition, he started it up, and sent the truck backing quickly toward the street.

Midway down the driveway, a thudding jolt behind him reverberated through his spine. The tires screeched against the pavement as he stopped the truck. Phil silently looked in the mirror outside his driver's window. He could see nothing in the fading light behind him.

While his left hand hurried to find the handle and open the door, his eyes darted frantically around the front yard, desperately hoping to find what he couldn't.

He jumped out and ran to the rear of the truck. With his heart in his throat, he stared at the ground behind the truck, where he found Otis lying motionless with a stream of blood flowing from his mouth.

Phil dropped to his knees beside his friend, who lay on his side, eyes open, but struggling for each breath. Phil felt like he'd been the one hit by the truck. He wished it were him. He desperately, helplessly tried to think a way to save Otis, but didn't know how. The nearest veterinarian was a good five miles away. Fearing he might do more damage trying to move him, all he could do was gently stroke the top of his head and down the back of his neck.

"I'm so sorry, buddy," Phil sobbed in a shaky voice, as a tear escaped his eye and rolled down his cheek. His bottom lip quivered uncontrollably. "I'm so sorry."

Phil laid down on his side so he could be face to face with the family member who had nursed and healed him and Willie through their times of trouble. He'd been present for everything the past seven years, the celebrations and the misery. He'd been their counselor, their guardian, their confidant. His breathing slowed.

Otis, showing his ever-trusting, ever-forgiving nature, extended his paw, resting it on Phil's shoulder as they lay face to face on the cold pavement of the driveway. With his warm, penetrating gaze into Phil's eyes, he conveyed his love and gratitude. In Otis's deep brown eyes, Phil could do no wrong.

And then he was still.

In that moment, Phil's heart broke so profoundly that he wasn't sure he could continue, even though he knew he had to.

He had failed Otis. He had failed Jill. Mostly, though, he had failed Willie. Not only had he now taken away Willie's guardian and best friend, he would most likely lose his job, and ultimately Willie's custody, handing him over to morally bankrupt Belinda. And right now, more than ever, Phil missed his mother.

Phil's aching body was like a sponge, soaking the cold out of the concrete up into his body. Perhaps it was appropriate that he found himself lying on the ground. This must be the bottom. He was hurting inside and out. He wanted it that way. He had it coming, he believed.

As the stars began to emerge above him, Phil laid on his side, still stroking his lifeless friend. What had brought him to this point in his life? How had he been spending his God-given precious time here on Earth? Certainly, he could do more with his life. More. Better. More of what, he wasn't sure, but certainly more and better.

He didn't know what was happening to him, why he was being pursued, or even who his parents really were. Was he the fruit of admirable blue collars or noble American royalty? It was then, right there on the cold hard concrete of his driveway, the notion struck him that maybe the most virtuous seeds of both were imbedded in him. He hoped it was true. It was a rare optimistic notion he'd just have to cling to in order to carry on.

After his time of reflection on the driveway, then giving Otis a proper and emotionally trying burial in the back yard, Phil felt compelled more than ever to take some kind of action. *More.* Like the epiphany on the driveway. It was 9:00 PM now. Willie was at Kara's for a few days. Charlotte was in the hospital for another couple of days.

He wasn't completely sure what to do next. He couldn't think of any avenues to pursue in Dover. Something inside him, though, was pulling him out of town. The time for it seemed to be now. Right now.

So, Phil went in the house, hurriedly showered, and threw some clothes in a Kroger bag. He reached toward his night stand and picked up the list of Spanish instructions he'd found in Charlotte's attic, folded it, and slid it into his back pocket. Maybe he'd show it to Ann. Maybe he wouldn't.

Before heading out the door, he stirred some instant coffee into a travel cup of microwaved hot water. His once muddied mind was clearing as he locked the front door behind him, went out to the driveway, and settled in behind the wheel of the little white truck. He reached up and hung Otis's collar around the rearview mirror, then pulled out his phone and dialed.

"Ann, it's Phil. Can you go to Connecticut tomorrow?"

"Yes, dear. We can fly out in the morning. Would you like for me to make your reservation?"

"No, thanks. My budget's a little tight at the moment," Phil said. "By the way, this guy who's like me, who did he murder?"

"A member of the Manson Family."

"Good Lord," Phil said. "In what way is he like me?"

"Well," she said, pausing, "he claims he was the child of—brace yourself—Sharon Tate."

Phil was silent, trying to absorb it all.

"Why don't you let me buy your ticket, Phil?"

"That's very kind of you, but I couldn't let you do that. I'm driving up tonight. Besides, I'm going to need my truck for another appointment."

"And who might that be with?"

"I'll tell you more about that tomorrow. Which airport will you be using?"

"Meet me at the Hartford airport. I'll call you in the morning with the arrival details," she said.

And with that, they ended the call.

Ann's new Tate-Manson development was reason alone to take this trip. But after he and Ann explored what it had to offer, Phil had an even more compelling mission in mind: New York City and Kristen Minnows—the girl on the plane.

# CHAPTER TWENTY-EIGHT

THE HUM of a mid-sized airport on a Friday morning can be more sleep-inducing than the cushiest of beds. After driving five hours overnight, Phil had found himself in a comfortable chair—by airport standards, anyway—sleepily awaiting the arrival of Ann Culpepper's flight.

He'd drifted in and out of a light sleep ever since he'd arrived at 2:15 that morning. One eye opened momentarily to see the clock on the wall rounding 11:00 AM. He'd forgotten the exact arrival time, but had heard Ann say eleven something. A few more minutes of shut-eye.

"Phillip Murphy, I presume?"

Phil opened his eyes to see Ann and her ever-smiling face standing in front of his chair. He supposed 11:02 was just as "eleven something" as 11:59.

"Pretty sure that's me," he said. "I don't think anybody else would claim to be."

"I'd hoped you might be waiting for me with a sign that had my name on it," she said with a chuckle.

They took a serpentine route from the arrival area to the baggage claim, through a snack bar, then out to Phil's little white truck, the tires of which had never touched New England pavement prior to this trip.

"Oh, if this little truck could talk," Ann said, "the stories I bet it would tell."

"We've had some good times, I guess—not so much lately, though," he said in a melancholy tone, with Otis having never left his mind.

Phil maneuvered through the traffic of the parking area, out onto the four-lane, and began the hour-long trip to their destination.

"You said on the phone, New London, Connecticut, Doc. What prison?"

"The New London Federal Correctional Institution."

"How imaginative," Phil said.

"Well, dear, it *is* the government."

"I take it that having the word 'Institution' in the title may be key here. Am I right?"

"Well, this facility does specialize in housing prisoners with psychological issues."

"So the fellow we're going to visit has had some difficulties, I assume," Phil said as he checked the mirror on his door in preparation to move over to the fast lane. "What's his name, anyway?"

"Yes, I would think that's a safe assumption," Ann answered. "And his name is Hinkle Bare Skann."

"Why are criminals called by all three of their names?" Phil asked.

"I would think it's to differentiate the criminal from innocent people who might share his first and last names," Ann said.

"Well, that's understandable," Phil said. "It would be a shame to smear the good names of all of the other Hinkle Skanns in the world."

As Phil zigged-zagged through traffic in the noon-time sun, shadows clung tightly to the cars he passed. His mind was so cluttered with recent occurrences, he wasn't sure what questions to even ask Ann.

"So why are we going to see Mr. Skann?"

"It's actually Doctor Skann," she answered.

"So, what did Doctor Skann do?"

"He appeared to be a good citizen, until right before he murdered a woman who was marginally connected to the Manson Family."

"What happened?"

"Well, I hope he's open enough to fill in some of the blanks for us, but from what I was able to gather from my research, he said he was trying to gain retribution for the death of his mother, who he claims is Sharon Tate."

"Good God," Phil said, as he continued to slice his way through the crowded highway. Patience could not be counted among his possessions at the moment.

"Everyone just assumed he was mentally unbalanced. He admitted to the crime, so they locked him up. There was never a trial, only a sentencing hearing."

"Do you believe him?" Phil asked.

"Well, in my research, I was able to see the transcript of the sentencing hearing. He spoke of details of the Tate murder that had never been discussed in the media, nor by the police—like he was there when it happened."

"Couldn't he be making it all up?" Phil asked.

"Couldn't *you* be making it all up, dear?"

"I suppose, of all people," Phil said, "*I* should be more open-minded."

"It's a lot to take in, dear," Ann said, patting him on the shoulder.

"How were you able to find him, anyway?"

"Thankfully, in this day and age, the internet makes it possible to search relentlessly using endless combinations of words and phrases," she said. "I'd click on a link, read a story that contained another link, and just keep going. Finally, I stumbled across a man claiming to be the unborn child of a deceased actress—our Hinkle Bare Skann."

As they continued on their way, Phil considered the notion of showing Ann the paper containing the instructions for Charlotte's quest. However, he thought better of it, not wanting to answer questions about where he'd gotten it. So, he left it tucked away in his back pocket.

Upon arrival at the prison, Phil parked the truck and they proceeded to the entrance. After passing through security, they entered a room with the typical security glass wall, seats on each side, and several visitors having conversations with prisoners through the glass. Phil advised the guard that they wanted to speak to Skann, then took a seat at one of the stations, which were divided by small partitions to provide some minimal privacy from the people in the next stall.

Ten minutes later, a bespectacled, slender man, thirtyish, appeared at the door on the other side of the glass. He approached his visitors and timidly sat down, crossing his legs in a rather feminine way.

"Hello, Doctor Skann," Ann offered.

"Hello," he answered, a look of bewilderment on his face.

"My name is Doctor Ann Culpepper, and this is Phillip Murphy. I suppose you're wondering why we've come to see you," Ann said.

"I don't really care," Skann answered quietly, coldly. "I've come to embrace any disruption of this facility's unceasing monotony."

"I'm a professor of psychology at Delaware Bay College in Dover, Delaware. I've been helping Phil, here, with a problem he's been having, and I think you two may have a lot in common."

"Is that so?" he said. "Who did you bump off, Mr. Murphy?"

"Nobody...yet, anyway," Phil answered.

Ann interjected, "We appreciate you taking the time to sit down with us."

Then the sleep-deprived, patience-impaired Phil cut in. "Listen, we don't have time to tiptoe around, and we sure don't want to waste your time, Dr. Skann. What makes you think you're the son of Sharon Tate?"

The mild-mannered Skann appeared taken aback.

"Why should I discuss that with you?"

"Because maybe we can help each other," Phil said.

"I'm beyond help, Mr. Murphy. I am... here," he said, motioning like a show model displaying a new sports car. "For the rest of my days."

"You know, Dr. Skann, they say misery loves company," Phil said with a sad smile.

"What kind of company can you provide me with, Mr. Murphy?"

"What if I were to tell you that I've been going through some things that have led Dr. Culpepper and I to believe I may have been originally destined for different parents than those who raised me?"

All in one motion, Skann uncrossed his legs, leaned forward in his chair, and took off his glasses. He said nothing for ten seconds.

"Well then, Mr. Murphy, I would heap all of the pity upon you that I could muster."

"Well, it's true," Phil said. "And Dr. Culpepper has been doing some research about it."

"Klaus Clavos?" Skann asked, looking at Ann.

"Yes," she said, with a look of mild astonishment.

"Don't look so surprised," he said in his dry manner. "What do you think I do here all day? I *am* an MD, and this place has a library and internet access."

"Dr. Skann, forgive me, but you seem as sane as anyone I've ever met," Ann said. "Why do they keep you here, as opposed to a more traditional prison, especially considering the nature of your crime?"

"Because my explanation of my actions gave them no other choice but to brand me a lunatic."

"I'd really be interested to know," Phil said, "how did this all start with you?"

"The crime or the Conception Reassignment?"

"The reassignment," Phil answered.

"My life was normal—I'd even called it a good life—until I was finishing up med school about three years ago. I was twenty-five, and I started having exquisitely real daydreams involving a beautiful woman who was my mother."

He sat upright again in his chair and placed his glasses back on. He quietly continued.

"I was having about an episode a week. The visions weren't in chronological order. In one, I would be a teenager, and in the next, a young child. I only got a glimpse of myself in a mirror in one vision, and I could clearly tell it wasn't me. I was still a male, but beautiful."

"So interesting," Ann murmured.

He uncrossed his legs momentarily, then crossed them back, switching them over.

"After about three months, I had the strangest episode of all. I was in the womb of my mother, bathed in darkness and bliss. I could hear what the fetus heard, albeit muffled, but at the same time, I also had the thoughts of me, Hink Skann."

"That's what happened to me!" Phil blurted out, recalling his store-window vision in the alley.

Skann appeared irritated that Phil had interrupted.

"I'm sorry, go on." Phil said.

"There was an extremely tense ambience that came over me. I heard the voices of a strange man and a woman, speaking slowly and very forcefully. My mother's voice was much louder to me, and desperate."

Skann was now visibly uncomfortable. His voice grew unsteady.

"The adult me that was temporarily residing in the body of the fetus heard everything. Every word, every scream, every gasp for breath. I also felt every sensation of excruciating pain endured by the fetus."

His face went blank, and he became quiet. Reliving it appeared to be too taxing for him.

"So you not only saw visions of the life you would have lived, but also the event that terminated the pregnancy," Ann said. "Phil, here, did too."

"Yes," Skann confirmed.

"Thank you, Doctor Skann," Ann said, trying to ease his discomfort. "We've put you through enough."

Gathering himself, he said, "I'm fine, Dr. Culpepper. Our time is limited here. They'll probably be taking me back inside soon. Is there anything else you want to know?"

"If you don't mind my asking, how did you determine Sharon Tate was your mother?" Ann asked.

"In one of my briefer visions, I was a child at a dinner party with my mother and a man. A person addressed them as Sharon and Roman. After I emerged from the vision, it was as simple as doing a search on the internet for 'Sharon and Roman'."

"And that worked?" Phil asked.

"His name was unusual enough that, being coupled with hers, it produced results. The moment I saw their photographs, I felt a bitter chill run up my spine."

"The fact that you recalled a vision from your flash forward that included your mother," Ann said, "confirms Dr. Clavos's theory that the flash forward shows your life as if the pregnancy-terminating event never happened. In this case, your mother's murder."

"How did you get here?" Phil asked.

"Let me say, at first my journey was odd and confusing, but somehow almost pleasant. However, after learning my mother's identity, and then researching her life and death, I became consumed with perpetrating vengeance upon my and her murderers, Charles Manson's followers."

He again removed his glasses, this time polishing them with a handkerchief he had pulled from his pocket.

"But they were all either dead or in jail for the rest of their lives. So, I found someone who had spent a short amount of time with them as part of their 'family', researched her, learned that she was not a model citizen, and sought her out to confront her."

"Confront her?" Phil asked.

"Yes. I knew this person wasn't responsible for what had befallen my mother, but I just wanted to give her a piece of my mind. I'm not a violent person."

"Okay," Phil said.

"I went to her home, overcome with emotion, and began to berate her at her front door. She disappeared back into the house for a moment, then reappeared with a handgun. Not being of stable mind, I tried to take it away from her. We struggled, and the gun went off, killing her."

He replaced his glasses.

"Because the gun was unregistered, the prosecutors were alleging *I* had brought it to the scene. I suppose I was the aggressor because I'm the one that showed up at her door. Both of our prints were on the gun due to the struggle, so I would have been easily convicted. They wouldn't even entertain the idea of a plea bargain, and I couldn't handle the thought of a trial. So, I just plead guilty. After all, it was my fault she was dead. I couldn't handle the guilt. In my mind, I believe my punishment is justified."

A prison guard approached Skann and motioned for him to wrap up his conversation.

"Murphy, let me stress something to you," Skann said. "I feel like I could have embraced the good of all of this, but I chose the bad. Don't make that mistake."

"I won't," Phil said, as he and Ann got up and headed toward the door. "Thank you."

"One thing I'm thankful for," Skann said as the guard came to usher him away, "is that I had parents who were easily identifiable. I think I'd really have gone crazy if I couldn't have figured out who they were. Do you know who yours are?"

"Still working on it."

Phil held the door for Ann as she exited, then started through himself.

"Murphy." Skann called out.

"Yeah."

"Use what you've learned, what you've seen, to your advantage."

He nodded to Skann, then left.

Phil and Ann made their way to the little white truck, and it took them back to the Hartford airport passenger drop-off area, where they said their goodbyes.

"Are you sure you don't want to stay the night in a hotel? You've got your extra clothes and everything," Phil said, pointing to her overnight bag.

"No, dear, I'm going to catch a flight home. Are you heading home?"

"I've got one more errand to run while I'm here," Phil said.

"Is that so?" she asked. "Where are you going?"

"Manhattan," he said, "to call upon a Miss Kristen Minnows."

# CHAPTER TWENTY-NINE

THE WAIL of a siren passing by stirred Phil from the light, sporadic sleep he'd found in the driver's seat of his truck. He was beginning the day parallel parked on West 49th Street, near 9th Avenue in Manhattan. He'd found it true that this city never slept, and was stingy with what it allowed its visitors.

His three-hour, traffic-fighting drive after leaving Hartford on Friday afternoon had placed Phil in Manhattan well after the business hours of George Magazine. He was banking on a magazine like George, being under constant deadlines, would have staff in the office working on Saturday. So, Friday night, he had found a place to park on the street near their office and set up base camp there. He had done a little exploring on foot, gotten something to eat, then slept in his truck all night. There was no room in his budget for a night in any motel, particularly one anywhere near pricey Manhattan.

Sleep in the little white truck had been fitful, but still good enough to get some rest and gather himself before setting out to find Kristen Minnows. He'd picked up a copy of *George Magazine* at a convenience store outside of the city, and learned it was headquartered on the forty-first floor at 1633 Broadway, just a few blocks from where Phil had parked for the night.

He exited his truck, locked it up, and paused to stretch a little. More driving, coupled with a night of uneasy sleep in a confined space, was not the medicine his fractured ribs called for. It was nearing 9:00 AM as he made his way down the sidewalk on the south side of West 49th. When it intersected with Broadway, he took a left, crossing West 49th, maneuvering his way through the crowd until he found himself in front of the 48-story behemoth at 1633.

He paused for an instant. Even though he'd had hours alone in his truck to plot what he might say if he encountered Kristen Minnows, he'd made no such preparations. Instead, he seemed guided by instinct.

Up the concrete steps from the sidewalk he went, across a small plaza, finally entering the building through one of several glass doors. He found his way onto a crowded elevator, saw that 41 was already pressed, and settled in for the ride up.

Finally, the belled tolled at 41, and Phil stepped off the elevator, pausing to see where to go next. Fortunately, to his left was a glass door and windows that revealed the lobby of George Magazine. Looked like he was right about them working on Saturdays. He entered the lobby to find several people sitting and a fiftyish, bespectacled brunette receptionist behind a desk on the phone. Phil stood in front of her and patiently waited for her to conclude her call. Finally, she did.

"Welcome to George. How can I help you?" she said, in a relatively warm but rehearsed tone.

"I'm here to see Kristen Minnows, please."

"May I tell her who's here to see her?" she asked, picking up the phone to call for her.

"Well, sure," he said with a tired smile, "go ahead and tell her."

"Oh, that's cute," the woman said with a heaping of big-city sarcasm.

"Sorry," he said, "Just tell her—"

He was abruptly interrupted by the opening of the door beside the receptionist's desk. Phil felt a chilling jolt hit him.

It was her. He knew it immediately, and she looked exactly as she had in his experience on the doomed plane.

"You can tell her yourself, hon," the receptionist said. "There she goes now."

The receptionist then called out to the briskly-exiting Kristen, "Ms. Minnows, this gentleman is here to see you."

"Come on," she said curtly, without even looking at Phil, only motioning with her head for him to follow her out the door. A purse strap over one shoulder and a leather portfolio under the other arm, she leaned against the glass door to leave the lobby. Phil quickly thanked the receptionist, then followed Kristen out the door toward the elevator.

By the time Phil caught up with her at the elevator doors, she was already engaged in a discussion with another woman. So, Phil waited patiently behind her.

Before she had finished talking to the other woman, the elevator doors opened. The other woman walked away, and Kristen, seemingly forgetting about Phil, walked straight onto the crowded elevator. When she turned around, she saw Phil face to face for the first time as he stood outside the elevator door.

Her mouth opened a bit, and her eyes widened ever so slightly. Gathering herself and passing it off as just some vague familiarity, she said, "Well, are you coming?"

Phil saw it. Her reaction told him he wasn't crazy after all. While he knew he didn't look like Davis Kennedy, something sent Kristen the signal of Phil's connection to her. He stepped onto the elevator.

"So, what can I do for you?" she asked.

"Well," he started, but then paused due to the lack of privacy, "my name is—"

"Kristen, are you going to your meeting with Horowitz now?" asked a female voice from the back of the elevator.

"Yes," she answered, "are you coming?"

Then ensued a business chat between the two that lasted through all of the elevator stops, shunning Phil like he was a GDI crashing a frat party.

Finally, the doors opened to the lobby, they all exited the elevator, and the two women parted. Again, seemingly forgetting about Phil,

Kristen proceeded at a quick pace toward the doors leading to the street.

"There was something I was hoping to talk to you about," Phil said from behind her.

"Okay, but you'll have to make it fast."

Phil wasn't used to the hurried pace of an urban professional. They passed through the glass doors, walking out onto the plaza in front of the building.

"I'm not sure this can be done fast," he said.

"It's going to have to be."

"Okay," he said, then paused, not sure of what he even wanted to say to her.

"Listen, we're going to have to do this another time," she interrupted. "I just don't have time right now."

She turned from Phil and started across the plaza toward the sidewalk. In desperation, Phil blurted out the first thing that came into head.

"The plane!" he yelled from across the plaza. "Why weren't we on it?"

She stopped in her tracks and turned back toward Phil.

"What?"

Phil walked toward her.

"Why weren't we on the plane? We would've been, but we weren't." He knew he wasn't making sense, but at least it was a conversation starter.

"What plane?" she asked.

Still ten feet apart, Phil paused before answering her. He knew he was about to sound like he'd lost his mind, but he answered her anyway.

"John Junior's."

As she stepped toward Phil, he could almost feel the sting of her glare. There had been so many people on the elevator before that it had been a potpourri of scents. But now, even though they were outside, she was close enough that Phil recognized the soft sweet fragrance of the expensive perfume she'd worn on the plane. The aroma hovering about her, along with her emerald eyes and dark flowing hair, had nearly put Phil back on the ill-fated aircraft once again.

"I don't know what mental facility you've escaped from, but you aren't funny."

"I'm not trying to be. Just listen to me for a second."

"No," she said, turning away to leave.

Without thought, Phil grabbed her arm, causing her portfolio to fall to the ground. This drew the attention of a nearby police officer, who approached the two.

"Everything okay here?" the officer asked, his belly straining the buttons on his shirt.

"Yes," Phil answered.

"No," Kristen said from her stooped position, picking up her portfolio.

The officer grabbed Phil by the arm.

"What's your name, buddy?"

Phil hesitated, because at the moment, no one knew his name, and he wanted to hang on to his anonymity.

"*Davis*," Kristen said. "His name is Davis!"

Phil's head spun, trying to grasp onto what was happening.

"How did you know that?" Phil asked.

"You told me."

"No, I didn't," Phil said, "I never got to tell you my name."

"Okay," interjected the cop, "so, Davis what?"

"My name's not Davis," Phil said.

"You just said it was," replied the cop, sounding increasingly annoyed. "You asked her how she knew your name."

"Officer," she said, "I work for George Magazine, and he comes into our office nine months after we lose John Junior, saying he's Davis Kennedy, and talking about us being on the plane that crashed. Then he grabs my arm and make me drop my portfolio."

"Think hard, Kristen," Phil pleaded, "You never heard me say my name, did you?"

She paused, her confusion showing on her face.

"Then how did I know it?"

"That's why we need to talk," Phil said as calmly as he could.

"No!" she said; then, turning to the police officer, "Get him away from me."

"Buddy, you can't be grabbing the lady's arm," the cop said.

Still holding Phil's arm with one hand, the cop reached for his cuffs with the other. Phil would have none of that. Anonymity still intact, he jerked his arm loose from the cop's grip, and ran across the plaza with the officer giving chase.

Down the sidewalk steps and onto the busy sidewalk, Phil zig-zagged through pedestrians like pylons on an obstacle course until he had disappeared into the morning Manhattan crowd. Even though his aching ribs and state of exhaustion slowed him down, he still rather easily eluded the overweight cop.

A block away, he looked back to see the officer, well behind, scanning the crowded sidewalk. To avoid being spotted on the street, Phil scurried down a nearby set of steps to the subway. He quickly bought a single-ride ticket from the vending machine and boarded the first train he saw, aiming to let his fogged head clear and get lost for a while beneath the streets of New York.

# CHAPTER THIRTY

THE RUMBLE of the subway had put the exhausted Phil to sleep. He slowly awoke, forgetting where he was for a moment, seated next to a middle-aged woman holding a bag of groceries.

Phil caught her eye as he stirred from his position leaning against the window. She looked at him, and he at her. He offered a tired smile, but she turned away. He wrote it off to life in the big city. Phil wasn't sure how long he'd been out or where he was. He figured, though, he was heading away from his little white truck, which was no doubt nervously awaiting his return, all alone on a side street in the urban jungle.

So, at the next stop, he got off the subway and ventured up the stairs to be among the street dwellers. He found himself on Lexington Avenue, at East 103$^{rd}$ Street, still in Manhattan, in the barrio district of East Harlem. Rather than go back down the stairs, find the appropriate train, and return to the little white truck, Phil felt the urge to stretch his legs a bit and explore.

It was almost 11:00 AM now, and the streets of Spanish Harlem were vibrant. East 103$^{rd}$ was brimming with small businesses, markets, and some beautiful old churches. He began to walk, heading east toward the East River. He strolled past the shops and slalomed through the pedestrians. As he continued, he began to feel more purpose in each step, as if he were seeking a destination.

With no clouds impeding its effort, the mid-day Manhattan sun blazed down with the best it could offer on a late April day, serving as a heating pad on Phil's sore back. At a moderate pace, he strode with ambition toward something, though he didn't know what.

He felt his senses dulling as he continued forward. Finally, he happened upon a shabbily adorned storefront, with a large vertical "Lotto" sign sticking out from the building above the door, and "*Mercado de la Carne*" painted in red upon the display window glass.

Without thought, instinct told Phil to pull the door open, which caused the attached bell to clang loudly. Passing through, the door closed behind him. He paused to take in what one might expect to find in a meat shop in a Spanish-speaking neighborhood.

Behind a counter to his left, a goateed man in an apron waited on a heavy-set, middle-aged woman, while a teenage boy waited in line behind her.

"*Buenos Dias, señor,*" the man behind the counter said.

"*Buenos Dias,*" Phil said, in an accent laughably American.

With Phil's dialect giving him away, the man kindly offered some English.

"I'll be with you soon, *señor.*"

"Thank you. I'm in no hurry," Phil said, still having no clue as to why he'd entered the shop in the first place. He stood in line, dumb-founded, until he felt upon him the dark eyes of a beautiful young woman sitting alone at a table to his right.

Evidently doing some sort of paperwork, her eyes were locked on Phil. He looked at her, offering an uncomfortable smile, which was only met with a penetrating stare. Phil's allergy to extended eye contact caused him to turn away to feign interest in some strange meat hanging behind the counter.

"*Papa, me voy a tomar un descanso.*"

Papa, I'm taking a break, Phil translated in his head.

"*Bien,*" replied the man behind the counter.

The young woman arose from her chair and walked slowly toward Phil.

"You have something to learn?" she asked Phil in a thick Hispanic accent.

"Excuse me?"

"Come with me," she said, taking his hand and leading him to a door in the back of the room. Phil was glad to see her father had his back turned, running ham through a slicer.

Through the door and down a short hallway, saying nothing, the young woman gently pulled Phil along behind her, her long dark hair gently bouncing off her shoulder-blades with each step she took. Her dress was so long and flowing that Phil had to be careful not to step on it.

At the other end of the hall, she opened a door with her free hand and led Phil into a dimly lit room with a small, round table and two chairs in the center. The table was topped entirely with a round mirror.

"Sit," she said, extending a hand toward one of the chairs.

Still feeling a bit glossed over from the sleepy subway ride and the uncertainty of why he'd felt compelled to enter the meat shop, Phil went along with her direction.

"What—" Phil started, but she interrupted.

"You will learn. That's why you are here."

"What's your name?" Phil asked.

"Candita," she said, finally surrendering a smile. She then proceeded to another door in the room and knocked softly upon it.

"*Mama, el esta aqui,*" (Mama, he's here). She then took a spot standing in a corner of the small room.

Before Phil could formulate a question, the door opened. There stood a woman adorned in a long, forest-green dress and a maroon scarf which held back thick silver hair from her lined face.

Phil said nothing.

Then ensued a Spanish conversation between Candita and her mother, only a few random words of which Phil recognized. He'd absorbed some of his Spanish For Dummies lessons on CD, but these women spoke too quickly. It was one thing for a novice like Phil to espouse some well-planned sentences in a foreign language, but quite another to be on the receiving end of a rapid-fire delivery. After about four exchanges between the two, the old woman walked silently to the table and sat down across from Phil.

"*Tiene algo suyo?*"

Phil looked over to Candita, in the corner behind her mother.

"Do you have something belonging to her?" Candita translated.

"Who?"

"From the woman who torments you," Candita said. All the while, the old woman stared directly at Phil. Feeling her eyes upon him, he momentarily glanced her way, then turned his eyes back to Candita.

"How does she know there's a woman tormenting me?"

"Why are you here?" Candita asked, answering his question with a question.

Phil paused for a moment, then reached for his back pocket, pulling out the folded paper he'd taken from the trunk in Charlotte's attic. He had decided not to show it to Ann but was glad now he'd brought it along. He unfolded it.

"I've got this," he said, offering it to the old woman.

As the paper passed from Phil's hand to the vein-ridden hand of the old woman, she let out an audible gasp and her eyes widened. Candita rushed to her mother's side.

"Is she okay?" Phil asked Candita. Before she answered she conversed with her mother in Spanish.

"Yes, she is fine."

"Are you sure?"

"Yes. She says that this paper is alive with *el diablo*."

"The devil?" Phil asked.

"Yes."

"What does it say?"

Still at her mother's side, Candita looked at the paper, careful not to touch it. After a brief conversation with her mother, she spoke to Phil.

"This is a recipe for finding a person that you want to harm. It is very old."

"What do you mean, finding a person?"

"You are descended from royalty. I am correct?" Candita asked.

"No," Phil said. But after a pause, he added, "Actually, there are a lot of things I'm not sure about right now."

The old woman interjected a flurry of Spanish lasting at least a minute, during which she pointed at Phil a half dozen times.

After a pause, Candita spoke in slow, measured words.

"You are in much danger. This person who hunts you is using these steps to consult an evil authority."

"What steps?"

"A series of rituals," Candita said, "so strong that while they are in progress, they change the weather. With each ritual, the storms grow more powerful. A foul mood is cast on all of the people in the village. They don't even know why."

"I saw that!" Phil said, excited that someone else was now confirming what he'd experienced. "The storms, the mood swings. My sweet sister, me, and even my dog became very agitated."

"In her ritual, she kills a sacrifice," Candita said while glancing down to refer to Charlotte's paper. "First, a small animal, like a rabbit. Then a bigger animal," she said in her thick accent. "After each sacrifice, she is rewarded with a vision. In that vision, a strong, very bad power tells her what to do next, where to go, who to look for. She gets closer to her prize after every step."

"There was a dead dog in her garbage. I saw it," Phil said, the urgency in his voice growing. "And I saw her try to kill a man. I stopped her." He paused, and with some embarrassment, added, "They were having sex." He felt the need for full disclosure because he believed they could help him.

"That is the last step," Candita said. "After killing a simple-minded man during the sex relations, her vision will reveal to her the identity of the person she is seeking. All of them, the man and animals must die by the piercing of a blade, even the person she seeks."

"Wouldn't she already know it's me?"

"Perhaps, but she can't complete her task until it is confirmed by the evil one in her vision."

"Why would she be coming after me?"

"That is what we will now find out. Just do what my mama tells you to do."

And with that, Candita returned to her corner in the dimly lit room. The old woman laid her hand, palm up, on the mirror-topped table. She then placed Charlotte's paper on top of her open palm. With her free hand, she placed Phil's hand, palm down, on top of the paper, resulting in the paper being sandwiched between her and Phil's palms. They slid their hands and the paper over to the edge of the table, so that most of the table top was in view.

The old woman closed her eyes, instructed Phil to do the same, and another flurry of Spanish ensued. After about a minute, she paused and added one more sentence.

"*Abre tus ojos*," the old woman said.

Immediately from the corner came Candita's translation. "Open your eyes."

With their hands still sandwiched toward the side of the mirrored tabletop, the old woman motioned down toward the table.

"*Mire estrechamente*," she said.

"Watch closely," Candita said, without missing a beat.

And they all stared intently into the mirrored tabletop as it began to gloss over into a mystical, multi-colored haze. Slowly the fog began to lift, and as it did, the three spectators were now immersed in a strange, dark world inside of the mysterious tabletop, privy to Charlotte's thoughts, feelings, and actions.

# CHAPTER THIRTY-ONE

JULY 16, 1999. Out of the thick night air, she exploded through the doorway into her empty apartment, slamming the door behind her. She leaned heavily upon it, trying to catch her breath. She had used more energy forcing herself to walk casually, resisting the urge to run the four blocks from the bus stop, than if she'd actually sprinted. Her job was now done.

Hair matted against the back of her neck, her heaving slowed as she gathered her thoughts. This state of exhilaration and flightiness was worlds away from her cold, rational self. Ninety minutes had passed since she had landed her small plane and left the airport. Certainly, there must be some report of it by now. Hurriedly, she scrambled to the couch, grabbing the remote and turning to the news.

There it was. The solemn night-time anchorman bearing the most bereaved face he could muster, announcing the news. Who was he kidding? Those leeches reveled in this stuff, she thought.

At this early stage, all the anchor could announce was that the plane was considered missing because it had failed to land at its scheduled destination. No one could yet confirm a crash, particularly when it was the ocean that had swallowed up the little six-seater, and not dry land. But she knew now that the deed was done, and her time in New Jersey would come to an end.

She would thank God, if she were of that ilk. Religion, she felt, was for the simple-minded, the unsophisticated, and she looked down upon them. Why would she honor a god who would allow her father to be killed while she was still in her mother's womb? She'd lived four decades of life, all without her father, and tonight she had completed the ghastly quest to avenge his death.

If she had ever allowed herself to partake of libation, now would be the time, as a celebratory glass of wine would be in order. However, she never allowed room in her life for the lack of focus that alcohol brought. Not that she didn't use alcohol, she just didn't ingest it. Many times had she out-maneuvered, manipulated, and coerced business competitors, co-workers, and clients who were handicapped by the cloudiness induced by liquor, all while she remained coldly sober.

She would celebrate in her own way, for tonight she had taken life from the only living son of the thirty-fifth president of the United States, thus extinguishing John F. Kennedy's surname from future lineage. While others might wear the Kennedy name, none of them would be direct descendants of John F. Kennedy. The name "Kennedy" was over, as far as JFK was concerned. What better and more final way to punish him?

From the time she was a doll-toting darling in Cuba, when her mother first told her of her father's heroic skirmish against American soldiers at the Bay of Pigs, she began to incubate a hatred for the man who had sent the invaders. Her mother, a practitioner of a particularly vile strain of Caribbean voodoo, had so poisoned her against America and their sainted leader that a deep-seated obsession had taken hold of Charlotte by her adolescent years. Years that would be spent, in part, by herself, due to her mother's institutionalization by Cuban authorities for pursuit of witchcraft.

Perhaps in a way only a child can, she twisted her mother's incarceration into being the fault of JFK, too. Watching the passing of time turn Kennedy into a martyr only fueled her desire to exact revenge. No matter that JFK was already dead before she even learned of her own father's demise. She felt betrayed by fate that she herself couldn't execute her justice upon JFK. Damnation on Lee Harvey Oswald...or whoever did it.

This evening's achievement was the culmination of four years of painstaking planning and work. She'd accomplished the feat by completing a series of malevolent tasks, after each of which she would enter a trance-like state in order to summon a baleful master who gave her directions and cryptic clues on how to perform the next task. She had learned well from her sorceress mother. Her ultimate goal was not just to punish Kennedy. Upon completion of the final task, she would be spiritually reunited with her long-dead mother, a reward brought by her dark master.

She'd already grown tired of the television. With so little yet to report, the anchorman's prattle had grown redundant. It had been a long day. Her eyelids were heavy. The time had come to reap her reward. However, as a brutal reminder of the reason for her retribution, each of her meetings with her master began the same way—back at the point in her life when her mother had departed.

She arose slowly from the sofa, pressed the "off" button on the remote, and walked toward the front door to shut off the lights. She pulled the curtains closed, found a vacant corner in the darkened room, and sat cross-legged in the floor.

The room was so dark, closing her eyes yielded no different a view than if they were open. After a minute of stillness, dark blues and rich greens began to seep into view behind her eyelids. Her breathing slowed. She inhaled deeply through her nostrils, taking twice as long to exhale through her open lips. Silent, empty, vacant-minded, tranquility ensued.

Her time of silence had now reached its end, however. Almost inaudibly at first, unintelligible words began to escape her lips. Words over which she had no control. Short, repetitive phrases, foreign to any human who might hear them, but not to their intended recipient. This was a call to her master, a being of great darkness, which manifested itself in her visions as a shrouded figure hovering above the nighttime ocean water. An entity whose face she'd never seen, but who had cryptically directed her with each task in her mission. Tonight, though, there were no more instructions. No more piecemeal hints. No more seemingly nonsensical directives that she would blindly follow. That was over. With her mission complete, tonight she would see her mother. Meanwhile, she drifted deeper into her self-induced hypnosis.

The swirl of colored fog behind her eyes began to clear, and as it did, she found herself in a familiar but haunting place. This was the place she'd started every journey to meet with her master—the night-time, desolate waters of the Florida Straits.

The moan of a stiff breeze chilled her wet skin, and the lapping of waves against a wooden raft filled her ears. The salt of the Florida Straits lingered on her lips. Why must she relive this hell over and over?

There she was again, just as it happened back in the summer of 1980. She, her mother, and a half dozen others had found themselves unwilling refugees, forced from their own country, helplessly drifting and paddling with futility toward a country that didn't want them.

Eventually the pounding of the waves and repetitive undulations of the swells took its toll. The craft broke apart in the dark of night, each passenger falling through the separating planks into the darkness of the ocean. She desperately grabbed onto whatever floating piece of wood the quarter moon's light allowed her to find. Her eyes burned from the saltwater as she hung on to a door-sized piece of wood, only her head and shoulders above the water. She cried out for her mother, to no avail. The screams of another mother, searching for her lost children, obscured any response she was hoping to hear. Seconds turned into minutes, and all she could hear was the sobbing of the suddenly child-less mother clinging to another remnant of their fractured raft. With only a sliver of light, all she could do was listen to the mourning mother drift away into the dark of the night.

Each time she had completed a task and sought a visionary meeting with her master, Charlotte was forced to undergo this cruel ritual, reliving the moment in 1980 when she had lost her mother at sea during their crossing to America. Her master appeared to her that night on the lonely sea, promising a reunion with her mother, but not until

Charlotte's thirty-fifth birthday. After sixteen years of acclimating to life in the United States, as instructed, she had called for her master the day she turned thirty-five in order to begin her quest. Tonight, though, would be the last call to the master, as all of her steps were now complete. Tonight, she would see her mother.

Crawling up onto the floating remnant as best she could, she sat on her knees, with her feet under her, and held the edges of the makeshift craft. She watched what little light the moon provided disappear behind cloud cover, and she then began an intense monologue in a call to her master.

In a moment, the sea became still. The steady breeze died completely. She sat alone, quietly floating in total darkness. Above her, the last cloud obscuring the moon passed, allowing its faint light to shine down, reflecting softly upon the motionless water. The slim moon's glow had now revealed what she'd hoped for.

There, hovering just above the dark water only thirty feet in front of her, was a shadowy figure, cloaked in a black hooded robe, face obscured. Her master knew no gender. It was only evil, willing to offer gifts in exchange for eventual bondage. It was a hulking, beastly sight, never speaking, and answering her questions only with hologram-like images created in the air by waving its cadaverous hands.

"My tasks are complete, Maestro," Charlotte said. "Can I see my mother now?"

The evil one slowly waved the back of its weathered hand horizontally across the air in front of it, like some sort of miscreant car show model, revealing moving imagery of a building, with cars and people passing it by.

"What is that?" Charlotte screamed. "No more clues! I want to see my mother!"

With that, her master again brushed its hand across the air, this time wiping away the building and street scene. Now it extended its right hand out in front of it, limp-wristed, swirling it in a small circle until the sunken-eyed face of her mother appeared, floating above the water.

"Mama!"

"Charlotte, my dear, your work is not complete."

"Mama, come to me!"

"I can't, *mi pequeño melocoton* (my little peach)," her mother said, "until all are extinguished by order of birth."

"There's another?"

"Follow the maestro's direction, and we will be together," her mother said, as her tired face began to fade away.

"Wait, mama! Don't go!"

Then the hooded master placed both hands around her mother's face, covering it like a ball, and blew mightily into its hands, dispersing the contents like a puffy dandelion out over the dark ocean.

"No!" Charlotte screamed. "I will destroy you!" For just an instant, she had forgotten to whom she spoke.

At that moment, the faceless master slowly raised its right hand up, pointing it directly at Charlotte. Her defiance had now turned to fright. The boney, pointing hand turned its palm toward the night sky and slowly began to curl its crooked index finger toward itself repeatedly, drawing Charlotte to come closer.

Still on her knees, she clenched the sides of her makeshift raft and cried, "No!" However, she was powerless, as the craft slowly began to creep toward the beckoning finger that was pulling it forward.

The thirty-foot buffer between them had dwindled to twenty-seven, twenty-two, fifteen, eleven. And then it stopped. The master's finger was now still.

Now, the floating, hooded behemoth extended its hand toward Charlotte. She was frozen with terror. The master slowly caressed her cheek with the back of its raspy hand, leaving a stinging scrape behind. Its once beckoning index finger made slow, wicked circles around her ear. Charlotte's heart felt as though it would pound its way out of her chest.

Just when she had surrendered to the thought that eternal death was inevitable, the master retracted its cold hand, and again waved it across the space between itself and Charlotte. Again, the street level scene of the office building appeared in the air. This time Charlotte paid close attention to it, noting details such as signs and car licenses, then burning a mental picture of it in her mind. The instant she had it committed to memory, it and the master were gone.

Abruptly, Charlotte found herself back on the carpeted floor of her darkened New Jersey living room, sweat streaming down her temples, pulse pounding and chest heaving. Evidently, she wasn't done after all.

---

NOW, in the small back room of a Spanish Harlem butcher shop, the three spectators lifted their eyes from the tabletop.

"I know that building," Phil said. "It's the building I work in."

"That completes the puzzle," Candita said.

"It's me she's coming after," Phil said as he stared blankly at the wall.

"Well, yes," Candita said, "but not only you."

Phil turned toward her with a sense of newly realized dread. Candita read the question in his eyes and responded.

"It's your baby. He is the last in line."

# CHAPTER THIRTY-TWO

THE FIRST THING Phil Murphy did when he got out on the street outside of the meat shop was make two phone calls. The first was to Gus Austin at the bank, to find out if Charlotte was still in the hospital. She wasn't. She'd been released that morning. The next call made was to his sister, to check on Willie. He was fine. Phil told her he was on his way home. After making his way back to his vehicle, Phil got out of Manhattan as fast as traffic would allow, then settled in for an uneasy ride home.

As the little white truck crossed into Delaware, zig-zagging through the late afternoon traffic, Phil's phone rang.

"Hello?"

"Phillip, I'm just checking to see that you made it home safely."

"Thanks, Doc. I'm just crossing into Delaware now."

"So did you have any success finding Kristen Minnows?"

"More than you'll ever know."

Phil then recounted his encounter with Kristen, and how she had told the police officer that Phil's name was Davis Kennedy, even though he'd never mentioned his name at all.

"Something extraordinary is certainly afoot," Ann said.

"I haven't even told you the weirdest thing that happened."

"There's more?"

He filled her in on the meat shop women who'd seemed to be expecting him, and the strange sights they had witnessed in the back-room table top.

"You're in uncharted territory, Phillip."

"I sure am, Doc," he said. "While it's all too much to absorb, I'm a bit relieved that I know what's happening now, and why. How, is a different matter. But at least I know now that Charlotte's goal is to end JFK's contribution to the Kennedy name. And now I know that I've got to protect Willie at all costs."

"Have you spoken to your sister? Is the child safe?"

"Yeah, I called her as soon as I got out of the meat shop. He's fine, but I can't get to him fast enough. I'm still not sure how I'm going to tell him about Otis."

"When the time comes, dear, you'll find the right words. He's very young. Children that age are resilient. He'll bounce back."

"I hope *I* can," Phil said. "He was so much more than a pet to us."

They said their goodbyes, and Phil promised to keep her updated. He continued to push the little white truck as hard as it could go. As the four cylinders strained and the bald tires roared, something occurred to Phil. So much had happened, so many focus-shifting events had transpired, he'd forgotten something vital.

After the fire at Charlotte's house, his breakup with Jill, Otis's death, the prison visit with Hinkle Bare Skann, his encounter with Kristen Minnows, and the exhausting look into Charlotte's vision with his meat shop hostesses, Phil had forgotten that Russ Curry was in mortal danger.

Charlotte had already tried to kill Curry in order to have the next step in her quest revealed to her. Granted, the ceremony instructions called for sexual congress with a simple-minded man, so it didn't necessarily have to be Curry specifically. But with how many such men did Charlotte already have a carnal relationship? Phil was convinced she was going after Curry again.

A twinge of ache was bubbling up in Phil's temple now. The rough ride and two nights of sporadic sleep in his truck were taking a toll. Seemingly out of nowhere, sparse droplets of rain found his windshield. His dry-rotted wipers only made things worse, smearing the bug-spotted glass into a blur. And, of course, he was out of wiper fluid. He found himself getting more irritable with each rotation of the wheels.

"Piece of shit," Phil uttered. The roar of bald tires pounding the rough pavement masked his words, sparing the feelings of the little white truck. Right now, it was the little engine that could, chugging Phil ever closer to Willie.

Even though everything he was griping about was his own fault—bald tires, worn wipers, and no fluid—Phil still felt like bitching. The rain was picking up. The onset of Phil's irritability was swift. He suddenly realized he'd experienced this combination of bad weather and crankiness before. Just a few minutes ago, the weather was fit for a picnic. His pulse quickened and his cranium felt like a grapefruit in a vise.

He knew what was happening. Charlotte was starting to brew her big pot of Curry stew. His eyes darted side to side as he worked his way between traffic, looking for a place to pull over.

He was too far from Dover to get there before the climax of Charlotte's ceremony, and even if he could, he wouldn't know where to go to stop it. They couldn't be at Charlotte's house—the fire had turned it into a pile of smelly char. The rain was steady as Phil found his way over to the emergency lane and pulled the truck to a stop. He hurriedly picked up his phone, and his shaking finger punched the pre-programed number for Gus.

"Hey, what's the weather there like now?" Phil asked.

"What, no 'Hello'? No 'How you doin'?"

"No shittin', what's the weather like there?" Phil barked.

"It's beautiful. Why?"

Phil's pulse began its descent from triple digits.

"I'm going through some rain, my head hurts, and everything's bugging me," Phil said. "I thought maybe Charlotte was up to her tricks again."

The rain was easing back to a sprinkle now, and the sun began to scare off the clouds.

"Relax, doofus, you're probably just going through a spring shower," Gus assured him.

"I guess so," Phil said. "Hey, have you heard anything about Curry?"

"Only that he's out of the hospital."

"I've got to talk to him. He may be in deep trouble," Phil said.

"What the hell happened up there, anyway?"

Phil merged back into traffic and rehashed the events of the last two days to Gus. Even though he'd just told it all to Ann Culpepper, he didn't mind doing it again for his best friend. Their conversation broke up the lonely trip. Explaining it to Gus also helped Phil sort it all out in his own mind.

"So, let me get this straight," Gus said. "Since I last talked to you, not even forty-eight hours ago, in addition to all the shit that happened in New York and the prison in Connecticut, you also managed to burn down Charlotte's house, screw things up with Jill, and back over Otis."

Phil's extended silence told Gus that he'd stepped out of bounds. After a pause, "I'm sorry, man," Gus said, with genuine remorse for his lack of empathy. He had seen first-hand what Phil and Willie had gone through, and what a great part Otis had played in their lives.

"Don't worry about it," Phil said, quick to accept his apology.

"You know, Otis is the worst part of all of this, so far," Gus said. "I couldn't give a rat's ass about Curry, but Otis, I'm gonna miss."

"What do you mean, so far?" Phil asked, knowing the answer, but not wanting to acknowledge it as a possibility.

"You know..." Gus said, his voice trailing off. "You and Willie."

"I know."

A rare moment of silence ensued between the two.

"But anyway," Phil said, breaking the awkward pause, "As long as Curry's alive, then I'm just on deck, and not in the batter's box. And something's gotta happen to me before it can to Willie. Plus, right now, I know more than she does."

"What do you mean?"

"Well, she won't know it's me for sure until she has her vision after killing Curry. Even though she suspects it may be me, she still has to confirm it all by completing all the steps in her ritual; from the rabbit, to the dog, to the simple-minded man. And it all has to be done by the blade of a knife."

"She didn't kill *John, Jr* with a knife," Gus said.

"Yeah, but she wasn't using this ritual yet. The purpose of this ritual is to find someone. In John Jr's case, she knew who she was looking for and thought he was the last in line. She was just trying to *kill* him – it didn't matter how." Phil said. "She didn't need to use the ritual, which calls for a blade, until she learned there was someone else that she needed to find. If she doesn't do everything exactly that the ritual calls for, it won't tell her who she's looking for."

"But once she kills Curry, then learns that you're next, can't she just shoot you or something, since you and Willie are the end of the line, and she knows Willie is your son?"

"I don't think so," Phil said. "I mean, sure, she knows Willie is my son. But for all she knows, I may have fathered another kid."

"You didn't, did you?"

"Nah, I'm sure of that. But she's not, and she *has* to be sure before she can move on to Willie because she has to eliminate JFK's descendants *in order*. From what I saw in her vision at the meat shop, if she doesn't go in order then she doesn't get her "reward" in the end – being reunited with her mother."

This exchange with Gus was helping Phil sort things out even more.

"You know, she kind of got burned, in her mind anyway, with John Junior, thinking he was the last one. So, she'll definitely feel the need to go through the ritual when trying to kill me to make sure there's not another kid of mine out there that she has to deal with before Willie."

"I'll see if I can find Curry," Gus said. "Or better yet, Charlotte."

"Watch yourself," Phil said with a laugh. "She may try to substitute you for Curry. All she needs is a simple-minded man."

"That hurts."

# CHAPTER THIRTY-THREE

IT WAS 7:30 when Phil wearily lifted his size thirteens up the four steps of his sister's porch. The sun was about to clock out for the day, but was making a last glorious splash across the western sky, pinkening the bottoms of the few white clouds that were hovering.

Never having to knock on Kara's door, he merely pushed it open and stuck his head in.

"What's goin' on in here?" Phil said loudly.

"Daddy!" Willie shouted from the floor, his hoarse little voice was good medicine for Phil. The little guy dropped his toy and ran into the open arms of his dad, who was now squatting like a catcher.

"You're here!" Kara said, coming out of the kitchen. "I saved you some dinner."

"That sounds great."

Phil picked Willie up, carried him to the kitchen table, and sat down, holding his son on his lap. He wasn't even aware, but he was already unconsciously keeping Willie close. During the course of Phil's meal, Kara kept him abreast of Willie's time with her family. Willie was basically Kara's third child, particularly since he'd had no mother present for a big chunk of his three years.

"So are you at liberty yet to debrief me on all the excitement in your life?" Kara asked.

During the drive home, Phil had concisely told Kara on the phone about some of the significant, but less weird, events of the last few days, namely about Jill and Otis.

"I'll fill you in when there's more time," Phil said. "It's going to take a while to explain some of these things. I'm just getting a grasp on them myself."

"You take your time, Beavis," she said. "I'm sure you'll get it right with Jill if you'll just honestly tell her how you feel." She was careful not to mention Otis in front of Willie. She knew that would have to fall within the scope of Phil's fatherly duties.

As Kara's words hung in the air, a low rumble found their ears.

"Was that thunder?" Phil asked, placing Willie in the chair next to him as he got up to walk over to the window.

"Couldn't be," Kara said, "it's beautiful out."

As Phil parted the blinds, his eyes found light raindrops accumulating on the outside of the window glass, and the sky starting to cloud.

"That's weird," Kara said, "an hour ago, the TV weather guy said the chance of rain was zero this evening."

Another rumble of thunder, louder now. The trees had begun to sway. From the living room, Phil could now hear the bickering of Kara's kids about who had control over the TV remote. Pressure began to mount in his forehead.

"Listen, I think I'd better get home."

"Just going to eat and run again?" she said, with no hint of her usual playfulness. Willie was now starting to sniffle.

"No," Phil said, "I'm just beat, and Willie's getting cranky."

At first, Phil had thought he might just be a bit paranoid. After all, he'd felt a little silly after his reaction to driving through a spring shower earlier that day. But this was different. His saint of a sister had just been spiteful, the kids were fussy, his head was splitting, the weather was growing ever bitchier—and he was back in Dover now, presumably in the same area as Charlotte.

As he grabbed Willie's belongings, Phil hugged his sister and told her, "You're going to be really crabby for a little while. Just cuddle up with the kids for a bit and wait for it all to pass."

"Wait for what to pass?"

"The storm and your headache," Phil answered.

"How do you know I've got a headache? And how do you know it's going to storm? This is just a little rain."

"Well, you've got a headache, don't you?" Phil's tone told him he was starting to be a bit of a turd himself.

She reluctantly conceded he was right. "Well, yeah, I do."

"Okay," Phil said as he picked up the sobbing Willie and made his way toward the front door. "And a storm is coming," he said. "A really big one. Trust me. Find a safe place away from the windows, and all of you stay there. I'll call later to check on you."

With that, Phil, carrying Willie in one arm and his night bag in the other, ran through the escalating wind and rain to the little white truck in hopes of getting home before the meat of the storm set in.

If what he thought was happening was really happening, Charlotte was in the last phase of her mission. If she was successful, she would finally know that Phil was the reassigned conception of JFK and Jackie. Also, and it wasn't just an afterthought, Russ Curry would soon be dead.

As he made his way through the stoplights on the way to the four-lane, the rain became heavier, coming down in sheets. The wind was starting to push his little truck around. He couldn't just do nothing while Curry was slaughtered. But where were they? He didn't know where to begin. Or did he?

Charlotte's house was destroyed by fire. There were too many motels to consider. On the other hand, motels could probably be ruled out, as too many other people would be in close proximity. If they were in town, they must be at Curry's house, Phil figured. Phil had given Curry a ride home from work about a year before and knew where he lived. Ideally for Charlotte, she would have him on her home turf, but with it indisposed, Curry's house, set back from the street, provided enough distance to soundproof her deed.

At the last moment, Phil sharply turned right on Magnolia Avenue, intent on making his way to Curry's house. Thunder shuddered the little truck. Everywhere, cars were pulled over, waiting out the storm which was now in full torrent. The shrill sound of Willie's crying filled the cabin of the truck. *If* they were at Curry's, and *if* he could get there in time, what would he do with Willie?

The windshield wipers couldn't keep up. Vision was poor before, with the pavement shiny and wet. But now the rain and wind were so heavy, the lightning so blinding, it was almost impossible to press ahead.

Abruptly, a ground-shaking rumble shook father and son. A flash of lightning lit up the roadway long enough for Phil to get just a glimpse of a thick sycamore lying across their path. He stomped his right foot down on the brake pedal, nearly shoving it through the floor.

"Shit!"

Even though it was in the presence of his kid, Phil was a bit relieved that only the synonym for fecal matter was the word that emerged unfiltered from his mind under such dire circumstances. How bad of a guy could he really be?

The past-their-prime brake pads on his patient companion tried their best to keep Phil and Willie from running into the tree that lay across the road in front of them. But its best wasn't enough. The little white truck did manage, however, to skid to a stop, using the leafy branches to soften the impact, rather than ramming the tree's trunk. Willie's sobs filled Phil's ears.

"It's okay, buddy," Phil said with all the gentleness he could. He stroked his son's head as he sat safely strapped into his car seat next to Phil. Although, he was trying to save a life, there was a nugget down inside of Phil that was relieved that he didn't make it to Curry's house while he had Willie with him. What would he have done, stormed into the house, carrying Willie? No. Would he have left him in the truck by himself? No. He hadn't thought out a plan, that's for sure.

There was no going forward, and with no wiper on the rear glass, he couldn't begin to see backward. He grabbed his phone. As he held the phone in his left hand and steadied the shaking index finger of his right hand in preparation to dial 911, Phil wondered how he would explain to the police how he knew there was trouble at Curry's house.

He'd have to think of something, because he had to try to save Curry and stop Charlotte from officially learning that Phil and Willie were the pot of gold at the end of her wicked rainbow. His thick finger did its work: 9, 1, 1.

A quick-paced repetitive buzz blared in his ear.

He hurriedly pressed the button to disconnect, then tried again: 9, 1, 1. Same result.

"Damn it," he let out under his breath, as Willie's crying softened now.

He again gently stroked his son's head, leaning over to get as close to him as possible. The storm was quickly diminishing. He was starting to accept the fact that he was powerless to stop what was occurring.

"I love you, buddy," Phil said softly, his face nuzzled into Willie's cheek. The child could only quietly sob.

The wind was gone now. Only a mild drizzle fell across the once bug-spotted windshield of the little white truck. Rain was good for that —washing away debris.

Able to see behind him now, Phil turned the ignition forward, put the truck in reverse, and slowly backed out. The branches seemed unwilling to relent, clinging and scraping across the hood. However, they eventually let go, like a mother dropping her son off to start college.

Phil's headache was gone. Willie was calm. The storm was over. Curry was dead.

# CHAPTER THIRTY-FOUR

Phil sat comfortably in his bed, legs stretched out under the covers, back against the headboard, staring at the television across the room. Willie lay next to him, out like last year's cell phone.

Phil's shower had been medicinal, soothing his aching frame after forty-eight tortuous hours away from home, the great majority of which had been spent in the little white truck. The 11:00 PM news was about to conclude. He was beyond exhausted. After all, he was at the end of a day which began with him waking up in his truck on a street in Manhattan. His mind was full, but starting to glaze over.

All the way home from the tree blocking the road, Phil had struggled with whether to call 911 and send them to Curry's house. He would have either appeared crazy or involved in the matter. Neither of those alternatives would sit well with a family court judge whenever Willie's mother was eventually released from prison. If he used his own phone to call, he'd be identified. Perhaps he could find a lonely pay phone and make sure no one was around. Still, he could be sending the police on a wild goose chase because for all he knew, they weren't even at Curry's house, or that Curry was even the victim.

The small television sitting atop the dresser provided the only light in the room. Phil cast a glance toward Willie. He was motionless on his back next to his dad, who out of habit wouldn't look away until he saw his son's little chest expand and deflate.

The Weather Channel's on-air talent were being put through their paces, although Phil had silenced them with the mute button. The Weather Channel was a potent sedative, as they seemed to recycle their reports about every twenty minutes. Ordinary shows weren't an effective tranquilizer because Phil constantly wondered what would come next.

His mind was starting to drift away, finding the random, mundane thoughts that told him sleep was waiting around the corner: chopping down a tree, mowing the yard. As he took one last look at Willie, a bright flash came from across the room. He turned his head back toward the television, which now was emitting only a light gray screen. Before he could wonder what happened, another bright flash temporarily blinded him.

When his pupils had dilated enough to refocus, the television screen was displaying a picture—a suburban street scene, at night. The view was jostling ever so slightly, as if the camera was situated from the perspective of the eyes of a person walking down the sidewalk of a tree-lined street full of small houses. Phil found it uncomfortably familiar, not only in that something similar had occurred on this same TV the week before, but this time the neighborhood looked familiar.

On the screen, the headlights of a car appeared in the distance. As they approached, the walker's eyes turned quickly to the right, scanned the trees and bushes, then quickly scurried into a yard and down behind a waist-high holly bush.

Through the twigs of the prickly holly, the lights of the car came nearer, finally arriving, and then rolling on past. A look left and right, then the view was elevated again, and moving back toward the sidewalk.

After forty-five seconds of steadily moving down the sidewalk, the movement ceased. The view lifted upward toward two perpendicular street corner signs. One read *38th St.*

The view on the screen then moved slowly around to the left to display the words on the other sign—*McHenry St.*

Phil's eyes widened, and suddenly his jugular was trying to jump out of his neck again. He tried to push down on the mattress in an effort to get up, but his arms wouldn't respond to his brain's command. He was unable to move.

No wonder the scene had look familiar to Phil, even in the dark. The corner of 38th and McHenry was only four houses away. His eyes darted over to Willie, who was still sleeping quietly.

"All right, wake up," Phil said internally, hoping he was dreaming. "Wake up, damn it!" But he knew he was already awake.

He looked back to the screen to find that the view was now in motion again, turning right onto McHenry. The pace was picking up. Faster and faster the owner of the perspective moved down the sidewalk, passing 3801, 3803, then 3805.

Phil struggled with all of the energy his drained body could summon, only to sit completely frozen. The only movement he could muster was internal, as his heart was pushing the blood through his veins at a frantic pace.

He knew who was coming. He knew why. Yet, he sat paralyzed on the bed, unable to move. He wondered if this was perhaps part of her ritual and she'd somehow frozen him.

The "3805" on Stanley's house filled the screen, but then the view moved up into his lawn and through its lush grass. It seemed ages ago that carefree Phil had covertly fertilized his neighbor's yard.

The scene on the screen had now found the little white truck, sound asleep in Phil's driveway. Quickly, the view lowered, moved up beside the truck's fender, then glanced left and right.

Phil felt sweat form on his temple, accumulate, then roll down his jaw in a bead. Internally, he was frantically struggling to free himself, only to remain physically motionless. He turned his attention back to the screen.

Up from behind the truck, the view moved swiftly toward Phil's porch, then to the front door. There was a downward glance at a potted plant on the porch. A slender foot then knocked the pot over, revealing a key. For the first time now, a hand, a woman's hand, was on the screen, picking up the key, then working it into the knob, turning it, and opening the door. If only Otis were here.

Still unable to turn his head, Phil darted a glance toward the bedroom door. Did he hear something from the living room? He frantically tried to call out but couldn't get words to emerge from his lips.

The screen now revealed a slow advance across the living room, turning down the short hallway, and then coming to rest in front of Phil's bedroom door.

Phil's fluttering eyes shifted from the screen to the door. He felt his eyes might jump out of their sockets as he watched the doorknob slowly turn.

The fusion of panic, adrenaline, and desperation ignited an eruption inside of Phil, severing whatever hold Charlotte had on him, allowing him to break free and exploded off his bed, springing toward the door. He grabbed the knob and flung the door open, nearly ripping it from the hinges.

Nothing.

He checked the bathroom, then ran down the short hall, checking Willie's bedroom and closet. Nothing. Running into the living room, he found the front door ajar. He leapt through the front door onto the front porch, eyes darting to find the intruder. He glanced down to see the overturned potted plant, and the key in the door knob.

He quickly decided against a search, and ran back into the bedroom to stay close to Willie, still sleeping soundly in the soft glow of the television, which now displayed the Weather Channel.

# CHAPTER THIRTY-FIVE

THAT WAS IT. Consequences be what they may, Phil was going to the police. Right now. He was no longer concerned with anonymity. He needed help protecting Willie. Midnight was almost upon them, but he pulled on some jeans, slipped on a hooded sweatshirt, put the slumbering Willie in one arm, tossed his blankie over him, and headed for the door.

As he negotiated the empty streets of Dover, the thought entered his mind to ask Kara to watch Willie, but it quickly vacated. Anyone who had Willie was in harm's way. He wouldn't do that to his sister. But mostly, Phil wasn't letting a sliver of daylight come between himself and his son.

The little white truck pulled into the parking lot of the Dover Police Department just past midnight. Phil pulled Willie from his car seat.

"Hey, buddy," he said to the stirring child. "We took a little drive and we're going in here to talk to a friend."

Up the concrete steps and through the large revolving door, Phil entered the lobby of the police station. To his right was a woman behind a counter, on the phone.

"Excuse me," Phil said, to which she replied by holding up an index finger to him.

"Yeah, maybe you should talk to a mental health professional," she said with an air of sarcasm to the person on the other end of the call. She hung up the phone.

"Kooks," she said.

"Beg your pardon?"

"People with their anonymous tips. Gimme a break," she said, confirming to Phil his suspicions about the reception an anonymous call might get, particularly one with the weirdness his would involve. "So, how can I help you, sir?" she asked without looking at him as she shuffled some papers.

"I need to talk to somebody," Phil said, realizing he hadn't put any forethought into his actions. "A police officer."

"What type of matter is this regarding?" the woman asked, still not making eye contact with Phil.

"There are people in danger," he replied. "A co-worker, me...my son."

"Your son?" she asked, finally looking Phil in the eye.

"Yeah."

"What kind of danger?"

"Well," Phil said, pausing, "Are you the person I need to speak to?" He didn't want to waste time spilling his guts twice, or to the wrong person.

"I need to know what kind of issue is involved in order to direct you to the person who can best help you."

"Okay," Phil said, "It's about a possible murder."

"Hold on," she said, picking up the phone. Phil turned from the counter while she was conversing. Not a lot happening on the station floor at this time of night.

"Have a seat over there, sir. Detective Foley will be with you in a moment." Phil, still holding the groggy Willie, took a seat on a bench across the room.

In a moment, a large wooden door opened, and a stout man in his forties followed his protruding belly through the door. Dressed in a brown suit that was both tight and loose, depending on where you were looking, he waddled across the floor of the lobby toward Phil.

"Ted Foley," the detective said, extending his right hand.

"Phil Murphy."

Phil arose from the bench and offered a reciprocating right hand of his own. The two men stood eye to eye.

"Who's this little man?"

"My son, Willie."

"Come on back."

He led Phil and Willie through the wooden door, into a large room full of desks, with offices in the corners. The scene reminded Phil of the space where he spent his days at the bank. The room was sparsely occupied, as one might expect on the midnight shift in a relatively small town like Dover. It was a friendly city, after all. They arrived at Foley's desk near the middle of the large room and sat down in a chair in front of it.

"Thanks for seeing me, Detective."

"Our receptionist used the 'M' word, Mr. Murphy. That gets our attention."

"Well, I don't know if a murder has actually occurred, but I've got a strong indication that it has."

"Who do you think is the victim?"

"His name is Russ Curry, a co-worker of mine."

"What has happened to Mr. Curry?"

"Well, I don't know exactly. I'm not really clear on what's happening. Some very, very strange things have been going on."

"Okay," Foley said. "Do you know who may have killed Curry?"

"I believe it's a person named Charlotte Timpkin, our boss at First Collateral Bank here in Dover."

"Let me ask a couple of questions, Mr. Murphy. Do you know that any harm has come to Mr. Curry? And what makes you think your boss killed him?"

Phil knew from this point on, he was going to sound like a crackpot. Ever mindful of an upcoming custody battle for Willie, he was struggling with how much he should divulge to the police. He shifted Willie from his right knee to his left and chose his words carefully.

"To answer your first question, no, I haven't seen that Curry has been harmed. As for the second, in my time around Charlotte, I've come to believe she is practicing some kind of witchcraft or satanic worship."

"Is that so?" Foley asked. Phil could already hear the skepticism in his voice.

"That's what I think," Phil said, trying to sound as reasonable as he could. "I believe she's in the midst of a ritual in which she has to kill, in succession, Curry, then me, then Willie."

His words were met with silence. Foley pecked on his computer and gazed solemnly at it.

"I know it sounds crazy," Phil said, "but I'm a little bit desperate, as you can see by me coming down here with my son in the middle of the night. Somebody, and I think it was Charlotte, just broke into my house about a half hour ago."

"You were at home at the time?"

"Yeah. Willie and I were in the bedroom, and I didn't get a look at the intruder, but considering the context of things she has said, I'm sure it was her."

"So what makes you think she's a ritualistic murderer?"

"Well, for one thing, you guys have already investigated an incident at Charlotte's house where she and Curry were hurt and the house burned down."

"I was just finding that on our system here, when I entered Curry and Timpkin's names. Says here though, that was due to a breaking and entering."

"That's what I heard," Phil said, doing his best to hide his involvement.

"Is there anything you might know about that, Mr. Murphy?"

The detective's voice had taken a decisively more biting tone toward Phil.

"Only what I heard at the office," Phil said, trying his best to control his pulse rate.

"Tell me now, Mr. Murphy, why *exactly* do you think Curry has been murdered?"

"Listen," Phil said with sternness, "I came down here to get some help because I'm sure that my son and I are next. All I'm asking is that somebody go up to Russ Curry's house and see if he's alive or not. And maybe ask Charlotte some questions."

"Mr. Murphy, I'm not sure you're in a position to be making demands," Foley said. "Besides, we're very busy here."

"Busy?" Phil blurted out, as he looked around the slumbering room. "The only thing I see here are some people waiting for their shift to end so they can go get some biscuits and gravy." He knew immediately he shouldn't have said it. These were the good guys, after all, and Phil respected their work. But he was operating on an empty tank and his thoughts were beginning to emerge from his mind unfiltered now.

Seeing that he was not going to get any help, and maybe get himself arrested, Phil pulled Willie from his lap to his chest and stood up. He'd better get out of there while he could.

"Where do you think you're going?"

"I can see I'm on my own here," Phil said as he turned from Foley's desk.

"I think you'd better stay here," the detective said forcefully.

"You've got no grounds for holding me, Foley. Unless you've got some help to offer, I'm leaving."

Holding Willie tightly in his right arm, Phil turned away and strode as briskly as his aching body would allow toward the large wooden door in hopes he'd hear nothing from the mouth of Foley. Fortunately, the detective was mute.

Phil went through the door, past the woman behind the counter, out the revolving door, and into the parking lot, keeping his eyes peeled for Charlotte. He hurriedly fastened Willie into his car seat, and they scooted away in the little white truck before anyone inside could think of a reason to detain them.

# CHAPTER THIRTY-SIX

PHIL AND WILLIE meandered around the streets of Dover in the truck until the clock on the dash read 12:57 AM. There would be no help or protection from the police. If they went about their lives as usual, they'd be sizzling in Charlotte's frying pan. Phil knew now that he had to find a secure place for Willie, then go on the offensive to end things once and for all. He'd spent the last half hour mulling over the options.

Any person he left Willie with would be in grave danger. He wouldn't do that to his sister, his dad, Gus, or anyone else. He had no out-of-town relatives with which he had a close relationship.

As the possibilities were eliminated one by one, Phil finally settled on his last remaining option. A week earlier he would have scoffed at the idea. But in this particular circumstance, it actually seemed to be the very best option. So, he pulled his phone from his pocket, and hit a number on his list of programmed contacts. A woman's voice answered the call.

"Norfolk Federal Detention Center, how may I direct your call?"

"I need to speak to the person, uh," Phil stumbled, "in charge of the program where an inmate's child can stay at the prison."

"That's the Second Home program, sir," the woman said. "The

person to speak to is Ms. Shipley. She won't be in until 7:30 AM, but I can transfer you to her voicemail."

"Yes, do that. Thanks."

After hearing Ms. Shipley's recorded greeting, Phil left his message.

"Ms. Shipley, my name is Phil Murphy. I'm bringing my three-year-old son to stay with his mother for a couple of days. Her name is Belinda Murphy. It's about one AM right now and I'm in Dover, Delaware. I'll have him there first thing in the morning, and you can have me sign whatever you need then. Thanks. And let Belinda know, please."

As outrageous as Phil thought the program to be when Belinda first told him of it, it was the perfect answer to Phil and Willie's current predicament. What more secure place to keep Charlotte away from Willie than inside of a federal prison? He'd be safely inside, but away from the prisoners, in separate quarters with his mother.

They would leave for the prison now, under the cover of darkness. Phil wasn't going to risk a stop at his house to get clothes for Willie's stay. He'd just pick him up something at a twenty-four-hour Wal-Mart or such on the way. There was, however, one quick stop to make before leaving Dover.

Phil guided the little white truck toward the north side of town, and Jill's apartment. He didn't know what he'd say, much less how it would be received, but his heart was dragging him to her. And most importantly, he had to warn her to beware of Charlotte. With Willie slumbering beside him in the car seat, the scent of honeysuckle floating in through the half-open windows brought Phil's mind back to the first time he'd driven to Jill's.

Phil and Willie reached the parking lot and brought the truck to rest in a spot in front of her building. Phil unfolded his aching body from the driver's seat, went around the truck, and pulled Willie from his car seat and out of the passenger door. He put the still-sleeping child in his right arm and lumbered up the stairs toward Jill's door. Each draining step upward seemed to shorten his life by a week.

Upon arrival at her door, he paused in an attempt to formulate what he might say. He couldn't. He'd been up nearly twenty-four hours. The last bit of fitful sleep he'd gotten was in his truck on a street in Manhattan. It seemed like days ago. He rang the bell.

In half a minute, a soft light shone through her window draperies. A few seconds later, he heard the deadbolt slide, and then the door opened, revealing a half-awake, robe-adorned Jill.

"Phil," she said quietly, brushing her hair from her eyes, "What are you doing here? Is everything all right?"

"Yeah," he said, then changing his mind to, "No." Men do that, too, sometimes.

"Is Willie okay?"

"Willie's fine."

"What's wrong?" Her sleepy eyes and tender voice were turning him into a puddle of goo.

"Everything," he said. "Everything's wrong." He was starting to disintegrate. "I've got...a really big problem, but I'm taking care of it."

Jill stood quietly, choosing not to speak yet.

"Before I do anything, though, I..." He was so drained of energy, he could hardly get any more words out.

"I just want...."

There were no more words inside of him. Surrendering, he just emptied himself. He reached his left arm out and placed it on the side of her neck, under her soft falling hair. As she looked up into his indigo eyes, his baby in one arm and the other reaching out to her, she could feel his tired desperation—the desperation of trying to hold together the pieces of a life that was falling apart right in front of her.

It wasn't a matter of forgiving Phil. She knew whatever his missteps, they weren't born of malice or deceit. Deep down, she knew that Charlotte's words were only meant to incite her and to drive a wedge between her and Phil. She had also come to regret her confrontation of Phil in his driveway, if only because she had given Charlotte exactly what she wanted.

Jill knew Phil was flawed. He had problems, some of which he couldn't compel himself to share with her yet. But she would wait until he was ready to include her. Until then, she would just be there for him, with him.

Without words, Jill brought her right hand up to the side of her graceful neck, placed it over Phil's hand, and gently massaged it with her thumb. He moved his hand around to the back of her neck and leaned down toward her, all the while keeping the still-slumbering Willie snug in his other arm.

She gently placed a palm on each side of his square jaw, cradling his face with her hands. Finally, they came together in a soft kiss, parted momentarily, and then came together again. With their lips still engaged, Phil let a tired, cleansing sigh escape. With it, some of his burden was also expelled.

When they eventually separated, he spent a quiet moment looking deeply into her big brown eyes. And then she spoke.

"What can I do?"

"You've already done it."

"Can I keep Willie for you?"

"God, no," Phil said. "Whoever has Willie is in real danger. I won't do that to anybody."

"Where are you going?"

"It's better that you don't know any details, but just be on the lookout for Charlotte. She's dangerous."

"Is there anything I can do?"

"I'd feel better if you weren't alone. Maybe you could spend some time with your parents."

She didn't answer him. Jill was strong-minded, independent, and wouldn't just hide away with her parents. Phil accurately read her silence.

"Just think about it, okay?" he asked.

"Please take care of yourself," she said, placing her hand upon his cheek.

"Don't worry about me. You'll be seeing me soon enough."

# CHAPTER THIRTY-SEVEN

SUNDAY HAD COME. Phil wasn't sure if the whine that filled the cabin of the little white truck was the tires or Route 13. In the absence of either, he supposed, the sound wouldn't be there at all, so it must be both. An obvious deduction, but such was the state of his sleep-deprived mind. Random thoughts scurried in and out.

The digital clock on the dash would soon land on 4:30 AM. He and Willie had just left the Delmarva Peninsula, and were now on the causeway of the Chesapeake Bay Bridge-Tunnel, where they would soon work their way in and out of the Atlantic Ocean.

After leaving Jill, his last stop before leaving Dover was his father's house, to swipe the pistol hidden under the driver's seat of his father's car. With his dad languishing mentally in recent months, the gun had been a source of worry for Phil. So taking it with him on this trip served two purposes.

Over the years, Phil had an occasional dalliance with guns, but knew little about them. He knew a handgun from a rifle, and that the lower the number gauge of a shotgun, the more powerful. Other than that, he only knew to aim and squeeze the trigger. He'd found the gun loaded in his dad's car, and now it was resting under his seat in the little white truck.

In daylight, an ocean view would surround them, but at this hour, there was only darkness. Father and son had spent the last twelve miles fifty feet above the waves, on a road supported by spindly legs that were forced to endure the rigors of the Atlantic.

They were approaching the first of a pair of mile-long tunnels that would send them diving down under the ocean. The tunnel had a five-acre manmade island at each end where vehicles entered and exited.

As the truck came down off the causeway and into the tunnel, Phil gave a glance over toward Willie, who was sound asleep in his car seat. Other cars were a scarce sight. The concrete walls on each side of the entrance rose quickly and seemed to swallow up the little white truck as the road steeply sloped downward into the tunnel.

The roar of worn tires and the static of a lost radio signal were causing Phil to gloss over—again. There was something mesmerizing about the tunnel, with its series of lights mounted on both walls. Passing by faster and faster, the lights soon became a blur to the already zombie-like Phil. He could feel it happening again. He'd been through this enough times now that he could recognize when things were about to get bizarre. Then it happened—everything turned into a flash of brilliant white.

Temporarily blinded, Phil squeezed his eyes tightly shut and held them for a moment. He felt a very cool sensation in his upper body, while he felt nothing in his legs. Everything was dark, and he was adrift.

Slowly, he reopened his eyes to see the severed hull of the crashed Kennedy Piper lying below him on the floor of the ocean. The seat cushion was still serving as a floatation device, pulling him toward the ocean's surface.

Suddenly, there was another flash of bright light, again rendering him temporarily sightless.

"Sir! Sir!" a man's voice called out sternly. "Can you hear me?"

He couldn't respond. All he could do was cough violently.

Again, he squeezed his eyes tightly shut for a moment, then reopened them to see the ceiling of an ambulance, and the faces of two people bustling frantically to render aid to him.

"Mr. Kennedy, welcome back, sir!" said a smiling young man at his side.

He still didn't have voice with which to respond.

"Don't worry about talking, sir," said the attendant, "you've had a lot of water in your lungs. A helicopter spotlight found you draped over a seat cushion and a floating oxygen tank. We're on our way to the hospital now."

Phil was stunned, and like before, he could feel, see, and hear what Davis Kennedy sensed, but still maintained the thoughts of Phil Murphy. As the siren wailed away, he felt the to and fro of the ambulance speeding down the road. He felt sensation in his arms, but nothing in his lower body.

Then a noisy jolt threw them sideways.

"Shit!" yelled the attendant to the driver. "What the hell was that?"

"Somebody's trying—"

Then another strong impact from the left side of the van threw it to the right, brushing against the guardrail.

"Somebody's trying to run us off the road!" screamed the driver, who'd now hit the brakes to get the attacker to pass them by.

"Who the hell is that?" yelled one of the attendants.

"I don't know! Some crazy woman," answered another.

Medical supplies were falling off the shelves, and the scene was chaos. Davis was strapped in, so he was going nowhere, but the attendants were falling all about the rear of the van.

Just then, another jolt hammered the ambulance, so the driver sped back up to try and gain some separation. It did no good, however, as the ramming had now become repetitive. Phil had no idea what was happening, but certainly the ambulance couldn't hold up under such an assault. Davis had closed his eyes, and now Phil was in darkness.

Then, the sound of a child screaming found his ear. The child was Willie.

One last impact caused Phil to open his eyes to find himself back in the tunnel, trying to maintain control of the little white truck. Willie's screams filled the truck's cabin, while to Phil's left a large SUV was pounding the driver's side of the little white truck.

Phil's truck was no match for the behemoth smashing him into the side of the tunnel. Somehow, though, the little truck kept moving forward.

Now a pair of oncoming headlights approached in the two-lane tunnel. The SUV, still in the oncoming lane, seemed undeterred by the approaching car. Over Willie's crying, Phil heard a horn blaring. The SUV was still to his left, scraping the driver's side of his truck. The little white truck was being pinched between the SUV and the wall, slowing it down. Phil jerked the wheel hard to his left, giving him a sliver of separation. He punched the accelerator and lunged slightly ahead of the SUV, allowing it to swerve back into the right lane behind Phil, and letting the oncoming car pass, avoiding a head-on collision. Phil would've liked nothing more than to use the oncoming car to peel the SUV off him, but couldn't do that to its innocent occupants.

"It's okay, buddy," Phil said to Willie. "Just hang on."

Although he couldn't see who was driving the SUV, Phil knew what was happening. Charlotte was using the isolation of this road and the time of day to finish them off. He also knew that she couldn't just merely kill them in a car wreck. There was a sequence to be followed. First Phil, then Willie. It had to be in order of birth, just as the ghostly image of her mother told her that night on the ocean. He was also sure that the woman in the most recent vision, ramming Davis's ambulance had also been Charlotte, trying to finish off what the plane crash hadn't.

The SUV bumped the rear of the truck. The little white truck was giving it all it had, but Phil could feel at least one flat tire, maybe more. The passenger side fender ground against the tire, too, slowing the truck down considerably.

Phil could see the end of the tunnel up ahead. Just then the SUV swerved back into the oncoming lane. Phil did the same, keeping it behind him. As the SUV shifted frantically back and forth between lanes, Phil managed to keep it behind him long enough to emerge from the tunnel intact.

"Hold on, buddy. Everything's okay," Phil said, stroking Willie's head with his right hand, while his left kept a grip on the severely vibrating steering wheel.

Once out of the tunnel, the road widened from two lanes back to four, and Phil kept the hammer down, trying to create some space between him and the SUV. But the hobbling little truck had no chance, and the extra lane made it easy now for the SUV to pull out around the truck.

This time Phil took the offensive, and swerved as hard as he could to his left, into the side of his attacker. The SUV spun out of control and came to a stop.

Phil used the opportunity to put distance between them. He also slid his hand frantically under his seat in search of the gun, but in all of the jostling, it wasn't there anymore. A cloud of smoke billowed from where the fender was rubbing the left front tire. The stench of burnt rubber was ungodly.

While still forging down the road, he pulled his phone from his pocket and hurriedly did his best to press 911 with his thick fingers. In his rearview mirror, he saw the headlights of the SUV in the distance. They were closing fast.

After a couple of attempts, he finally managed 911.

"911. What's your emergency?"

"I'm on the causeway, and I'm being attacked by another car."

"Which causeway, sir?"

"The Chesapeake—"

Before he could finish his sentence, a colossal impact hammered the driver's rear corner of the little white truck, pushing the vehicle into and partially over the protective wall, leaving it dangling by its left rear tire over the turbulent Atlantic below.

Willie's screams pierced Phil's ears, but the boy appeared uninjured. This would've been the best commercial ever for car seats. Phil knew they had to get out of the truck before it plummeted into the ocean fifty feet below. He couldn't be concerned with Charlotte now.

The whole truck was leaning at a forty-five-degree angle, with Willie below Phil. With the truck so precariously out of balance, Phil couldn't just lunge toward Willie and pull him from his child seat.

He carefully unlatched his seatbelt and reached over toward Willie, causing a loud creak. He immediately froze. Being careful not to lean, again he reached over, this time slowly, unlatched Willie's seat, and smoothly pulled the boy out and into his chest.

The dark waves pressed relentlessly against the causeway legs down below. With the sobbing Willie in his right arm, Phil leaned cautiously against the driver's door and pulled its latch to open it. Nothing. The pounding administered by the SUV had jammed the door. Phil had no choice but to lift Willie up through the open driver's window, allowing him to climb out onto the pavement.

"Stay right there, Willie. Don't move."

As Phil began to slither out of the window headfirst, his peripheral vision caught a glimpse of the SUV, no Charlotte. He continued cautiously on out of the window, first his hands on the concrete, then his knees, and then he sprang to his feet and scooped up Willie.

A quick scan around found no one, only the SUV, grill smashed in and headlights on, pointing at Phil and Willie only fifty feet away. No other cars within sight.

A dilemma entered Phil's mind. Should he and Willie run for it, and hope a car came by and that he could convince it to stop? Or should they stay put, and use the little white truck for the small amount of shelter it might provide?

If he did run down the road, there would be no cover at all. Charlotte hadn't emerged from the truck yet. Maybe she she'd been injured when she rammed the truck. Both his phone and the gun had been scattered inside the truck during the last big collision. And with the slightest shift of the truck's weight probably dropping it into the ocean, Phil couldn't afford to go rummaging through it.

At that moment, the driver's door of the SUV opened. With Willie clinging to his leg, Phil shaded his eyes to soften the glare of the headlights. A figure then emerged—Angela Boatright. Her forehead bloodied, she was shakily pointing a handgun at Phil.

"Angela?" Phil yelled, in equal parts bewilderment and relief. "What are you doing?"

"Quiet, Phil," she said in the firmest tone she could summon as she wiped blood from her forehead. "You need to say your goodbyes to Willie now."

"Angela, why are you doing this? What's wrong? Let me help you."

"Your interest in helping me now is touching, Phil," she said, the sarcasm dripping from her words like the blood from the gash on her head.

Never letting the gun drop, she pulled her phone out and dialed.

"I've got them. Both of them. Where are you?" Angela asked the person on the other end of the line. "Okay. I'll just stay on the line until you get here."

"Oh, Angela, tell me it's not true," Phil said in disbelief. "Who are you talking to?"

"That's right, Phil. It's Charlotte."

"Good Lord, why?"

Then Angela turned her attention back to the phone.

"Okay, I won't. Just hurry."

Speaking to Phil now, Angela said, "Just shut up, Phil. Don't talk anymore."

"Angela, why are you being Charlotte's puppet?"

"I'm not her puppet!" she yelled. "We're in love. You never had any use for me, Phil."

"Good God, Angela, Charlotte's not capable of love. She's only using you to help her kill Willie and me."

"Shut up, Phil. She told me what you did, and why you have to die."

"I didn't do anything, Angela. She's lying to you!"

Turning her attention abruptly back to the phone at her ear, "I can't help it. He keeps talking." After a short pause she said, nearly crying, "Then just please hurry up and get here!"

"Angela," Phil said, taking a step toward her, "it's not too late. You can stop all of this. Put the gun down, and let's just get in your car and leave."

A look of sadness came upon her face as she tilted her head slightly to the side. Phil could sense he might be getting through.

"Angela," he said, "have I ever lied to you?"

She stared blankly toward him as he edged closer to her.

"Have I?" he asked again.

"No." She'd let the hand holding the phone drop to her side.

Phil could see car lights approaching in the distance behind Angela. Was it a passerby, or could it be Charlotte?

"Nothing she's told you is true," he said.

"But she loves me, Phil. You never did." Although the phone was at her side, her tiring right arm was still pointing the gun toward Phil and Willie, who was still clutching Phil's leg.

The headlights were within a hundred yards now, and starting to slow, either for the SUV parked in the road or because it was Charlotte.

"I've always cared for you, Angela. Our timing just wasn't right," Phil said with an eye on the approaching car. "Angela, how far away is Charlotte?"

The words had just floated off Phil's tongue when a set of bright blue lights flashed from the top of the approaching car. It was a police cruiser.

Phil exhaled with the greatest relief he'd ever felt. The car slowly passed the SUV, then the dangling truck, and parked next to the four-foot-high concrete barrier wall, ahead of the truck in the emergency lane. The driver's door flew open, and an officer squatted behind it, pointing his gun at Angela.

"Drop your weapon, now!"

She just stared blankly at Phil but didn't lower the gun.

"Put it down, Angela. It's over."

She lowered the gun to her side, dropped the cell phone, and smiled sadly at Phil.

The officer called for assistance on his radio, then eased out from behind the door and walked steadily toward her.

"Drop the gun now," he ordered.

She complied.

"Lay on the ground, face down, with your hands behind your head."

She did.

Another police vehicle was now approaching. The officer walked cautiously up to Angela in the right lane of the road, straddled her, cuffed her, then lifted her up to a standing position. Phil and Willie stood beside the little white truck.

The second police car pulled up alongside of the SUV and stopped, angled toward the retaining wall. Phil heard the engine rev. Like a cannon shot, the car lunged forward, directly at Angela and the officer holding her arm.

Phil saw terror overrun their faces as the police car swiftly struck them, knocking them first into, and then over, the retaining wall, and down into the dark Atlantic.

# CHAPTER THIRTY-EIGHT

IT WAS ALL SO TIDY. With one quick swoop, the cop car had cleaned up the Inconvenient. Phil wasn't surprised when the car door opened, and Charlotte emerged brandishing a handgun. A rumble of thunder trumpeted her arrival, followed immediately by a few drops of sprinkling rain.

"Long time, no see, Phil-boy," she said, standing thirty feet in front of him.

"Charlotte," Phil said, having lost his breath at the sight of Angela and the police officer being wiped away, "what are you *doing*?"

"I'm completing my life's work, Phil. That's what I'm doing."

"You make it all sound so noble," he said with disgust.

"But it *is* noble, Phil. Your life has been made worthwhile by becoming a tool in my little project," she said. "Isn't it nice to get together outside of work like this? I suppose the last time we got together was when you popped in on Russ and I. Me, all unconscious and without a stitch on, either. I hope you were a gentleman and didn't try anything inappropriate.

"Why did you tell the cops it was Gus?" Phil asked.

"That was just for my entertainment, Philly."

Phil could only shake his head.

"Now here's how this is going to go," Charlotte said.

Then she pointed her pistol toward Phil's right thigh. Simultaneously, Phil heard a loud blast and felt a burning bite in his thigh. Instantly, he found himself down on one knee, while Willie clung to his other leg. The wind whipped against his face.

"We've got some business to take care of, Phil, and I can't have you running off. Now you just stay put, and we'll get through this soon enough."

Phil struggled to his feet, his right thigh bleeding profusely. The rain was picking up.

"There's a certain order to what must be done," Charlotte said.

Just minutes before, Phil had heard the cop call for assistance on his radio. So he needed to buy time.

Figuring Charlotte would want to prolong his suffering, "Why don't you just get it over with?" he asked, his mouth agape, doing his best to bring air into his burning lungs. His thigh sizzled like a branded steer.

"Quiet now, Phil. I've got work to do."

Charlotte began a Spanish monologue, only a little of which Phil could decipher. She was now in the course of her ritual. If Phil was right, she couldn't kill him before she'd completed her soliloquy, and it had to be by a blade. And as long as he was alive, then she couldn't kill Willie. Phil hoped he could stall her long enough for the police to reach them out on the isolated causeway. Lightning flashed through the sky now.

"How'd you get a cop car, Charlotte?"

She let out an exasperated sigh but couldn't resist the chance to pat herself on the back.

"You must've been pretty convincing to that detective at the Dover Police Department, because he had cops everywhere looking for me. One of them pulled me over, but he wasn't as prepared as I was," she said. "Since they were looking for my car, I just decided I'd take his."

It wasn't lost on Phil that Detective Foley had taken action after their meeting. Lesser cops may have let ego consume them and would've either arrested Phil as he tried to walk out, or merely laughed the whole thing off after he left. Turns out Phil had spoken to the right man.

"You know, Charlotte, Angela thought you were in love with her."

"She was a means to an end, Phil. You need a little help in a project this size, and she fit the bill. You breaking her heart played right into my hands."

Phil could see the headlights of a car approaching from the direction of the Virginia mainland. At this hour, only the occasional car would be passing by. With there being two wrecked vehicles and two cop cars with flashing lights, it just looked like a run of the mill accident scene. Drivers might slow down for a little rubbernecking, but no one would be stopping since they figured the cops were already on the scene.

"Now Phil, don't you get any silly ideas about trying to flag down these passing cars," she said as she lowered her gun to her side, out of sight of the approaching car. "If you do, the next bullet goes right in to Willie's little ass."

The car passed, and she resumed her ritualistic rambling, all the while keeping the gun pointed at them. Phil took a quick glance at the dead cop's car that was still behind him. The driver's door was still open. Maybe the keys were still in the ignition. He needed more time.

"How'd you crash John Junior's plane, Charlotte?"

She paused, visibly irritated, but commenced with an answer. Phil could see she enjoyed having someone with which to share her genius. After all, he was really the only person she could tell.

"Two-way radio and remote manipulation of his instrument panel gauges from my plane," she said with an air of pride. "You'd be surprised how much access to a hangar a hand job to an airport night watchman will get you, Phil. Now, shut up."

She resumed her ritual. Phil was losing blood and getting light-headed. He had to do something soon. He let her get about ten seconds into it, scooped Willie up, turned, and ran only a few steps toward the police car before hearing another blast. This time his left butt cheek was aflame. At least, for the time being, he didn't notice the pain in his thigh or ribs anymore. He fell forward, Willie coming out of his arms and hitting the pavement, too.

"Get in the car, Willie! The police car! Run!"

The little fellow scrambled to his feet, ran to the cop car, and climbed in the driver's door.

"Stay there, buddy!" Phil yelled, laying on his stomach.

"You had enough, Phil?" Charlotte asked. "That's fine if you want the little bastard to stay in the car," she said. "I wouldn't want anything to happen to him anyway...yet. You, my friend, must die by the blade. I've shot you to keep you from running off. If you try it again, I'll shoot that little brat of yours in the ass before I slice *him* up."

Phil said nothing. He was still on his stomach, losing more blood each moment. Meanwhile, Charlotte resumed her ritual. A real storm was engulfing them now.

Phil's blood loss was affecting his brain, changing it, but maybe in a useful way. As Charlotte's words faded into the background, the words of Hinkle Bare Skann entered Phil's mind. Just before Phil walked out the door of the prison, Skann had told him, "Use what you've learned, what you've seen, to your advantage."

Seizing upon that thought, still lying face-down on the ground, Phil slowly reached around behind his neck and pulled the hood of his sweatshirt up over his head. He had quit thinking. His brain was functioning in a different manner now. Suddenly the Spanish he'd studied in school and had been working on in his truck the last few months had all fallen into place.

He pushed himself up off the ground, his pants drenched with blood, and managed to stand, albeit wobbly. He turned and faced Charlotte, who was still reciting her dark prose thirty feet away. From under the hood that shrouded his sullied face, he spoke.

*"Por que el pequeno melocotin de tu madre le permitio ahogarse?"* (Why did your mother's little peach allow her to drown?)

Charlotte became immediately mute.

*"Permitanme caricio de neuvo la mejillo como lo hice en las ondas,"* (Let me caress your cheek again on the ocean waves.)

*"Que?"* the stunned Charlotte asked.

*"No hiciste nada y permitiste que tu madre muriera,"* he said. (You did nothing and allowed your mother to die.)

Using the only inside information he had from Charlotte's vision, Phil was recreating the hooded master who had hovered above the Florida Straits. He kept the hood pulled down, so as to obscure his face all he could.

Slowly, he raised his right hand and pointed directly at her. Charlotte was confused and entranced. The storm above poured itself out upon them. He turned his palm upward and slowly pulled his index finger toward him, just as her dark master had beckoned her on the lonely, still sea.

*"Acercate' mi a pequeno melocoton,"* (Come closer my little peach), Phil said in a chillingly devilish tone, again using her mother's pet name for her.

*"Que passe?"* she asked.

*"Su balsa no es beuno para usted ahora, mi pequeno melocoton,"* he said. (Your raft is no good to you now, my little peach.)

Stunned as to how Phil would know these things from *her* vision, Charlotte actually began to wonder if she was indeed facing her hooded master.

At that moment, a faint female voice from out in the ocean called out, *"Charlotte!"* It was barely audible over the fury of the storm, but there it came again: *"Charlotte!"*

It could only be Angela. She was alive. Pouncing on this opportunity, Phil played this last and unexpected card he'd found up his sleeve.

*"Llama a su madre desde el mar,"* (Your mother calls out from the sea,) he said. *"Por qué su pequeno melocoton dehar que se hogara?"* (Why did her little peach allow her to drown?)

"Mama!" Charlotte cried, and she ran over to the retaining wall, leaning over it to look for her mother. "Mama!"

Phil recognized this as his only opportunity to save Willie. He was much closer to Charlotte than he was to Willie's police car. If he ran for the car, Charlotte would have plenty of time to gun him down. Even if it meant sacrificing himself while taking her out, he knew he needed to end this now in order for Willie to live.

So, with his last ounce of energy, Phil commanded his bullet-ridden body to get to Charlotte as fast as it could. His legs churned furiously, pumping as hard as they were able, but it seemed an eternity trying to cover the thirty feet between himself and her.

Halfway there, she still had her back to him, but it wouldn't stay that way. Hearing his heavy footsteps and breath bearing down on her, Charlotte spun around, raised her pistol, and squeezed the trigger.

The ringing blast filled Phil's ears, but his momentum was unstoppable. He plowed into Charlotte's chest, hearing the sound of breaking bones as he drove her into the waist-high concrete retaining wall. Her lower body was stopped by the wall, but Phil's weight drove her upper body over the wall, forcing her legs to follow, as she did a backflip into the turbulent Atlantic fifty feet below.

Phil nearly went with her but came to rest leaning over the wall. His stomach was ablaze.

"Angela! Hang on!" he called out weakly, even though he couldn't see her.

He collapsed backward from the wall, landing on his lead-filled buttocks, then falling onto his back.

"Willie!" he cried in desperation, but it exited his lips as not much more than a gasp.

He placed his hand on his stomach, then lifted it up in front of his face. It was drenched with blood. Bullet number three had done the most damage yet.

Phil Murphy lay quietly on his back, staring up at a late April sky. The sun was just beginning its daily resurrection from burial beneath the Atlantic Ocean. Charlotte's sinful storm had already subsided, and a few stars could be seen trying to hold off dawn's arrival.

He no longer felt the slugs in his thigh, buttock, or even his hemorrhaging abdomen. He was numb to any pain, and too tired now to hold his eyes open. As his lids gently fell, he became at ease with what was happening. He knew he couldn't stop it.

Behind his resting eyelids, his evermore blissful mind now envisioned the wondrous sight of a vast, beautiful meadow. In it, Phil saw two infinite single-file lines of people heading toward each other. One coming from the left; one from the right. A line of mothers and a line of new souls eager to begin a mortal existence. Meeting in the middle, the head of each line stepped forward, both joyful over the sight of the other. Joining hands, they walked away together, as the mother escorted the soul into corporeal life. This pairing of souls to mothers would repeat as the new head of each line stepped forward.

Your place in line is nothing more than chance, Phil realized. When he was a billion spots away from the front of the line, and his mother the same distance back in the other, the two of them knew nothing of who they might be paired with. A speck of a speck is the difference between a life of privilege and a life of destitution; elegance and disfigurement—a difference of one measly place in an infinite line of souls.

The image of the meadow then darkened and evaporated from his mind. As Phil lay still under a sky giving birth to dawn, a thought seeped into his tranquil mind. Whether the soul is assigned to a body of elegance or disfigurement, a life of privilege or poverty, the soul itself is still one of beauty—even the soul whose body may have been hijacked by evil. The body is just a shell, and whether that shell is one of the vast common, or a son of Camelot, it doesn't matter.

In a final moment of clarity, Phil realized the crux of life was as his mom and dad had always taught him. Everyone should be offered respect, even before they prove themselves worthy of it—no matter where their place in line. His satisfaction in knowing that he had, in large part, abided by that principle during his time here, comforted him in these final moments.

His body was slowing down. His heart was beating at a quarter of its usual pace. His ever-cooling blood crawled through his veins slower and slower until his faltering heart could no longer push it along. And then he was still.

However, he didn't find darkness behind his closed eyelids now. What emerged was a beautiful, brilliant blanket of silver fog that soothed and embraced him. The pain in his shredded trunk was gone. He felt complete comfort and peace now.

The soft fog began to clear, and he found himself on a familiar deserted beach, looking up at a stately white house on a knoll. Then, a glance down the beach revealed a most glorious sight. In the distance, running at full gallop toward him, came his precious Otis. It was the most beautiful spectacle ever to bless Phil's thirsty eyes. He was covering ground with such splendor and ease, it was as if he had wind filling his sails. In moments, he was within a few strides of Phil, who had dropped to one knee. When he arrived into Phil's waiting arms, their two minds melded momentarily into one, at which time they had a complete exchange of consciousness, leading to wholly reciprocated understanding. The love they'd shared on Earth had now been confirmed.

Phil arose from his knee and set his sights on the house on the hill. A beautiful soft glowing light was in the distance behind it, as if it were coming from a shimmering city. On the lush green lawn overlooking the ocean, sat a man and a woman, side by side in Adirondack chairs, holding hands. Phil turned toward them, and with his faithful friend at his side, walked across the beach and up onto the lawn. He couldn't feel the ground beneath his feet, and there was no Earthly landing as each step fell. With each glorious stride toward them, he felt a warmth and love that he'd never experienced. A relaxed, joyous smile overtook his face.

Their faces were clear now, and the adoration they conveyed was evident upon them. These were his parents, his true parents, whose union conceived him. Doc Culpepper had been right all along.

Within a shadow's distance now, he found them adorned in white, with a soft luminous glow seeping from them. He dropped to one knee immediately in front of them. A warm tingle spread throughout him. This feeling of utter harmony and serenity was unlike anything he could describe.

His mother, with her raven locks shining, gazed into his eyes and placed her palm upon his cheek. Gone were his Earthly scars, bruises, and abrasions he'd accumulated in recent weeks. She lovingly caressed his face. Without words, she revealed the love to him that only a mother can.

He turned his eyes toward his handsome father, who reached out and stroked the head of his last child. Each time his father's hand passed over his scalp, he could feel volumes of knowledge being transferred into his mind—worldly wisdom of the ages dispensed from his father's hand and soaked into his consciousness.

As he gazed upon his parents, he noticed their smiling faces turn slightly to their right in unison. When he turned to see the focus of their attention, he found the mother who raised him, Lisa Murphy, now seated in a chair of her own next to the couple.

"Mom," he exhaled with quiet joy, and he went from one knee, down to two in front of her, resting the side of his head in her lap. She was like a priceless portrait. He'd never seen her so vibrant and beautiful. She stroked the side of his head, caressing his temple with her thumb.

This was the sight of four souls in complete harmony, all of them nourished by this reunion, but knowing that it was not to be eternal. Not yet. Then his father spoke.

"There is more for you to do, son."

"We'll be awaiting you," his mother added.

Then, the saturating sound of a soft voice drenched their senses. It was all around them. One word.

"Daddy."

The hoarse little voice of Willie beckoned. This heavenly reunion would have to be something to look forward to. Phil arose from his knees, touched all of their hands, stroked Otis's shining coat, then backed slowly away from them. His eyes upon them, he drifted backward toward the beach and the dense silver fog until they were only small, faceless figures on the lush green knoll. He was consumed by the fog, and then everything went white.

"Daddy," the hoarse little voice whispered in his ear.

He opened his eyes to the flashing lights he thought he'd left behind. His gut burned and his body shivered. The sound of sirens was in the background, growing nearer. Still on his back on the cold, wet concrete, his head was cradled in Willie's lap, and the boy was gently rubbing his father's scalp.

Phil reached up and eased his son down to his face, kissed him firmly on the cheek, and kept him nuzzled close.

# CHAPTER THIRTY-NINE

THE SECOND OF June found Loockerman Street buzzing with down-towners anxiously making their way to their cars to get home for the start of their weekend. Phil, his dad, Willie, and Jill stood among the passersby outside the massive wooden double doors of the Stumble On Inn.

"Can't believe it," Phil said, "but I'm actually a little nervous."

"You, Phil Murphy, are nervous?" Jill asked.

"Well, this is the first time I'll have walked through these doors as the owner."

"I would think this is a walk in the park compared to what you've been through," she said as she squeezed his hand.

"Let me tell you, no joint venture with Gus Austin is going to be a walk in the park," he said with a smile.

With Phil still nursing a stomach wound and sporting an obvious limp, Jill lifted Willie up, and they all proceed through the entrance. Gus had assembled a few friends to celebrate their journey into entre-preneurship. The Friday night crowd hadn't made it in yet, and the place was only sprinkled with customers.

"There he is!" Gus yelled, as he was flanked by Missy from HR. "Get in here, you miserable cripple."

Friendly faces, both old and recent, were good medicine.

"You're looking fit as a fiddle, Phillip," said Ann Culpepper. "My, that's a bit of a tongue twister. I'd better make this my last glass of wine!"

"Come on, Doc, let the good times roll. I'm just really glad you're here."

Kara lunged out of the crowd to give her little brother a hearty but cautious hug, ever mindful of his recovering frame.

"My baby brother's going to be a captain of industry!"

"Well, it's a start," he said. "We're lucky the owners were looking to retire and willing to finance it for us themselves."

Gus chimed in, "We're gonna make a killing."

"With a little fine tuning, we should do okay," Phil said, trying to reel in Gus's majestic expectations.

"You know, Murf, gettin' shot in the ass like that is scary stuff," Gus said with a big grin. "That was probably really tricky work for your surgeon, havin' that bullet lodged so close to your brain."

A good time commenced, though Phil partook of only a ginger ale, as he was still rattling with antibiotics. After all that had happened, antibiotics or not, he was ready to slow everything down a bit.

He nursed his drink at a table with Ann Culpepper. Gus, meanwhile, had taken the stage with the house band, and was pouring out a gibberish rendition of "Semi-Charmed Life."

"It's just such a shame about the girl from the bank," Ann said.

"Angela, yeah. She never had a chance, really, especially with the cuffs on."

"Poor thing," Ann said. "It seems odd that they found her fairly quickly, but they couldn't find the police officer or Charlotte."

"I understand it, I guess," he said. "By the time they found Angela, she was almost four miles away."

"Yes, I suppose rough currents, particularly after a storm, could wreak havoc on a search mission."

"One of the Virginia State Troopers who's been investigating called me on Tuesday to say that Charlotte's now been declared legally dead."

"That was nice of him," Ann said.

"It was. Gives a little closure to the whole thing."

"Oh, I would imagine she just became fish food," Ann said.

"I would say you're right," Phil said. "The police think with land being so distant, she couldn't have survived, especially since she probably had some broken bones or maybe even spinal cord damage."

"And still no word on the Curry fellow?"

"Can't find him. The police checked his house right after Willie and I left the station that night, and couldn't find anything out of line. Nobody's seen him. I'd bet Charlotte made sure there's nothing to find."

"So, Phillip, what about you?"

"What do you mean?"

"What kind of plans do you have?"

He paused for a moment, took a sip of his ginger ale, then looked back over his shoulder at Jill, who was chatting it up with Kara at another table. Those two had become quite close during Phil's month-long recovery. Jill felt Phil's eyes upon her and returned his glance with a soft smile.

Turning back to Ann, he said, "Just gonna heal up, then try a little harder, you know?"

He took another sip from his glass, then added, "I've been told that I've got more to do."

It was approaching 8:00 PM, and Phil was in no physical condition for a long night. He rounded up his dad, Willie, and Jill, said his good-byes, and headed toward the door.

"This was fun," Jill said.

"It was."

As the door closed behind them and they found themselves on the sidewalk, a low rumble of distant thunder caught Phil's ear. He turned to Jill and spoke.

"They callin' for rain?"

# ACKNOWLEDGMENTS

Thank you for taking time to read this story. I hope you'll come visit me at PatPaxtonBooks.com. If you're looking for someone to blame for this atrocity to literature, look no further. I owe all of these nice folks a thank you.

- *Sara Marian,* for her keen eye and insights in looking over my manuscript.
- Fellow author, *Tara Cromer* for her encouragement and advice.
- Misters *Tony Acree* and *Stuart Thaman* at *Hydra Publications*, accomplished authors as well as top-drawer publishing gurus. Thank you, gentlemen, for giving a first-timer a shot.
- Although, I've not met him, thank you to the closest thing I have to a writing influence, *Gary Larson*, whose *Far Side* work beautifully illustrates the dictum, "Brevity is the Soul of Wit."
- My lifelong best friend, *Bill Mullins*, who always has an ear available. In this same vein, my head is full of tales inspired

by my time spent with *Scott Mattson, Jim Tippie, and Gary Bush*. But that's another book (which won't be written, for fear of incarceration).

- Early test readers, encouragers, and good friends *Angi Cooke* and *Katherine Gillis*.
- Dear friends *Steve* and *Cathy Hanley*, just because.
- My mom, *June Paxton*. Although she didn't hatch me, she helped raised me from age seven.
- The best and sweetest sisters anyone could ask for, *Teresa Callahan* and *Beth May* (especially for her encouragement).
- My brother, *Lorn Paxton*, for always cheerfully offering help and support over the years.
- My eldest brother, *Howard Paxton*, the silliest person I know. That's about the highest compliment I can pay anyone. Thank you for teaching me how to "act a fool".
- My mother, *Joan*, who's not been with us since I was five years old. I'm looking forward to our reunion.
- My dad, *Howard C. Paxton*, the most generous and dependable person I've ever known. I miss you.
- My daughter, *Katie*, who always, always has words of support and encouragement for her dad, no matter what crazy new thing he's trying next.
- My son-in-law, Keith for his friendship and desert-dry sense of humor.
- My son, *Ben*, whose example, even as a child, has always inspired me to try harder.
- My granddaughter, Evie. I hope when you think of G-Pap, it will remind you that it's never too late to try something new.
- The best thing that ever happened to me, *Polly,* for thirty-five years and counting. I'm so thankful to be the beneficiary of her questionable taste in men.
- *God*, for never having allowed me to feel alone.